BAD TO WORSE

Acclaim for *Bad to Worse*

'Satan circles and eternal triangles endlessly intriguing.' *Euclid*

'Most compelling description of Hell I have read.' *Dante Alighieri*

'Loved the pendulum motif.' *Galileo*

'A new, new testament for humankind. A holy book.' *St Ignorius*

'Literature reimagined ... may prove to be history's fabled End-Novel.' *S Vestry*

'Ceci n'est pas un roman.' *R Magritte*

'Irresistibly draws us to rational, moral, and heroic life choices.' *F Godwilling*

'Simultaneity in climax appears achievable.' *A Einstein*

To Three Children

**Published with support from the
Fremantle Press Champions of Literature**

BAD TO WORSE

Robert Edeson

 FREMANTLE PRESS

O Lord

I am lost in my enemy's forest.
His quarrel darkens to the Counting Owl
winding the curse of his father's ruin.
Now a shadow lengthens upon me.

My Son

Listen to the thriced.
Then is deliverance yours, the Owl become
gracious, the tyrant stopped in his shadow
and the infidel turned, if from bad to worse.

Leonardo di Boccardo
Conversaziones e Silenzio

FOREWORD

Before you lies a book of truths, and I start with a very peculiar one: I do not know the author of this work. Not even his or her name.

From internal evidence of an emotional intelligence and refinement of sensibilities that could hardly be masculine, I thought at first the author to be a woman. However, based on textual and stylistic similarities to another work entitled *The Weaver Fish*, and the crass transparency of attempted subterfuge, I now incline to believe this is the writing of A B C Darian in masquerade as an anonymous recluse.

Whatever the case, by some entwinement of circumstances beyond my understanding and a natural ineptitude for tactical avoidance, I find myself in multiple roles as that person's literary agent, power of attorney, editorial correspondent, and briefly his *nom de plume*. Even more onerously, the responsibility has fallen on me to excite in total strangers, by means of my following remarks, a compulsion to continue reading until the last veracious full stop.

How should I do that? At least I have prepared conscientiously, by reading the manuscript five times. Forward quickly, forward slowly, once aloud, once backwards, and once upside down (a convent skill, never explained). Five times I entered his dissenting universe, where every fact seems fallibly familiar and every falsehood impossibly erased. Only once before has this reviewer's frocked composure been so tested by the reasoned sensual. (When Monsignor Papaduomo visited our

Order to speak on 'Constructs of Celibacy', and remained at the abbey as tutor-in-residence.)

If, like me, you prefer to know what a book is about before committing to read it, I shall tell immediately. This is the account of a century-long vendetta; true, tragic, and so transcendent in its special evil that the Inferno itself was visited on a small frontier town in America. It is a record of generational human misfortune and ambiguous redemption, unequalled for malice and tenacity in the whole miserable world history of feuding families.

But it is so much more. Informative asides are unexpectedly grammatical, or arithmetical, sometime crustacean, sometime chemical, aeronautical, oceanic, theological, or ambivalently poetic.

I give examples: Here, in a discreet footnote to an unexceptional endnote in a commonplace appendix, you are confided the identity of the Supreme Being ... Learn the true number of the Trinity ... Expose Luciferans secreted in your family ... Why is the Circular Sea so shaped? ... Know what crabs think upside down in z-bends ... Who first thought of zero? ... What are Satroit's tenses? ... Break out of the Couplet Prison using only the power of thought ... Why is the Inferno hot? ... Where will you find a Secret Chord? ... What is Theta Collapse? ... How do waitpersons vanish? ... Return from the dead ...

Yet all the time we are never distant from the sickening criminality of the beautiful Regan Mortiss, her executive killer known as Glimpse the prospector, and a witless half brother codenamed Haberdash. Nor, we can be thankful, are we far from the moral certitude and discerning ruthlessness of Richard Worse, opposing them.

Every modern chronicler of Ferende history, Dr Darian included, has observed that nothing should surprise us about that country. Even so, I was intrigued by the geological marvel of volcanic josephites. Nor could I anticipate the terrifying events that unfold deep inside the Medallion Caves. Or the astounding scientific and anthropological findings concerning Rep'huselans, the presumed Neolithic ancestors of today's Ferendese, who left their people's likeness memorialized in sacred caverns unknown to posterity until now.

I am aware that anglophone readers, and Westerners generally, lack a familiarity with the Ferendes that historically they enjoy with Singapore, say, or Hong Kong. There are many reasons for this, not the least being revolutionary tumult that has regularly punctuated the sham tranquillity of civic repression. Nor, geopolitically, does that nation sit restfully on earth, being centred as it is in the South China Sea over inestimable hydrocarbon prospects openly coveted by a rapacious, expansionist and militarist near neighbour.

Nevertheless, I feel I have done my homework here as well. Earlier this year I visited the parish of St Alonzo's in Madregalo where, in my capacity as a former abbess, I was invited to address their deconsecration working party. This was an opportunity to learn more about Ferende culture, meet with theologians, and venture far into the suburbs to hear about ordinary life under their new and mysterious monarch, Prince Arnaba.

Of course, for the academically curious, the main excitement out of the Ferendes is not to do with the Shuffler, or liquid-core geodes, or Stone Age roadworks. It is about language. And the world's foremost authority on birdsong linguistics, Nicholas Misgivingston, happens to base his swint field studies at the Cambridge-administered Language Diversity Initiative research station in that country's remote Joseph Plateau. In this volume, you will find the latest science expertly summarized, along with informal reflections by Dr Misgivingston and unpublished conjectures about the swint's thricing behaviour, multilingualism and capacity to count.

All this, I know, would be enough to draw you in; but wait! For those with the courage to embark, there is offered a chaperoned journey through the underworld in the company of American poet Monica Moreish. Hailed the Dante of our era, her acutely observed travelogue rendered in elegant cantos has enabled our own author to provide in the present work a modernized, practical and English cartography of Hell, highlighting previously unknown dangers and recommending realistic strategies for escape.

You have opened your personal book of change; now it dares you into destiny. But be warned: *This work contains implicit language.* (And some explicit.) It is safely read and internalized only by the sound in mind and pure of soul. If you are one amongst those, perhaps with ambitions to outwit Satan and even aspirations to immortality, take seriously our nameless author's prescription, which is to study probability and the geometry of circles. Also, do as I have: read his book five times.

Magdalena Letterby

1   TWICING BREAD

DANTE, ARIZONA. 1877

Keff leaned forward, squinting to read, one hand combing his horse's mane.

'Tom Worse, Baker. All ya k-neads met. What's k-neads mean, Rigo?'

'Jesus, Keff, ya dope, it says needs, spelled wrong. Smells good. Get's a loaf.'

Keff stayed mounted, slightly standing in the stirrups as he called loudly, 'Baker!'

A man stepped from the shadowed interior; he was wearing a blue-white striped long apron and a black bandanna scarf. He picked flour from his hands as he spoke. 'The name's Worse.'

'Hey Rigo. He dressed like a butcher. You wanna meat loaf? Could be worse.'

Keff folded over in mirth, recovering just enough to demand, 'Get the man a loaf, and I mean bread, mister.'

Worse looked at Keff unresponsively, then at Rigo, who returned a cold stare.

'I was a butcher once,' said Worse. 'Miss it, somehow. Miss the blood.'

Rigo's expression didn't change. 'What side was you, baker? Where was you butcherin'?'

'What's that to you? War's long gone.'

'Shut your mouth, baker. No one answers back to Mr Rigo.'

Keff's flare of temper made him tense in the saddle. His

horse felt it, moving sideways nervously. Worse read the animal, and the rider, and ignored them.

'Side of principle, where I could find it. Butchering mongrels, where I could find them. Service of humanity generally.'

Worse glanced at Keff, then back to Rigo. 'Reckon I missed some.'

Their gaze was locked for a few seconds, interrupted by Keff.

'Mister, folks die from passing insults. You wanna die in a fleck of a town called Dant?'

'Dant-tay, Keff,' Rigo shot at him irritably.

'Like the Inferno, Keff. That's where the Host gets baked.'

Worse turned back into the shadows, re-emerging with a wrapped loaf. He approached Rigo on the side away from Keff, and passed him the bread.

'I call this loaf a twicing. Enough for you both. That'll be a dollar.'

Rigo took the bread and looked at Keff, as if to an interpreter.

'Baker, nobody pays a dollar a loaf. And Mr Rigo, he don't pay nothing. You know who Mr Rigo is? Hey, baker?'

'I know. He's a Mortiss brother. I've seen a reward poster. Only, up close he's even uglier than an artist can draw without dying. That's a half-dollar for the bread, half for delivery. No credit.'

Keff stared at Worse, shocked. Then, deciding they were dealing with a simpleton, he began to laugh again. Worse was looking steadily at Rigo, who pulled sharply on a strap, causing his horse to round on Worse, snorting loudly. Worse didn't recoil, instead reaching up and stroking the mare's face, speaking softly. In return, the horse nuzzled, but Rigo pulled her away with the left rein.

'So that's a dollar, or the bread returned, or I'll take the horse in lieu, if that's your preference.'

'Go to hell, baker.' Rigo tore at the bread with rotten teeth, and spat a mouthful towards Worse.

'That doesn't qualify as returned. Now it's a dollar or the horse,' said Worse.

Rigo placed the loaf against the horn of his saddle, freeing his hand to hover above a right gun holster.

'Now, mister. I've killed better men for lesser talk. You get back to the kitchen, you hear me? I'll take the bread by way of apology.'

'I'll take the dollar by way of payment.'

Rigo straightened in his saddle.

'There's another payment I like to make, baker. I call it a bullet.'

Worse reached up to stroke the mare.

'No way that would cover expenses. I'd need to take the belt-full, in fairness.'

Keff required time to take in Worse's response, then burst into laughter. He was silenced by a glare from Rigo, and quickly recovered his role.

'Baker, no one talks back smart to Mr Rigo. You upset Mr Rigo, you upset the brothers. And the Mortiss brothers, baker, they don't forgive and they don't forget. You got family, baker?'

Worse ignored him, whispering horse words to the mare but looking at Rigo, who was the first to break the silence.

'Know what I think, baker? We're gonna turn our beasts and ride away, with the bread, with the dollar, with the horse, and less one bullet if you raise objection.'

'And here's what I think,' said Worse. 'You turn away, get yourselves shot as thieving mongrels. I take the dollar, the horse and the cartridge belt for my trouble. You get the bread and a pauper's burial, and the town benevolent fund has the leftovers.'

'You telling me you shoot customers? That ain't good business.'

Rigo's eyes were darting around the shopfront, assessing his risk, checking for witnesses.

'I'm selective, obviously. Just uncivil folk like yourselves, to keep up the bakehouse tone. And discouraging non-payers makes sense because it cuts losses and simplifies bookkeeping, which is definitely good business. Plus it's effective deterrence. Plus it eliminates reoffenders. Whole of Dante knows. You should have come inside and read the conditions of purchase. Pay or die, in summary.'

'Fuck you, baker,' said Keff. 'Kill him, Rigo.'

'Think I might just do that,' said Rigo slowly, eyes now fixed on Worse. He backed his horse up a few paces, testing the situation. It offered Worse a clearer view of Keff, but he spoke to Rigo.

'Your mare's uneven shod on the right foreleg. Be tender before long.'

'You saying you're a farrier now, baker?' Keff's tone was mocking.

Worse answered without looking at him. 'I keep a forge alight, out back. All part of Dante's inferno services. Just don't try raising a gallop, or she'll fall lame.'

'You mind your bad mouth over my mount, mister,' said Rigo.

Worse wrung his hands again, wiping flour onto the apron, at the same time loosening the tie at his waist.

'That'll now be two dollars, accounting for the delay and inconvenience, the expert veterinarian opinion, and the cost of conversation with the dimwitted across there.'

Keff looked stunned. Rigo continued staring, weighing up Worse. Eventually Keff found his place.

'You got a big mouth for a baker, mister. Kill him, Rigo.'

'I'm saying to you, baker, you make your peace real quick with the Lord, as there ain't no preacher hereabouts gonna help you along with a prayer of the departed,' said Rigo.

As if feeling the heat, Worse reached up to loosen his neck scarf, flicking it to the ground. Underneath was an ecclesiastical collar.

'Preacher says the baker's pure and deserving of Heaven. The

Lord tells the preacher two sinners on horseback will appear, each impossibly more stupid than the other, riding to the Inferno. The Lord wants only the horses spared. He's very particular: only the horses.'

Rigo and Keff stared at Worse.

'That'll be four dollars, being just two extra for the words of the Almighty.'

Rigo and Keff were silent.

Worse rubbed his hands together, then clapped, creating a small cloud of flour dust. 'There's something you may not know about flour.'

Rigo's right hand now rested within a fist length of his revolver. 'And what might that be, preacher?'

'Well, with all the understandable God-fearing nervousness and such, the shakes, the sweating and the like, it gives a better pistol grip on that lady-type pearl inlay you've got there.'

As he spoke, he casually pulled the apron sling forward over his head. 'I'd dust up my right hand, if I were you.'

Rigo's gun hand flinched slightly, and he moved it forward to rest on his thigh. Worse knew that he was drying his palm.

'You got a big mouth for a baker, mister. Kill him, Rigo.'

'You hear that, preacher? My friend here, who's a believin' man, finds the evil in your words deservin' of being shot, and I have to agree with him. Now you commune your last time with the Maker because from where I'm sitting I see two guns against the meek pickings of flour dough.'

Worse raised both hands in a sign of benediction.

'Behold the power of two. Now hear what the Lord says of sinners: In number is damnation, for the multiplicity expandeth wrong in the same measure it divideth good.'

'Kill him, Rigo.'

'Then for each among the many, his days to Judgement will become hours, even as the hours of his perdition will be made days.'

'You got a big mouth for a baker, mister. Kill him, Rigo.'

'Well, preacher, the way I see it we still have the power of two guns against the God-speaking, hand-wringing impotence of one pastry-baking mortal,' said Rigo.

'Hear again the lot of sinners: The weakness of one will ever surpasseth the strength of another, wherefore the power of two bringeth the downfall of both.'

'Kill him, Rigo.'

But Rigo had been thinking. His face turned even uglier as he smiled. 'We don't need to do that, Keff. We're too smart to be wasted on the labours of killin'. Better we just get the law to help out with an official town hanging, courtesy of the local justice.' Rigo lifted up the bread, displaying the missing bite. 'What have we got? We was sold a defective product; extortion, threatening behaviour, impersonating a man of the cloth, talk of horse stealing. What's the sheriff gonna say to all that?'

Rigo looked pleased with himself. He put the loaf back on the saddle, stealing a glance at Keff, who was grinning victoriously.

Worse's left hand pulled his apron right down, exposing a right-sided gun holster, and a tin star on his lapel.

'Sheriff's going to say: Pay or die, mongrel.'

Keff jumped with surprise, his horse responding with a complaining snort. Rigo's self-satisfied smile vanished.

'That'll now be eight dollars, to cover the humiliation of public disrobing, and time taken when the baker could be stoking the Lord's inferno. Plus another eight for the sheriff's impartial mediation. Plus sixteen in fees for the deeply considered jurisprudence determination in tort and mercantile law, as well as ongoing pastoral care from the preacher. Total thirty-two. For that you get complimentary flour dusting if the pearl feels damp. Judge Thomas M Worse will oversee collection of the dues and issue a receipt of the court.'

Worse held out his left hand for the money.

'Fuck you, baker.' This time it was Rigo; Keff had decided to stay out of the argument. 'Now, we gonna turn our mounts and ride away from here. You're not gonna shoot a man in the back, being a sheriff and a preacher and a judge, are you?'

'Well now, you seem to have forgotten. First off, I'm a certificated mongrel killer. In that event, where the lead goes in depends on which way the mongrel happens to be running, and I say that's all his choosing.'

'Kill him, Rigo. You can take him. Just kill him.'

Rigo wasn't so sure. He dried his gun hand on the denim again. 'You're saying we can't ride off, without getting shot front or back, unless we pay you thirty-two dollars?'

'Correct, but you're not keeping up with the invoicing. Sixty-four dollars, the advice of a mongrel butcher being highly priced around these parts.'

'Kill him, Rigo. You gotta kill the fucker.'

'Shut up, Keff. I'm thinking.'

Again Rigo's hand wiped along his thigh.

'While you're thinking, I'm asking once only that Keff here slowly take his weapon and drop it to the ground, then dismount on the side I can see him, hands in the air.'

'Now why would I do that, baker?'

'Because I'm arresting you for incitement of a felony, being soliciting a third party killing, as well as bad hygiene, general antisocial attitude and an unworldly ugliness sufficient to cause public alarm, all of which are in violation of town statutes. First the weapon, then get down.'

Keff suddenly found himself a leading actor, and he wasn't used to it. He looked at Rigo, who continued staring at Worse. Keff reasoned that he had nothing to lose and everything to gain by repeating the crime.

'Kill him, Rigo.'

But Rigo wasn't offering any comfort. He kept looking at Worse, and his right hand was now constantly wiping back and forward. Keff was left to find his own way out.

'Now what you gonna do if I just refuse, baker?' The voice lacked depth.

'Well, Keff, you're asking for your fortune told from a mongrel killer right now, and you know his talk is very expensive. Can you figure out what that question might cost you, Keff?'

'Christ. Fuck you, baker.'

Keff's right hand reached for his gun, but not slowly enough. Nor was it quickly enough. Before his weapon was completely drawn, he slumped forward in the saddle, his jaw anchored over the pommel and a point-45 bloodless roundel centred on his forehead.

The event took Rigo completely off guard. He turned to look at Keff and started, audibly catching his breath. Worse reholstered his gun.

'Resisting arrest. Cursing a lawman. Attempted murder. There's a sweet, uncomplicated judicial killing, I'd say, with a Churchman's blessing and the aroma of fresh-baked bread. What could be kinder?'

Rigo was unable to see Keff's head wound and couldn't know where he was hit.

'My friend needs a doctor, mister, plain as day. Call the town quack, for Christ's sake. Get him some help.'

'We're humane and caring folk in Dante. Doc always attends a shooting.'

Worse reached to a rear pocket with his left hand, producing a stethoscope that he slung lazily around his neck. He tilted his head sideways and studied Keff quizzically.

'Nothing I can do, sadly. I pronounce his life extinct. Cause of death: execrable depravity. An evocative final pose, you'll agree; doubled up like that in homage to the twicing, I expect. Reverend, should you say some words?'

Worse muttered in Latin, hands clasped before him and eyes downcast. Then he looked up brightly.

'Now, in the matter of payment. There's sixty-four dollars arrears, plus another sixty-four in sheriff costs, attending physician's comprehensive consultation, and the preacher's solemn Bible talk customized to the unredeemed. Within that, there's a one-off penalty for the final blaspheme which I determine offensive to the Divinity as well as all bakers. There are also burial expenses for one, plus retainer for a second anticipated. I should say those interment fees have been generously discounted by the town mortician, on account of the corpse not being too messy, supplying its own transportation, and the economy of a two-for-one excavation. So that's one hundred twenty-eight dollars owing, cash only, or the horse in kind.'

Worse clapped his hands sharply in the manner of using a gavel. '*Res judicata*, Judge Worse presiding. Be assured the offer of flour *gratis* still holds.'

Rigo, though looking at Worse, seemed to be staring trance-like into the distance. He hadn't even seen the gun draw, it was so fast. When he spoke, it was emptily, without emotional presence.

'You're telling me you're the undertaker as well in this stinking town?'

'As the sign says, all your needs met. Temporarily. Funny thing is I'm a stand-in, but it's lie-down easy compared with baking.'

Rigo continued looking absently at Worse, only half listening, his mouth fallen open. He was trying to understand how one small misjudgement about a dollar could come to this. But his thinking was blunted, circling ineffectually around intimation, incomprehension, and irrelevancy.

'What happened to the undertaker?' he asked flatly.

'Appetite for bread beyond his means.'

Keff's horse suddenly sensed her deadweight. She snorted and bucked a little, shifting her rump away. The effect was to point Keff in Rigo's direction. What Rigo saw froze his spine: only a supremely confident gunfighter would make a single head shot under pressure.

'As I was saying, one hundred twenty-eight dollars. It's an exceptional loaf, being the staff of the Lord's own inferno. And, of course, you get to eat both ends of it now, blessed be Keff.'

Rigo spent the following seconds in a chill turmoil of indecision and resolve. All his life, the weapon at his side had served to settle conflict. Now for the first time, when he had no choice, it looked too hard.

His hand stopped rubbing, and Worse noticed.

'You might want to close your mouth for the afterlife,' Worse advised, 'it being sulphurous where you're headed.'

'You're one son-of-a-bitch, baker.'

Rigo was fast. His hand, so near to his gun at the start, had a grip of the pearl inlay, the barrel fully drawn from the holster and almost aligned. But his cold-sweated trigger finger wasn't yet closed on the steel when his head jerked back with the impact of Worse's shot. At the same time, his horse reared up in fright, flinging rider and loose kit backwards from the saddle.

Worse stepped forward to calm the mare, speaking in the same reassuring voice as before, holding the leather down firmly, stroking her face. He would care for her, reshoe her, and rename her. 'Twicing', perhaps, in recognition of the day's exchange: this beautiful, spirited animal for the loaf now settled in the Main Street dust before its buyer's sightless stare and gaping mouth.

An account of the gunfight is given in the Dante *Judgment Daily* of June 11, 1877, under the heading '**Incident at Bakehouse**'. It had been witnessed from an open second-floor window in a lodging house by one Miss Baker, seamstress, whose attention was drawn when she thought she heard her surname called. Two weeks later, an unnamed wit penned the epitaph:

> Here lies one called Rigo Mortiss.
> Drank like a hare but drew like a tortoise.
> Couldn't shoot and couldn't spell
> Funny how he's shot to Hell
> Signing in with *Rigor Mortis*.

(Such crude and heartless parodies were common in the era.) In fact, the Mortiss grave would have been unmarked. The historic Boot Hill cemetery has itself long been buried, currently under a shopping emporium.

The hapless Keff is remembered only for a single utterance, because it proved prophetic, to the effect that the Mortiss brothers would never forgive and never forget. He was probably Kevin Dupain Fister, who was wanted in Hericho for horse stealing and multiple killings.

[**Editor's note** Readers are referred at this point to Appendix A. The author has advised that supplementary materials provided there ideally should be read concurrently with corresponding chapters in the text. Alison Pilcrow, UITA Press]

2 STATION BWRD (TRANSCRIPT)

[Music fade]

[Studio] That number was for Shirley from Duran who says 'Come back, baby; Haley's moved out and I love you again'. You are tuned to BWRD, the voice of Dante, Arizona. We'll be back with more requests after the traffic report, and remember, folks, our lines are always open. We want to hear from all the good citizens of Dante about your news, your troubles and your joys. Stay on BWRD, the station in Dante, for Dante.

[Traffic report. Commercials]

[Studio] This is Mike Pincher back with you on BWRD, bringing you your favourite music and talk-show program. Right now, we have some breaking news for you folks. Seems like an executive jet has disappeared from radar while transiting the Dante tracking sector, about eighty miles north of town. That would be deep inside the Bleacher Desert, so let's hope those airborne folk are okay up there. Our next number is from Duran, who dedicates the track to Marilyn with the message 'Come back, baby; Shirley's moved out and I love you again'.

[Music]

[Studio] Nice choice, Duran. Let's hope Marilyn is tuned to the best airplay in the west, BWRD, the station making wireless waves in Dante. Now we have an update on that missing airplane for you, folks. Our Flyover traffic reporter Dan Jammer is heading north with pilot Buzz Wingles to take a look in the Bleacher. We now cross live to your station BWRD's own search and rescue 'copter mission. Dan, what can you tell us about events. Is disappearing from radar necessarily a bad thing?

[Jammer] It is, Mike. Nearly always. According to Dante control tower, what we have here is radar dropout, loss of voice contact as well as transponder silence. The combination can't be good. It usually means a midair catastrophe, Mike.

[Studio] Dan, do you have information about the plane? Do you have ID on the crew and passengers?

[Jammer] We have preliminary information, Mike. The plane's an FC100 Condor, a new executive model. Apparently it was being ferried from White Sands to San Diego for its owner.

[Studio] And on board? Any ID on the folk on board?

[Jammer] Just the pilot, Mike. We have confirmation there was just the pilot and no passengers, Mike. At this stage we have no ID on the pilot but the indications are that he is an employee of the plane's designer. That's the Flight Control Corporation in New Mexico, Mike.

[Studio] Where are you now, Dan, relative to the possible down zone?

[Jammer] We're well inside the Bleacher, Mike, closing in on the coordinates. I can tell you it is barren and lifeless down there—Buzz! Over there! Something shining!

[Studio] Dan? What are you seeing?

[Wingles] Dante Control Tower. This is BWRD Gridlock Flyover in the Bleacher last contact zone. We have a visual north-west five miles. We're going in for a look. Permission requested one hundred feet over point.

[Dante Control] Dante Control to Gridlock Flyover. Roger that. Affirmative one hundred feet. Bearing north-west. Gridlock Flyover, you will be sub radar. Repeat, you will be sub radar. Maintain voice contact. Advise status two-minute parcels. Gridlock Flyover, you have Sheriff Bird tracking. State visual on Sheriff Bird.

[Studio] Dan. What's happening?

[Static. Speech inaudible]

[Wingles] Gridlock Flyover to Dante Control. Confirm radar advisory. Confirm two-minute parcels. Negative visual for Sheriff Bird. Approaching possible airplane wreckage. Four miles.

[Studio] Dan?

[Jammer] Mike, we can see something shiny on the ground, about four miles away. We're heading towards it. It's hard to make out. Doesn't look like an intact plane, unfortunately. You would have heard there's a sheriff's helicopter on the way as well. Buzz? Can you communicate with the sheriff?

[Wingles] BWRD Gridlock Flyover to Sheriff Bird. Do you read me?

[Static] This is Sheriff Bird. Loud and clear, Gridlock Flyover. What do you see?

[Wingles] We have visual, two, three miles. Confirm aircraft wreckage. One large component.

[Studio] Dan? You are streaming through to our listeners. What do you have for us?

[Jammer] Mike, we are closing in on the wreckage. Buzz is just pulling around and taking us down to one hundred feet for a better look. It's a big bit of the plane. Hard to see yet but I think it's the wings, still joined. There seem to be no other parts of the plane in view, no fuselage or undercarriage. Yes, it's the two main wings still joined but no fuselage between them. The rest could be miles away. There's a scar in the desert floor for about two hundred yards as if it came in on a shallow angle. [Shouting] Buzz! Buzz! Look! Jesus Christ! Oh shit, excuse me.

[Broadcast delay triggered: 4 sec. Six word deletion: -1 to -6]

[Studio] You're okay with that, Dan. What is it?

[Sheriff Bird] Sheriff Bird to Gridlock Flyover. Sheriff Thomas M Worse speaking. Station BWRD: maintain radio silence UFN. Gridlock Flyover: report what you see.

[Wingles] Tom, you're not going to believe this. A guy just stepped out from the shade under the wing and climbed onto it and he's waving at us.

[Sheriff] Buzz, are you saying there's a man down there waving at you? Where did he come from? Do you see a vehicle? Tyre tracks? Is he some crazy desert hiker?

[Wingles] None of that. You know hikers don't last six hours out here. He looks great. Tom, we're not graded to put down on sand. We'll drop some bottled water and stand off till you arrive.

[Sheriff] Roger that, Buzz. Good work, Gridlock Flyover. We have you on screen. Our ETA is three minutes. BWRD, you may resume communications.

[Studio] Dan! You can see a man on the wreckage? You think the pilot survived?

[Jammer] Mike. No way that's possible. We see the two main wings still held together by the spar. That's all. Nothing else.

[Studio] Except a man down there. Could he have parachuted down, then found the wing to shelter from the sun?

[Jammer] Well, I guess. He's got something in his hand, waving at us. Can you make out what it is, Buzz?

[Wingles] No way that's a parachute, Dan. Looks just like a ribbon or a necktie to me. Gridlock Flyover to Sheriff Bird, I see you closing.

[Sheriff] Roger that, Gridlock Flyover.

[Studio] This is Radio BWRD, Mike Pincher in the studio, bringing you news of an executive jet crash up in the Bleacher. If you've just joined us, I can tell you we have our very own Dan Jammer and pilot Buzz Wingles over the wreckage now. They have clear visual of a man on the ground. At this stage we don't know if he's a survivor or unrelated to the crash. The sheriff's 'copter is close to the scene. Unlike Buzz's, it has the sand shielding to put down in the desert and rescue the man. Dan, what's the latest?

[Jammer] Thanks, Mike. The sheriff's machine is just landing. The scene's a bit obscured by the dust blow at the moment. We're pulling away some as we don't have sand-proofed mechanicals, Mike.

[Studio] I understand that, Dan. Can you see anything yet?

[Jammer] Mike, Sheriff Thomas M Worse is walking over to the wreckage and the man on the wing has jumped onto the sand to meet him. He looks completely uninjured, Mike. It's amazing, if he came down on that piece of debris.

[Studio] Dan, we have reports from Dante Control Tower that the plane was at thirty thousand feet when it was lost to radar. There's no way that could be the pilot you're looking at down there.

[Jammer] You're right, Mike. That's a crazy thought. I wonder who he is though. Mike, Sheriff Worse and the man are just getting into the other helicopter. Buzz, can we see if we can get the story down there?

[Wingles] Sheriff Bird. This is BWRD Gridlock Flyover standing off. I advise you are open mike to BWRD listeners. Sheriff Worse, do you have an ID on the man? How was it that he was on the ground right there?

[Sheriff] This is Sheriff Thomas M Worse Sixth. The sole occupant of the FC100 Condor jet that disintegrated in flight north of Dante this morning was the pilot, Walter Reckles. I am happy to report that Walter Reckles survived and has been rescued from the desert crash site. He will be flown to Dante for a medical check. He states that his only injury is a bruised shoulder where he was hit by a water bottle. I will issue a comprehensive statement later today. Dr Reckles advises that when the plane broke up after colliding with a rogue drone he piloted the wing section down to a smooth landing in the desert. He says this was possible due to the good math and a spare necktie. I have nothing further to add at this stage. Over and out.

[Jammer] There you have it, Mike. The pilot, a Walter Reckles, is alive and well. The sheriff's helicopter is just leaving the scene to return to Dante. We can expect the Transportation Safety Board will have their investigators on the ground later today. They'll need to locate the rest of this Condor jet and recover the flight recorder. As well as search for the wreckage of the drone, I guess. But what we can say at this stage, Mike, is that we have witnessed a miracle up here this morning. This is Dan Jammer reporting from BWRD Gridlock Flyover up in the Bleacher. Over to you, Mike.

[Studio] Thanks, Dan. Well folks, you heard it first on Station BWRD. The air crash in the Bleacher has a happy ending. Let's hear some happy music to go with it. Here's a number requested by Duran and dedicated to a lucky lady called Simone. Duran says 'Come back, baby; Marilyn's moved out and I love you again'.

3 ANNA CAMENES TO RICHARD WORSE

Dear Richard

I don't think you ever met Walter Reckles from the US, but I know we spoke of him. He was the designer of Edvard's research balloon *Abel*, and I remember you commented on the ingenuity of the brim shape when Edvard and I were wearing his patent tornado-proof hats in Madregalo last year.

We have just heard that he miraculously survived a plane crash in Arizona, which we are all naturally very pleased about. I am including a link to a news report, partly because it's an amazing story, but also because I couldn't help noticing the local sheriff's name, and wondered if there might be a family connection to you.

You are probably unaware that I write occasional pieces for the popular aerospace press, and some time ago I interviewed Walter for a piece in *Aviation Reviews* on the very subject of surviving aircraft catastrophes. There's an abridged version in the book by Darian, but if you don't have that and are interested you can find the full interview at the second link below. *AR* has asked me to go back to New Mexico to reinterview him, but that will take some tricky scheduling for us both. I do think you and Walter would get on if you were to meet.

Rodney Thwistle tells us constantly what a fabulous time he had with you in Perth. He seems a much more talkative soul than when his radius of experience ended at the Cambridge ring road. Edvard says that in conversational word count, Australian wine may soon surpass mathematics, which I'm sure you will agree is a very surprising development for Rodney.

Edvard's monograph on Thomas MacAkerman and the early documentation of weaver fish is launching next month. After the events in Madregalo, he had to rewrite completely the Afterword, which took considerable time. I believe UITA Press is to make it available in Australia following release in the UK.

On the subject of weaver fish, we both read Darian's book with a mixture of delight and dismay. Granted, he's a balanced and meticulous historian, but it's still quite disconcerting to see one's own unwitting presence in those events placed on the historical record for all to see. We wonder what your thoughts might be.

Edvard and I are still trying to organize our lives so that we also can take up your offer of a guided tour of the Margaret River region. I hope it will be in the near future. Equally, should circumstances bring you to England, you must stay with us in Chaucer Road.

I expect you know that Millie has been offered a visiting professorship in Perth, though I am unsure as to when she will take it up. She recently re-joined Rodney's department, and has become a Fellow of Nazarene College.

Nicholas is back in the Ferendes now that the dreadful revolution business is over. Apparently, they have found an amazing complex of caves deep inside the Joseph Plateau, quite near the LDI station. The exciting thing is that there are prehistoric pictograms and possibly primitive alphabetic elements on the walls. Edvard has been studying photographs sent by Nicholas but, as you might imagine, he is beside himself with impatience to return and explore the site personally.

The other news from out there is that the swints have returned—presumably some of the very ones you released from captivity last year. Nicholas said there were hours of murmuration in the form of a cross over Madregalo before they roosted in the palace. I suppose the fact that the new prince is a man of the cloth has drawn them back. There's forgiveness, if ever there were.

Edvard sends his best wishes. He and I are well, and we hope you are also. Do tell us your news.
With kind regards
Anna

Anna Camenes is a research psychiatrist at the Compton Institute in Cambridge. She is the partner of **Edvard Tøssentern**, a linguistics professor who started the international **Language Diversity Initiative**. His special interest has been the insinuation of weaver fish lore into Ferent languages. An LDI field station in a remote part of the **Ferendes** is managed by **Paulo Cinnamonte**, and has as resident statistician and volunteer factotum **Nicholas Misgivingston**. **Walter Reckles** is an aeronautical engineer and founder of Flight Control Corporation, based in New Mexico. These five previously collaborated in a breakthrough study of the novel embryology and flight science of the Asiatic condor, which is native to the Ferendes. Their paper has not yet appeared but some details are given in the recent history from **A B C Darian**, entitled

The Weaver Fish, which documents events leading up to the Ferende revolution.

Richard Worse is a security analyst working in Perth. He knows personally Anna, Edvard and Nicholas, but not the others. **Rodney Thwistle** is a Cambridge mathematician who has enjoyed a long-standing correspondence with Worse on advanced cryptography algorithms, and recently was Worse's guest on a holiday wine tour of Western Australia.

Millie is **Emily Misgivingston**, Nicholas's sister and also a mathematician. People who know both her and Worse think they would make a good couple, and on occasions hint as much. In the first hours of the Ferende revolution, Worse and Millie together entered the deserted Palace L'Orphania in Madregalo and set free thousands of **swints** kept caged by Prince Nefari, whose violent death began the turmoil. The fact is briefly mentioned in Darian's book. Anna's remark about the newly acceded Crown Prince Arnaba, a theologian and cleric, alludes to the common belief that swints settle only on property that is sanctified in some way.

4 RICHARD WORSE TO THOMAS WORSE (1)

Dante County Sheriff's Office
Dante, Arizona, USA
PRIVATE: For Attention of Sheriff Thomas M Worse
Personally

My name is Richard M Worse, and I write to you from
Perth, Western Australia. I have recently become
aware of the news story about Walter Reckles, who is
the friend of a friend, but more intriguingly, I noted
your name in the online reports. Please forgive me
if I intrude in any sense, but I wondered if we might
be distantly related. If the 'M' in your name stands
for Magnacart (or perhaps, in America, it has been
phoneticised to Marnacourt, or something similar),
then that is definitely the case. If not, we are unrelated
and I apologize for imposing the enquiry on your
time. My only excuse is that, as my years advance, I
have become more interested in my extended family
and more attentive to the responsibilities of its
ancient motto.
Regards
Richard Magnacart Worse

Dear Richard
Your email was indeed an intrusion, but the most
interesting and welcome one in the working day of

a sixth-generation lawman. Definitely, no apology is required. I have often wondered about my southern hemisphere cousins, about whom my father seemed disappointingly uninformed other than to pass on a family joke about the 'Worse' branch of our ancestors settling in Australia rather than America (I'm sure you had the corresponding merriment down under). Let me express my unreserved delight that you have made contact, and I hope that one day we might meet in person.

Famille Oblige.

Thomas Magnacart Worse VI

For readers unaware of its history, the name **Magnacart** is pronounced Marnacourt. The motto, which dates from the thirteenth century, is shared with the **Misgivingston** lineage, and is a patrilineal oath to protect within and between the two families.

5 AREA PI

The operation to retrieve the Condor wreckage was conducted by the Transportation Safety Board with policing support from the Dante County Sheriff's Office. Convinced that the cause of the crash was collision with a drone, Walter Reckles was keen for the investigation to report promptly so that the reputation of Flight Control Corporation and its Condor design was not damaged.

Though forward orders for the FC100 tapered off pending a reassuring board finding, there was one unexpected benefit for Reckles from the disaster. His spectacular survival, judged miraculous by all in the press, had garnered national attention and his story and explanations were widely sought. Extraordinary, then, that he had already prepared a book on the very subject, *How to Walk Away from a Midair Collision*, which publishers previously had been reluctant to take on. Now there was an industry clamour to win the rights, with rumours of advance fee auction estimates exceeding two million dollars.

Eventually, a local Delegate Board of Enquiry was convened and a preliminary hearing scheduled. It was to be held in a hotel conference facility in Dante, and not expected to be a drawn-out affair. There would be a statement of facts, witness testimony, and presentation of interim findings from board investigators. Reckles was required to attend.

Walter agreed to a comprehensive follow-up interview with Anna for *Aviation Reviews*, and after much negotiation over dates they decided that the best place to meet would be in Dante during the hearing. Anna could attend using an *AR* press pass and obtain more background for her story. As well, she hoped to speak to people involved in the rescue, in particular Sheriff Worse. She flew to Dante and checked into her hotel.

Edvard
You will be pleased that you haven't come. I am staying at a place called the Boot Hill Emporium Hotel, known by the locals as the BHEH, pronounced Bee Hay. Walter is arriving later today. The hearing starts tomorrow afternoon and is being held in one of the rooms in this complex. I need to rest for a while, so will write later tonight.
Love Anna

Anna slept till 5.00 pm. She found an email from Walter saying he had arrived at the BHEH and asking if she were free for dinner. She replied, suggesting 8.00 pm. Then she showered and went for a walk, exploring the historic sites of Dante.

When she returned to the hotel, Walter was seated in the lobby in conversation with another man who was wearing a business suit. She waved and walked towards them. They both stood up, and Walter came forward to greet her. He asked about her flight, then turned to introduce his companion.

'Anna, this is Sheriff Thomas Worse. Thomas, this is Anna Camenes.'

Anna was astounded at his resemblance to Richard. When he spoke she was more astounded by how different were their accents.

'A pleasure to meet you, Anna.' Thomas reached out to shake hands. 'I hope you enjoy our finest Dante hospitality during your stay.'

'A pleasure to meet you also, Thomas. I believe I know your Australian cousin, Richard Worse. We shared some dramatic adventures in the Ferendes recently.'

'Oh yes. I was very pleased that he got in touch. You must tell me about him. Will you join us?'

Anna sensed that she may have interrupted an important discussion, and declined. She arranged that Walter would come by her room just before 8.00, and excused herself.

Anna returned to her room. When she entered, she found an unaddressed envelope slipped under the door. Inside was a single sheet of BHEH guest stationery and a handwritten message.

> I spy with my little eye
> Something ending with Pi.
> There are engines and wings
> And guidance and things
> But nothing to see in the sky.

She wanted to share it with Walter, and took the elevator back to the lobby. Walter and Thomas were still there, and as she approached they both looked at her expectantly. Again, she felt she was interrupting, and made her reason clear without delay.

'I found this under my door.' She held out the sheet to Walter. 'Why would anyone give me that? Who would know that I'm here about the investigation?'

'Any number of people could know that,' said Thomas without elaboration.

Walter handed him the message.

'It appears you have a secret corroborator,' said Thomas to Walter. 'It's obviously referring to an unmanned aerial vehicle.'

'But a limerick? How serious is that?' asked Anna.

'Oh, don't mind that. It's a Dante tradition from way back,' said Thomas.

'What is the Pi reference, do you think?' asked Walter.

'That's the most interesting part,' said Thomas. 'You probably haven't spent enough time in Dante to know about

Area Pi. It's a research establishment north-west of here, under federal regulation so my office isn't too involved. It has the same mythical relationship to Dante as Area 51 does to Vegas. Conspiracy, paranoia, alien experimentation, government secrecy, that sort of thing. Any cab driver will tell you about it, only they won't take you there.'

'Why?' asked Anna.

'They've heard stories and they're scared,' said Thomas.

'With reason?' she asked.

'Maybe,' said Thomas.

Anna looked at both men.

'Shall I take that?' she said, reaching for the sheet. 'I'll see you for dinner, Walter. I can bring you up to date with research in the Ferendes. Good night, Thomas. I hope I see you again.'

'I am sure you will. At the hearing tomorrow, if not before. Good night, Anna.' Thomas stood up as she left. 'Oh, Anna,' he added. 'Take my card, please. Call if you need any assistance.'

The mall space that formed the lower floors of the hotel had some very fine restaurants. Anna and Walter chose Commedia. After ordering, Anna brought the subject around to the board investigation.

'How are you feeling about tomorrow, Walter?'

'I'll be happier when my testimony is over. It's not all that easy reliving the breakup of the plane.'

'Are you sure you want to do our interview?'

'I'm fine with that. You're not going to be cross-examining me, pushing disbelief onto the facts.'

'Why do you think tomorrow will be like that?'

'Thomas has given me some warning. It seems there is a rather unpleasant individual who's managed to inveigle himself onto the board.'

'I'm sure you will be treated with the greatest respect,

Walter. Why should you not be?'

'We'll see.'

Anna changed the subject. 'What are you doing in the morning?'

'Nothing special. Maybe a walk. What about you?'

'I was thinking I might rent an SUV and head out to Area Pi. That's where our anonymous poet is directing us. Want to ride shotgun with me?'

Walter grinned. 'Can I have the AK upgrade?'

The rental car was delivered to the BHEH at seven o'clock the next morning. Anna could find no information about the location of Area Pi, and certainly no address to input to a GPS device. She asked the hotel concierge for directions.

'Ma'am, you won't find that name on any maps. Some folk think there's no such place.'

'What road would we take if it were there?'

'Ma'am, we don't recommend that route to our guests. It's not, ah, scenic, ma'am.'

Anna gently protested that everything in America was scenic to the English, and he gave her a map with a back road to Phoenix highlighted.

'Take water,' he said. 'When do you expect to be returning to the BHEH?'

'Midday, I would think. We're attending the safety board hearing at two.' She held up the map. 'Thank you for this.'

Anna turned to join Walter, but the concierge called her back.

'Ma'am. Dr Camenes. Don't go out beyond half a tank. You won't find gas in those parts, and there aren't folk willing to help.'

They walked out onto the concourse to their car. Walter drove while Anna navigated. Forty minutes later, they were well along the barren, unsealed Route 3141. Out there, it seemed like a road from nowhere to nowhere. Anna stretched forward to look in a wing mirror, watching the plume of dust erupting behind them.

'Walter. Do you find this country scenic?'

'It's always better from the air, Anna. Anyway, I'm not here for the scenery.' He leaned forward to peer at the road ahead, clenching the steering wheel with both fists, and adopted a yokel voice. 'I come for da shootin'.' Anna glanced across to find him grinning.

When she first interviewed Walter for *Aviation Reviews*, it had been a rather formal exchange, and she was sometimes regretful that she may have portrayed him a little unkindly to the *AR* readership. Her self-justification was that his ideas on survival really did seem somewhat bonkers at the time, though now his spectacular appearance in the Bleacher Desert was unarguable vindication. She felt this second interview was an opportunity to rebalance the sentiment of the first.

Besides, she had come to really like Walter, and respect his skill as an aeronautical engineer. When he joined their team in the Ferendes studying the flight mechanics of the Asiatic condor, he had brought enthusiasm, humour and theoretical rigour. She was pleased to see him.

'How's the fuel level?' she asked after a long silence.

'We'll make it to the horizon and back.'

They fell silent again. Anna was looking at the landscape, but thinking about her interview. Actually, she was starting to think about something quite different from a normal interview, more a story about Walter and his experience, with conversational passages and reportage on the board hearing. She would email a concept plan to her editor.

'Shall we try the radio?' she asked.

Walter fiddled with controls on the steering wheel. They came in halfway through an announcement, but it repeated constantly. Both found it difficult to believe what they were hearing.

Driver of silver SUV heading west on 3141. You are entering a restricted area. Proceed no further. Turn back. Turn back now.

Walter flicked through several stations, finding the same message on them all.

'They've hijacked our system,' he said.

Anna was frightened. 'I think we should stop.'

Walter was already slowing down. She looked around at the desolation.

'How can they see us?'

'Probably from a drone.'

Turn back now.

Walter was furious. 'Who do they think they are? It may be a dirt track, but it's a state highway. It's got a number. It's a public throughway.'

He began turning the car, under protest.

'Walter. Look.'

Anna pointed in the direction they had been travelling. Appearing from over a small hill, a vehicle dust cloud was coming toward them at high speed.

Walter briefly considered trying to outrun them, but remembered his right to be there. They were now facing back to Dante, and had driven half a mile before an SUV in camouflage paint came almost bumper-close to theirs, sounding its horn. Walter slowed and pulled over.

The other vehicle passed and stopped in front of them. Two men in militia fatigues got out and walked back to them, one on either side. They each rested a hand on a holstered pistol as they approached. It was an arrogant display of threat.

Anna applied an old lesson in personal security; she placed her smartphone, switched on to voice record, on the gear selector console between the seats. Walter lowered his window, but kept Anna's closed.

'What's your business in these parts, sir?'

'What's your right to ask that, and what's your right to stop us?' said Walter.

Anna was scared, and her natural impulse was to be polite and conciliatory, perfected over years of professional practice dealing with confrontational psychiatric patients, and their families. All the same, she was impressed by Walter's (typically American, as she saw it) asserting of his rights and challenge to authority. She would have said, 'We're tourists. On a daytrip. Is there a problem?' and smiled.

The man who spoke scowled. He held out a hand.

'ID.'

'No,' said Walter. 'You show me your ID. Then I'll know what authority you have. That's the law.' He added provocatively, 'You're not police, are you? Not state troopers. Not federal. What are you? Private security? Dressed up? We're on a public access road and we'll drive where we like. Right now we are going to Dante.'

Anna had always viewed Walter as mild mannered. She was astonished at his reaction. Astonished, scared, and admiring.

The man stared coldly at Walter.

'Getting back to Dante, you need a serviceable vehicle.'

He stepped forward and gave the front tyre a kick.

Just then, Anna saw something profoundly reassuring. A dust plume was speeding towards them from the direction of Dante. The others hadn't seen it. She looked at the second man, on her side of the car. He was staring at her. She lowered her window.

'But you people would help out if we had any car trouble, wouldn't you?'

She spoke lightly, as if there had been nothing disagreeable between them and a charitable act would be a matter of course in that remoteness. The second man made eye contact with the first, then looked at Anna.

'Men take care of themselves in this country, miss,' he said.

That was a 'No', and it was also menacing. Anna glanced

discreetly forward. The car was approaching very fast, and to her relief she could see flashing red and blue roof lights. She looked at the man beside her, nodded slightly, and raised her window in disapproval.

Walter at last seemed to understand that they were dealing with borderline criminals, and that civilian rights counted for little in the middle of nowhere. He had become quiet.

Not until the sheriff's office patrol car turned on its siren in the last few hundred yards did the militiamen realize it was approaching. They watched as it pulled up close to their own vehicle. The man beside Walter stepped away.

'Make sure you don't come back.'

Both walked towards their vehicle with what Anna saw as an exaggerated saunter, and stopped to confer on the way.

The police officers sat in their car for several minutes, lights still flashing. To Anna the delay was a statement of power. When two men got out, one was carrying a rifle cradled in his elbow, pointed at the ground. He held up a hand to indicate to the militias that they should stay where they were. Then he leaned against their vehicle to watch. The other officer walked up to Walter's window, tilting his head to look inside.

'Dr Reckles, Dr Camenes. Are you both okay?'

'We're okay, thanks. Very relieved to see you,' said Walter.

'I'm Deputy Lloyd. My partner is Deputy Wright. Do you have a complaint against these two?' He pointed towards them.

'They forced us to stop, harassed us, demanded ID, refused to identify themselves, threatened to disable our car. Yeah, we've got plenty of complaints. Especially against that short one.'

'I'm sorry to hear that, sir. Leave it with us.'

Deputy Lloyd walked over to the man who had spoken to Walter. Anna lowered her window to hear the exchange.

'ID.'

'Come on, pal. You see our uniform.'

'I see probable offender. ID.'

The probable offender was just a little slow in complying. Deputy Wright altered his posture, swinging the rifle to point upwards. The butt now rested on his knee, and his grip was around the trigger guard. It was another exhibition of power, and the short man understood it. He handed over a wallet. Lloyd opened it.

'Why did you pull these people over?' he asked without looking up.

'They were already stopped.'

Anna felt an instant frustration that the two would lie their way out. She need not have worried.

'You're lying, Butt. We monitored your broadcast. That was threatening and coercive and a violation of, maybe, fourteen statutes.'

Lloyd held out his hand for the other man's ID. He took both wallets to the patrol car and sat in the driver's seat with the door open and a leg stretched outside. Deputy Wright stayed leaning against the militia SUV, watching but saying nothing.

Anna picked up her smartphone and photographed the scene through their windscreen. It would be material for her *AR* article. A second later, Walter opened his door and the sound caused both militiamen to look towards them. Anna captured their sullen looks when they found Walter grinning broadly.

'Stretching my legs,' said Walter.

Anna thought she would do the same. She got out of the car, carrying her smartphone. Walter walked over towards Wright, who motioned him sideways from his field of view.

'You're Deputy Wright?' said Walter.

'That's me, Dr Reckles. How you doin'?' He was warm but never took his eyes off his charges. Anna joined Walter as he answered.

'Yeah. We're good, thanks. So, did you know we were out here?'

'Word gets around, Dr Reckles.'

'Say, you know where Area Pi is somewhere near here? We've just heard stuff about it,' continued Walter.

'Bad place. Bad people. Over the rise five miles to Pleno, then north nine.'

Deputy Lloyd walked up to them. He nodded silently to his partner, who stood up straight and held out a shepherding arm to move Anna and Walter well to the side. Lloyd took a few extra paces and called out.

'Step apart. Face away. Hands in the air.'

Butt spat at the ground. He looked up to find the rifle now levelled at him, and turned. Lloyd approached them from behind, removing their pistols and putting them down near Wright.

'Hands to back.' Lloyd handcuffed them both. 'Sit down.'

'Company's going to get you for this, you dicks,' said Butt.

'Company's going to write you off, more likely,' said Lloyd.

He caught sight of Walter looking at his watch. It was 11.00 am.

'Are you good with the time, Dr Reckles?'

'Oh yes. We need to be at the hearing by two,' Reckles replied.

'Easily managed,' said Lloyd. 'We'll escort you to the BHEH.'

Lloyd opened the door of the militia SUV and searched inside. He returned, holding the ignition key.

'Get up.

> You're under arrest for breach of the peace
> Public nuisance also. You have a right
> To attorney and quiet
> But I'm holding you tight
> Pending further enquiries.

Back seat. Move it.'

Trying to stand up from a dusty road while handcuffed behind is an awkward business. Wearing a uniform that projects power one moment and is worthless the next gives added humiliation. Walter was grinning as he and Anna returned to their vehicle.

'I'm loving this place,' he said as he settled into the driver's seat. 'They even arrest you with poetry. Are you happy for me to keep driving?'

'Yes,' said Anna. 'Do you think they make that up on the spot, or do they have to learn a whole lot from a manual?'

She turned off the voice recorder on her mobile. 'Wait.' Anna played with some dash controls to record their GPS coordinates.

'Good thinking,' said Walter. 'Route 3141 to this point, plus five west plus nine north, if the deputy's right. I don't know about the limerick thing. We'll ask.'

Thomas Worse chose not to explain that the **Dante limerick** is a serious poetic form considered by American literary cognoscenti as equal in gravitas and sophistication to the sonnet. It is rarely sexual, unless studiously so, and certainly never ribald. Appearing first in the late nineteenth century, and championed by the scholarly proprietors of the *Judgment Daily*, it became a preferred mode of private and civic discourse for the county. That the note to Anna was so composed would have been unsurprising to Thomas.

Visitors to Dante not aware of this tradition are frequently bemused at the limerick's place in ceremony, legislative wording, and the language of higher education. For example, it is common that marriage vows are so worded, as are welcoming remarks or introductions of dignitaries at public events. Occasionally, academic theses are written and defended, not fully but substantially, in the form. The key to understanding its place in Dante society is to appreciate its broad acceptance as the pinnacle of refinement and respectability. That is not to say it is wholly elitist; verse declaration has become an unremarked utility of the everyday, as Lloyd's coarsely manufactured statement of arrest shows. (This author is in possession of a notice of parking violation that, were it not for its acquisition cost, would be collectable for its charm.)

For the world beyond Arizona, the Dante limerick was discovered and popularized by the poet **Monica Moreish**, notably in her emulative masterpiece *Inferno*. (This work is credited with elevating the form in national literary consciousness, a task made easier by renaming the limerick as *canto*.) In her introduction to that volume, Moreish explains how conventions evolved to eschew much of the orthodoxy (such as forced rhyming scheme) of historical variants.

The reader should not for a moment imagine that the lines delivered to Anna reflect the norm for beauty and erudition. Their relative crudeness would have been noted by Thomas in the natural course of considering possible authorship.

6   ANNA TO EDVARD TØSSENTERN

Dear Edvard

Walter and I have had an absolutely shocking day, though it has been much worse for him than for me. The hearing this afternoon went very badly for him. One member of the board was needlessly aggressive and quite dismissive of everything Walter had to say about the crash, the drone collision and so on. The chair was a last-minute substitute and didn't really manage things well. He seemed not to listen to reason, as Walter put it. Poor Walter was left feeling devastated. It wasn't at all what anyone really expected, though Thomas Worse (the chief of police here, and the one related to Richard in Perth) had advised that there might be a bit of argument, but nothing like what happened. After all the unpleasantness, the hearing was adjourned with no date set. I've spent the last two hours debriefing Walter and trying to be supportive. Thomas and Walter and I are meeting for a late supper about 10.30 tonight. I think Thomas will be helpful in supporting Walter too.

This morning was weird as well. Actually, it was extremely scary at one point. We've been hearing about a very secretive research establishment of some kind out in the desert. They call it Area Pi, and no one knows what happens there. The locals are frightened of the place. It seems to operate above the law. In fact, they have a kind of private army with uniforms, guns, and military vehicles and whatever. I was given an anonymous tip-off (why me, I don't know) that it might be relevant to Walter's crash. Anyway, he and I decided to drive out there. We didn't see anything special but their security people stopped us and were most threatening. Fortunately, the real police came and rescued us.

Edvard, I think we need to help Walter. There seems to be a concerted move to disparage his evidence and destroy his reputation. It's so unfair. Walter is becoming convinced that Area Pi is somehow involved in the drone collision. That does seem feasible, and it is what the anonymous note was implying. I was thinking that Nicholas might be able to get some satellite imagery—he managed to do that for you with the logging business in the Ferendes. It would be a start, considering we can't get near the place by road, and no one will talk about it. Would you be happy to ask him?

I hope you are looking after yourself and eating well. I will phone late tonight to catch you at home in the morning. Walter was most interested to hear news about the LDI station. He says he very much enjoyed his stay there. Tell me the latest from the caves project.

Love Anna.

7   THE CIRCULAR SEA

The revolution (officially, orderly succession brought forward) that followed the death of Prince Nefari was over, and executive government in Madregalo had largely returned to normal.

Unhappily for Edvard Tøssentern, as chair of the Cambridge trust running the LDI programme, the Ferende bureaucratic norm slumbered on a scale from indifferent to incompetent. He informed the appropriate departments of the discovery of the caves, their evident anthropologic significance, and the need for a professionally managed survey along with some form of policing to prevent theft and vandalism. Apart from a polite but delayed acknowledgement, administrators had been unresponsive.

On the basis that the cave complex contained primitive hieroglyphs, Tøssentern decided that the scope of the original charter allowing LDI to operate in the Ferendes gave him a legal basis to proceed with exploration and documentation. He instructed his station manager, Paulo Cinnamonte, to apply whatever time and resources were available to the project. Paulo and Nicholas Misgivingston had made several visits, installed some lighting, and begun preliminary mapping of the cave geography with a photographic record of its wall paintings. Meanwhile, Tøssentern was assembling a multi-institution research team, hoping to include academics from the University of Madregalo who might expedite any necessary approvals within the government.

Despite their considerable expenditure in time and effort, the programme of study seemed frustratingly slow to Nicholas. Each visit involved a ten-kilometre round-trip hike through dense forest, carrying all their supplies. From the cave entrance to the first chamber was a thirty-minute descent that was not easy, and as yet had no safety railing or foothold supports. That first chamber was vast, and they had not fully explored its boundaries; they certainly knew nothing of its dome ceiling because their lights could not reach it.

They had, however, discovered the elevated entrance to a tunnel leading from the first chamber to a second that seemed even larger. The passage was difficult, often steep, with blind alleys, side caverns, and at one point a sharp z-bend that was hard to negotiate with bulky equipment. They had been through four times, and found wall paintings near the entrance to the second chamber similar to those in the first.

It was, of course, those wall paintings that mainly drew their interest. For Tøssentern, who knew as much as anyone living about the graphic symbology of past cultures, these were the most mystifying objects he had ever encountered. They lacked the stylistic primitivism and the subject content of animal figuration or the stencilled human hand that are common in the earliest cave art. But nor was there the precision or character definition and repetition found, for example, in later cuneiform or hieroglyphic scripts.

These were, for want of a better description, medallions; black foggy disc-shaped patterns on the pale rock, each about thirty to forty centimetres in diameter and arranged, wherever the flatness of the wall allowed, in extraordinarily disciplined matrices of ordered rows and columns.

When Paulo and Nicholas first discovered them and examined examples closely, they shared an impression that a form of chemical etching was involved in their making.

In several, the black contrast was also subtly tinted pink, though ascertaining true colour under torchlight was difficult. The conjecture about method was retracted after more detailed study, replaced by an admission of complete ignorance regarding manufacture and significance. Their bafflement translated into an *ad hoc* working terminology: the blotchy non-etchings became blotchings, though in serious correspondence with Tøssentern, they remained medallions.

For researchers in linguistics, there was an irresistible prejudice to interpret these palaeographically. The problem for Paulo and Nicholas, and Tøssentern working from Cambridge, was that the usual strategic pathways led no-where. A fundamental property of orthographic systems, alphabetic or otherwise, is repetition—no script would ever be rationally devised where every signifier was unique and non-repeating. (To discover such a string by chance, would be a very unfortunate instance of sampling.) It is this property, repetition, that affords a first-pass statistical analysis; namely, a frequency distribution that may be correlated with hierarchical information from other sources.

However, repetition was not apparent in blotchings. Grossly, medallions were similar to each other, but even under fairly relaxed metrics in discrimination software no two could be judged identical. Moreover, development of appropriate feature recognition algorithms, and investigation of possible classifications based on similarity and difference decision tools, required high-resolution digital reproductions. These they had not yet fully obtained, due to problems with access and lighting.

As well, the effort expended on this seemingly intractable decipherment compromised other urgent directions of research, such as blotching methodology and dating, or the larger questions of what civilization would produce such artefacts and why, and what was their people's fate.

There were other possibilities, of course. Paulo suggested that the medallion arrays had the appearance of an abacus, and their function might be in calculation, which in turn raised the idea of an exchequer or other number record, perhaps related to festivals or astronomical events. Unfortunately, in this case also, very little advancement was possible without a starting point of basic pattern detection.

Their objective today was to install generator lighting at the vestibule opening into the second chamber. Paulo was to carry an extension cord through the tunnel, while Nicholas stayed within the first chamber controlling its feed. They communicated using battery-powered two-way radio headsets.

When Paulo was satisfied that he had secured the new light in a stable and useful position, he asked Nicholas to make the connection to their power distributor in the first chamber, and switch it on.

'How does it look?' asked Nicholas.

'Fantastic, Nicholas. It's completely transformed from what we could see in torchlight.' Paulo paused. 'Stunning. The medallions here seem brighter, richer than the outside ones. Come through. Mind you don't trip on the cable.'

As he approached the inner vestibule, Nicholas could see the glow from Paulo's installation. He decided there definitely was something cheering about the proverbial light at the end of a tunnel.

When he arrived at the chamber, Paulo was setting up camera equipment that had been delivered on a previous visit. They both removed their headsets when Nicholas was close.

They had scheduled one hour in this chamber for Paulo to begin a systematic photographic record of the right-hand medallion wall. On this occasion, Nicholas was free to explore, and after conferring about the best way to sequence the filming, he set off into the darkness.

The ground was moderately rough, and sloping downward. Without warning, he reached an edge, a step down of about ten centimetres, beyond which the stone surface seemed completely smooth. He nearly lost his footing, as there was no shadow to reveal its presence.

Nicholas stopped, and shone his torch to both sides. The step extended evenly in both directions as far as his light would carry. He wasn't certain, but it appeared to have a slight curvature, as if it were the shoreline to a smooth stone sea. Ahead, his torch detected nothing. He looked back. The new mains-powered light was easily visible, but he couldn't see Paulo.

He continued walking. The incline was very gradual, and the surface featureless. From time to time, he checked Paulo's light. It became very small and faint, and he began to think about turning back.

Then he came to the water. So shallow and clear and smooth that he almost stepped into it. He stood at the edge, staring down, mesmerized by its stillness and what he imagined to be an ageless title to purity and secrecy. Again, he looked around. In every direction, his torch beam was lost in darkness. Behind him, he was no longer sure if he could see Paulo's light, and the uncertainty made him a little anxious.

He turned back to face the water, directing his torch downward in front of his feet. The slight anxiety was suddenly replaced by a gripping fear. Where there had been a mirror stillness of the water, perfectly reflecting his curiosity in torchlight, there were now ripples, miniature waves lapping at the rim.

It was in Nicholas's nature to find existence rational, to be confident in mechanistic explanation. But in that isolation and darkness, where his knowledge of the world extended only the range of a weak torch beam, he was instinctually alarmed. The deadness of the water, supposed undisturbed for perhaps thousands of years, had gone in the seconds of his watching. He couldn't see the cause, and he didn't know his part in it. He thought of weaver fish. He thought of Asiatic condors. In an instant his mind conjured up a menagerie of monsters sharing the one dominant importance of being invisibly threatening.

Nicholas swept his light around before turning in the direction he hoped would lead to Paulo. He persuaded himself that, as there was nothing to see, he should leave. But nothing to see could mean things unseen, and he knew that underneath the reasoning was a presumptive, undifferentiated terror. In setting off, he felt the slight dishonour of retreat.

He navigated by keeping his course uphill, and soon was confident of seeing Paulo's light. But it wasn't until he reached the stony shoreline and stepped from smooth to rough rock that he started to feel safe. He shone his torch first to the right, where the delineation looked as before. But to the left, the scene was changed, and it was clear that with the slightness of the incline he had wandered from his previous path.

His torch was reflected in a large sparkling boulder resting at the edge. He walked across, and found it to be one in a row of similar stones, placed about five metres apart, extending down toward the water and uphill into the cave. Beyond these, four metres away, was another row, equally spaced, and parallel to the first, the two giving the appearance of an avenue of sentry stones.

Nicholas reached the first and touched it. The surface was cold and faceted, and when he held his torch to it the whole rock body seemed to glow with ethereal transparency. At his feet he saw some smaller pieces, roughly spherical and about the size of a grapefruit. He collected one to study, and set off toward Paulo. When he was close enough to call out and hear a response, the anxiety was gone.

'You were a long time. What did you find?' asked Paulo when Nicholas entered his light.

Nicholas gave an account of his discoveries, showing Paulo the rock specimen he had taken. He omitted mention of his fear, which now seemed rather groundless. Paulo was unmoved by hearing of ripples in the water.

'There might be low-level seismic disturbance in the plateau. We've never thought about it, but we should monitor that. I'll tell Edvard, because it could be a safety concern for survey teams working down here. Or there may be other cave entrances, or chimneys to the surface. So, fresh water could be feeding in somewhere, perturbing the surface. Or likewise wind. That would be good, if there's ventilation.'

It was easier to be rational when you were safe, thought Nicholas. He knew he had felt no disturbance in the ground, sensed no movement of air, heard no falling water, but he said nothing.

'We need to bring in a canoe, or an inflatable maybe, to explore your lake,' continued Paulo. 'I'll organise water analysis. That can be done in Madregalo.'

It was a reasonable plan, but Nicholas had little enthusiasm. Although the terror was now passed, he did remember it.

'I think we need much better lighting down here, first,' he said.

After their evening meal, Nicholas sat alone in the office that he shared with Paulo. The amount of time they were now devoting to the exploration of the cave was affecting other work, including his private IT consultancy obligations with international banking and insurance clients, as well as the ongoing LDI modelling and analysis programme. He was also trying to keep up with the burgeoning research literature in avian linguistics, a field that he had pioneered.

At one stage he became aware that the office was completely dark except for the glow of his computer screen, and he switched on a desk lamp. Its light played on the cave quartz that he had positioned as a paperweight, and his attention was diverted periodically over the next few hours by its curious and beautiful optical properties.

Those hours were spent following up on the Area Pi request from Tøssentern. None of the commercially available geospatial imagery was particularly informative, unless one's interest was in the detail of roads and roofs. Nor were there online sources explaining the site's purpose. He decided that Walter's needs called for a more intrusive inspection, and he knew of only one person who combined the skills and discretion to achieve that effectively. He emailed Richard Worse.

When that was done, he closed his laptop and turned off the lamp. In the dark, his arm knocked the quartz; he heard it fall off the stack of papers onto the desk and roll to the edge. He felt instantly sickened that in these beginning hours of his custodianship an artefact appropriated from its immemorial resting place would fall to the floor and shatter.

But it didn't shatter. Instead, it flashed with light. Nicholas was confused; he found the switch of the desk lamp and turned it on. He picked up the quartz and sat in his chair to examine it carefully. It seemed undamaged, and he decided to experiment. He held it over a folder on his desk, switched off the light, and brought the stone down, gently at first, then more forcefully. With each impact, the quartz flashed, and the louder the sound, the brighter the light.

The **Circular Sea** in Ferende cosmogony defined both the possible world and the dominion of its founding queen, Rep'husela. Its perfect circumscription resulted from the limiting flight of servant condors restrained to calling distance from her Great Throne. Of course, it was conceived as oceanic, not subterranean. But when Edvard Tøssentern was informed of the find in the second chamber, he was quick to point out that archaic Ferent words for sea and lake were the same: any distinction resided in modifiers about size and potability. He boldly suggested that Nicholas and Paulo had discovered, if not the mythological expanse, perhaps its secular inspiration.

The earliest European maps to depict explicitly the Ferendes attach the name **Centrum Mysticum**. There is debate whether this referred to the land mass generally or to the actual throne of Rep'husela, for which no artefact or natural feature has been identified. Whatever its significance, the notion of *Centrum*, along with the Circular Sea, receded into myth when the imagined collided with the real: those same cartographers brought civilizational upheaval in the form of empirical geography and something even more unsettling, foreign language. (And with foreign language comes a higher order concept: translation error.)

The name Nicholas Misgivingston will be familiar to all who follow the literature of **mathematical linguistics**. Best known for his seminal contributions to our understanding of silence in human communication (his *Stochastic Signatures of the Parsan Gap* remains the standard reference), he was also the first to obtain statistical proof for punctuation signifiers in **birdsong**. In the case of the swint (*S. tinctoria*; US: *S. transmuta*), which is the species most studied to date, these include markers for *stop, question*, and *exclamation*. Current research is focused on whether swint grammar is structurally triadic. (Human language is polyadic. The idea that restricted grammars might be possible was put forward by **Tøssentern** in *Interlocutory Graphs: A Theory of n-Grammars*, but their existence had been assumed hypothetical. For readers untrained in linguistics, the concept is best explained by noting that any well-formed n-grammar statement is fully intelligible in a society of k individuals when $k = n$, and not otherwise. Tøssentern's theory has at its foundation the famous fifth postulate, customarily but simplistically rendered from symbolic notation as 'Language is cooperative'. The designation is a natural target for academic rivals who delight in drawing parallels with Euclid's fifth, but have failed to expose a weakness. Indeed, in numerical simulation studies, it is the cooperativity parameter γ in Tøssentern's equation system that is proving to be the main determinant of intelligibility, translatability, and—for unstable or negative γ—language extinction.) If so, this might relate to the well-documented but mysterious phenomenon of *thricing* in swints, in which flock counts without exception are exactly 3-divisible (but see Appendix A). Of course, there remains the historical, supernatural explanation that thricing manifests the swint's holiness, being a behaviour reverential of the Trinity.

The occurrence of *exclamation* is widely viewed as evidence that swints enjoy a sense of humour. In the field, this marker is almost invariably followed by a respondent song element (provisionally catalogued *mirth*) that is unisonous and perseverated, and identified with laughter. The proven connection of modern birds to their dinosaur ancestry provides an insight into the past. Far from the savage, terrifying environment fictitiously (and facilely) portrayed, life in the Mesozoic likely had a benign sociability, with a forest background of complaining chatter and comedic repartee little different from that of today's senior combination room.

8 NICHOLAS MISGIVINGSTON TO RICHARD WORSE

Dear Worse

I hope all is well with you in Perth. I know that Millie is very much looking forward to returning for her fellowship year, but I don't think the dates have been finalized yet.

I have a slightly complicated request of you, and you must say if you are too busy to become involved. Actually, the request comes from Anna through Edvard, and now through me. Anna tells me that you know about Walter Reckles surviving a plane crash just north of Dante in Arizona. There's an investigation under way into its circumstances. Walter believes that he collided with an illegal drone, and that a conspiracy is in place to suppress the truth. The theory is that a secretive research establishment called Area Pi near Dante is involved. The problem is, no one can find out anything about the place, or what goes on there.

Anna was in Dante recently to interview Walter for an article in *Aviation Reviews* (I believe). I think you are aware that it's one of her slightly eccentric non-psychiatry pursuits. She attended the preliminary hearing with him and thought he was given a very rough time by one of the board members (by name of Mortiss). While she was in Dante someone gave her an anonymous note suggesting that Area Pi was implicated. She and Walter drove out towards it and were terrorized by a couple of private army heavies protecting the place. That's about all we know at present.

Edvard asked me to get some satellite imagery of the site, which I have obtained from commercial suppliers. It shows the buildings and so on, but doesn't tell us about their operations. I was wondering if you might be able to access better sources for a more revealing look at the place. If so, Walter can give you exact date and time information in the hope that you can analyse activities on the day of the crash. I have attached the images that I could obtain conventionally. You will find the coordinates of the site on each frame. Walter's address is walterreckles@flightcontrolcorp.com.

I am still very involved in the Ferent language research programme here. As well, the swint studies have reached an exciting stage. It would be wonderful if you could come back to the Ferendes one day soon and visit us at the LDI station. (Perhaps a trip with Millie?)

We have discovered an incredible cave complex in the South Joseph Plateau that shows evidence of early human occupation and—wait for it—primitive semiotics painted on the cavern walls. LDI certainly landed in the right place when it came here. Not only that, there's a huge underground lake with two rows of precisely positioned henge stones leading towards it. I'm tempted to imagine they form some kind of *via dolorosa* used in prehistoric religious rituals. It's like an avenue of great clear quartz boulders and looks spectacular—and quite haunting, I have to say—even in our feeble torchlight.

Anyway, Worse, if you can help with the above Dante business, that would be greatly appreciated. But of course you should not feel under any obligation as I know you always have a lot on. The next public hearing of the crash enquiry is scheduled in a few weeks, and will also be in Dante.

Best wishes

Nicholas

Despite its superficial resemblance to clear quartz, Nicholas's rock specimen was something very different. An example of a petrocyst, it was formed by a process called igneo-capsular condensation. Typically spheroidal, the Ferende variety (now known as **josephite**, an origin term coined by Tøssentern) has a variably thick, irregular and very hard crystalline surface composed of oxides of silicon and **terencium**. This encases a core of colourless liquid terencium sulphide (evidencing a volcanic origin) with argon in solution.

The phenomenon of **sonoluminescence** has been recognized in the modern era for almost a century, though it has not previously been reported as a percussion response in a natural mineral. The acoustic pressure wave causes miliary cavitation; as micro-bubbles collapse, they generate extremes of temperature and pressure, emitting photons in the visible spectrum. In experimental models, the flashes are very transient (lasting fractions of a nanosecond), but josephite emissions are of the order of milliseconds. Moreover, because thousands of bubbles are formed over a single pressure cycle, each differing in dimensions and collapse kinetics, a semi-continuous luminescence can result. When used ceremonially, we might also suppose that a Neolithic percussionist would observe the responsiveness (natural frequency) of a particular josephite and attune his beating to stimulate resonant cavitation-collapse cycles, thereby maximizing useful illumination.

In a letter to Tøssentern, Nicholas described his mental picture of such a ceremony:

Out of the blackness in the second cavern, the avenue of josephites would suddenly be lighted as drummers, perhaps two or three per stone, were cued to start their beating. The striking implements may have been wooden or bone but were more likely smaller josephites that would themselves scintillate as the drummers' arms swung through the air. It wasn't solely a light show; the rhythmic sound might be musically directed and joined with flutes and human voice. This would echo through the cave, conduct along the tunnel to the first chamber, enthralling those not privileged to be present in the deeper sanctum. Then some holy rite would begin, a procession down the avenue of flashing stones, direct into the water. Perhaps there were sacrificial subjects, made numb with adulation and seki wine. Perhaps there was Rep'husela herself, or an effigy, carried on a chariot-barge, drawn by attendants representing harnessed condors. At the avenue's end, where the light of submerged josephites scattered in the depths, her acolytes would gladly breathe the water for their queen, while she was launched across the darkness to the centre of the sea, into the *Centrum Mysticum*. Then the furthest drummers would drop their striking stones to enter the procession, followed by the next, and each in turn down to the water's edge, till all were given likewise to the Circular Sea. It was the baptismal journey of their race, bequeathing to the centuries a heaviness of faith and fear. From time to time this re-emerged, to speak its testament as ripples on the surface.

9 RICHARD WORSE TO THOMAS WORSE (2)

Thomas
You will see that I am writing to you from a different address, which I recommend you use from now when contacting me. I attach a file that you should open in your email account when you write to or receive from my address. There are clear instructions contained within it. You can be confident that the encryption is effective. Please open that file now and the remainder of this email will present to you. There may be short delays as verification handshakes continue between us.

I wasn't expecting to be back in touch so soon, but I am seeking your assistance. I mentioned that the pilot you rescued, Walter Reckles, is known to a friend of mine. Apparently Reckles was given a tough time at a recent air crash enquiry in Dante, particularly by a board member named William Mortiss. Reckles believes that his plane collided with an illicit drone operating out of a place called Area Pi. Mortiss spoke forcefully against the claim, essentially ridiculing it without fair hearing, I am told. My friend (actually, more than one) has asked me to help uncover evidence to prove Reckles' case.

My early impression is that Reckles may be correct. I have established that whatever is going on at Area Pi, a Chicago-based company called Mortiss Bros has an interest, and may well be in full control. As William Mortiss is listed as a director of that company, there appears to be an unacceptable conflict of interest in his being involved in the investigation.

I was hoping that you might tell me what you know about Area Pi, and what happens there. Secondly, I would value any information you have about Mortiss Bros. They seem to have corporate interests all over the US, but I am especially interested in their presence in Dante and Area Pi.
Richard

Richard
Good to hear from you. Area Pi is as much a mystery to the people of Dante, including their sheriff's office, as it is to you. In fact, I was not aware that Mortiss interests were involved at all, though it doesn't surprise me as their economic (and, I would not be surprised, criminal) reach is far-flung. So on that score I can't help much at present, but I will do my best to learn more.

Mortiss Bros originated in these parts in the 1870s, and I can tell you a lot about them because it's personal. The family carries a generational oath to destroy the Worse line in Arizona in a feud going back all that time. I will send separately some of the history that explains its origins. Depending upon who's in charge, their wealth and power are periodically directed into the family obsession. It's a worry at the moment because the senior heir in waiting, Regan Mortiss, recently replaced her father Charles Mortiss as chair of the board and MD. Our information is that the changeover was involuntary, but no one's officially missing and no one's complaining, so neither Chicago nor we can justify going in. Anyway, that makes her the first matriarch of Mortiss Bros, for which she won't abide any jostle. The suggestion is she's taking on the revenge business as her special project, like a destiny thing. They say she calls herself Rego in private, after the original badass Rigo who started it all nearly a century-and-a-half ago.

I think in the case of Regan you can't be too careful. She's bad. She may well get the idea of spreading the hatred beyond Arizona, even as far as your parts. That would be the more likely if she finds out you are prying into her business. I already had some concern that our email contact might have been compromised and the jeopardy widened to you. I am pleased we now have a secure channel. Take care, cousin.
Thomas

10   REGAN MORTISS

The boardroom of Mortiss Bros overlooks the Chicago River, fifteen floors down. Regan stood close to the glass watching a top-deck architecture tour drifting downstream between the bridges. Periodically, a hundred interested faces would redirect as one toward a city landmark. When they stared at the Mortiss Tower, she glowered back.

Six directors filed in and took their seats. They might gesture a greeting to others, but the room was silent. Their view was of Regan from behind, clutching a manila folder at her back, tapping it slowly against herself. They knew she wasn't happy.

Under the company constitution they each exercised one vote, while Regan had seven. For decision-making, these meetings seemed unnecessary and their personal attendance pointless. But no one dared dissent, abstain, or be absent. Previous members of the board, including Regan's own father as chair, had been known to discontinue their directorships suddenly and without explanation. They all feared the tall woman at the window. She turned to them.

'What the fuck is going on?'

It was her standard expression of displeasure, and six hearts sank at the prospect of attack. She crossed the room to her seat, but remained standing. There was never any adherence to meeting protocol, like a call to order. Proceedings were understood to have begun with the question and the slap of her file onto the table. She glared at her IT manager. The others shuffled papers.

'This is your responsibility.'

Tony Saviccia was sullen but knew he must meet her eye. The others were relieved that responsibility had been assigned to someone else.

'And yours, asshole.'

Suddenly, the relief was looking tenuous. It was the chief accountant's turn to look up. Arnold Tweisser secretly desired Regan and his gaze hesitated at her breasts on its way to her face. He assumed the indiscretion would pass unnoticed, but it never did. Regan registered it. In her corporate world, beauty wasn't truth; it was power. She looked back at Saviccia.

'Well?'

'I'm sorry, Ms Mortiss.'

In that room, addressing the chair nearly always started with an apology.

'We know there have been two breaches, one at an Area Pi server, the other—'

'We're all aware of that. It's in your report. That's why we're here. Enlighten us.'

'With the Chicago system, we know there was an attack. We don't yet know how far it penetrated.'

Regan glanced at Tweisser, her lips slightly parted. She was playing with him.

'It's your job to know, and to stop it, Saviccia. How is it possible?'

'I don't know, Ms Mortiss. I don't yet know. We're state-of-the-art with defences. No one in our team knew this could happen.'

'What damage have they done?'

Saviccia was relieved that he could report something half positive.

'None, it would appear. No malicious damage. No theft.'

'Jesus, Saviccia. Of course they've done damage.'

Saviccia realized his mistake. Regan continued.

'They've damaged my confidence in you dumb-asses, for one thing. We've no doubt taken in a sleeper or Christ knows what kind of spyware. We're exposed, Saviccia. These fuckers have lifted our skirts and taken a look.'

She glanced again at Tweisser, and raised her eyebrows a millimetre. He was excited. Whatever she might shout at him, whatever she might call him, he wanted her the more.

'Tweisser, you idiot. Stop dreaming and tell us what you know.'

'There are no irregularities in the accounts, Ms Mortiss.'

Regan stared at him without responding. He wondered if she were secretly smiling. The others saw a savage scowl. She sat down, placing her leather shoulder bag on the table beside her file. Everyone looked at it; the rumour was that she always carried a pistol and wasn't loath to bring it out. Tweisser wanted her the more for that as well.

'Who's done this to us?' She was now looking at Saviccia.

'We can't identify the intruder. It was a very sophisticated attack. We don't yet understand it. We have outside consultants engaged urgently. We're not even sure if the Area Pi and MB incidents are connected.'

'Of course they're connected, you moron. Not good enough.'

'Ms Mortiss, if I may continue,' said Saviccia—rather bravely, the others thought—'although we cannot trace the hackers, we do have intelligence of unwanted interest in our Area Pi operation. It's an email intercept reported to me since I wrote that.' He nodded at the file on the table before her. 'I don't know if it relates to the hack.'

'Of course they're connected, you moron,' she repeated. 'Go on.'

'We routinely search on mentions of Area Pi. There was an email trail from Dante to England to the Ferendes to Australia. They weren't the usual vacuous mentions from gullible tourists. It seemed to stem from the investigation into our drone mishap out there in Dante.'

Regan looked at her brother.

'William?'

'I have that enquiry under control, Regan. It won't go anywhere,' he said.

'I'm coming to see that for myself, next time.' She returned to Saviccia. 'The emails?'

'The last one is the most interesting. It requests satellite intelligence of the installation at Area Pi,' said Saviccia.

'Fuck.'

'We shouldn't be too concerned, Ms Mortiss,' said Saviccia. 'They'll never get surveillance with the resolution they need to learn anything. We're well hidden on the ground. Trashy magazines are always buying that imagery to run sensation pieces on places like Area 51 and Area Pi. They go nowhere.'

'Jesus, Saviccia, you idiot. If they're inside our system they don't need high-fidelity imagery.' She breathed deeply. 'Who are we dealing with? Give me names.'

'In the Ferendes, it's a Nicholas Misgivingston. He's some kind of language researcher there, a mathematician, from what we can determine.'

'Why would he be interested?'

'Emails tell us he's doing a favour for a friend, named Anna Camenes, who was in Dante at the time of the safety board sitting. Evidently, she is a friend of Reckles; that was the pilot, Ms Mortiss.'

'I know the name of the pilot. It's been all over the news.'

'I saw her in Dante,' said William. 'She and Reckles hung out. We also saw her close to the sheriff.'

Regan took another deep breath.

'I don't want that bastard's name uttered in this room unless we're celebrating his grisly murder.' She returned to business.

'Where did that request go?'

Saviccia looked down. He expected a bad reception.

'Someone called Richard Worse. In Perth, Australia,' he said.

'Worse? Worse? It's a Worse?' Regan raised her voice, instantly leaning forward and rounding on Saviccia. After a few seconds she sat back in her chair.

'Fuck.'

She turned her head towards the window and stayed silent. The others looked down at their files, except Tweisser, who looked at her breasts. He was caught out as she turned back.

'What do we know about that Worse?' She spoke more soberly.

'It's hard to find out anything,' said Saviccia. 'We can't read anything ex-Perth. He appears to have no online presence.'

'Your people just need to work harder, Saviccia.' She scowled at him. 'Is he an M Worse?'

Saviccia reached into a briefcase as he answered.

'Our only source of information about him is contained in a documentary published last year, evidently unauthorized.' He held up a copy of Darian's book. 'Because of a connection to Misgivingston described there, we believe it is the same person.' Saviccia paused. 'In which case his full name is Richard Magnacart Worse.'

'Fuck.' Regan stared at the window again. When she spoke, her voice was hard and soft at the same time. 'We eliminate both. Those in favour?' She didn't move her eyes from the window. The motion would carry. She turned and addressed William.

'Who can handle Missington?'

'Misgivingston,' Saviccia corrected, but immediately regretted his interruption.

Regan ignored him and spoke ironically to William. 'Do we have anyone in the Ferendes who can overpower a mathematician?'

'We have Glimpse, the prospector, Regan,' said William. 'He was the one we used in St. John's last year.'

'The warehouse fire? That was good,' she said.

'Well, there were some innocent victims in that operation. It wasn't clean.'

'Misfortune definingly visits the bystander, William,' she said, and glanced at Tweisser, who had no idea what to make of the comment. 'Why is Glimpse in the Ferendes? Is he working for us on terencium supply?'

'Yes and no. Glimpse works for himself in the main,' said William.

'Set it up,' said Regan. 'What about Perth? Who do we have there? Where is it, anyway?'

'We have no one in Perth,' said William. 'We will need to send personnel.'

Regan looked around the table. Her eyes settled on a man she viewed as a pestilential twit barnacled to company largesse by virtue of being her illegitimate half brother.

'Can you handle it, Ben Jay?'

'No worries, Regan.'

The others winced silently. Regan was calculating that he would probably fail, but at least he might get hurt in the process. Ben Jay adjusted his baseball cap and placed a cigarette pack on the table. His tongue was loosened by his unexpected importance.

'We're not gonna take Worse shit in our seki ... ses ... sexi ...'

No one came to his rescue.

'... thing.'

'Ses-qui-centenary,' said Regan syllabically, 'and it's years off. Memorize it or don't say it, for Christ's sake. And if you want to smoke, leave the damn building.'

To defuse her irritation, she turned again to the window. All but its principal actor read her thought-play that here would be an ideal means for his leaving the building. She looked back at Ben Jay.

'That's settled then. Take two professionals from Security. People with kill CVs. William, you oversee selection. Financials to Camelline. I want a team in Perth by Monday, wherever the fuck it is. Do they speak English there?'

No one was sure if an answer was expected, but she kept looking enquiringly around the meeting. They read the signs of growing impatience, and William put himself forward.

'They're impossible to understand, but it is a basic form of English, yes,' he said.

'Perfect. A basic form of English is your language, Ben Jay. Twice daily reports to the GM, and a result by Friday latest. Remember, the Worse target is business but it's also family honour.'

'No worries, Regan. Friday latest,' interrupted Ben Jay.

'Don't mess up. All done.'

Regan pushed her file toward the centre of the table, and placed a hand on her shoulder bag. It was a sign that the meeting was over.

'Tweisser, stay behind.'

It was an instruction that the others would dread, but Tweisser felt special. As those dismissed left the room, she casually unbuttoned the top of her shirt, almost as if he weren't present.

Tweisser couldn't believe his good fortune. No matter what people thought of Regan Mortiss, she was acknowledged by all as extremely beautiful. He felt his heart thumping, missing beats, racing. Thank God he had that pacemaker–defib inserted earlier in the year. At least he could still pump blood to where it was needed at times like this.

Regan reached for her shoulder bag again. To Tweisser, it was a slow, caressing touch of the leather as she drew it towards her. He wanted to be dangerous too, to be touched like that, drawn close to her, pressed against the white lace border displayed for him. Now she was playing with a second button, looking at him, smiling.

'I was wanting to ask, Arnold. How is your wife?'

11 GLIMPSE

Dear Worse

I trust you are well. I was wondering how your enquiries went regarding that Area Pi business. The safety board hearing will resume sometime and Walter is certain that place is somehow relevant to his crash. Not to worry if you can't do anything. It's really up to Walter to present his case and convince the US authorities to investigate fully.

We have a rather strange visitor to the station. A big German-sounding chap (Paulo thinks he's Afrikaner) who calls himself Glimpse appeared in a 4WD truck a few days ago, saying he was a prospector heading west. He asked if he could camp near our compound for a while. Paulo said that was fine, and we've provided the odd thing for him. He doesn't seem to do much except sit around his truck all day watching what's going on. It's causing a bit of spooking in some of our teachers here.
Nicholas

Nicholas

My advice is to treat anything out of the ordinary with a high degree of suspicion. Take extreme care, Nicholas. I suggest you instigate a 24-hour discreet observation. Send me some photographs for an

Interpol face-rec search in case he's on record. Just don't let him see you pointing a lens in his direction. Also send the registration of his truck. I will check payment channels. The Area Pi matter is progressing. Worse

The cave work was suspended for the next three days as torrential rains made the five-kilometre hike through the jungle too unpleasant. Paulo used the time to catch up on administrative duties, which included negotiations with the new government in Madregalo about provision of basic medical services at the LDI station. Nicholas immersed himself in programming.

As station manager, Paulo became increasingly concerned about the presence of Glimpse. Much of the conversation at the shared canteen meals was about their visitor's strangeness, and increasingly disturbing fantasies were aired about his identity and purpose in being there. He was becoming a morale issue, especially among the women. Paulo also felt a growing unease about their security.

After breakfast on the first fine day, when they were planning to resume the cave survey, Paulo told Nicholas that he had resolved to confront the issue, and he set off towards Glimpse's truck. When he returned to their office hut, Nicholas was keen to hear how the exchange went. He asked what Paulo had said.

'I said I would like to know what his plans were about moving on, that some of the staff found his presence distracting. Actually, I told him frankly that people here didn't like the feeling that they were being constantly watched. I asked him what he was looking at all day.'

'What did he say?' asked Nicholas.

'Nothing. He just sat on the running board staring up at me. Totally cold. I gave him several opportunities to speak, to explain himself, but he was completely unresponsive. In the end I lost patience and told him LDI had administrative leasehold for a radius of forty miles, and to leave the station within twenty-four hours.'

'Good for you, Paulo. Did he say anything then?'

'Votzefock.'

The next half hour was spent packing and checklisting items into two weatherproof rucksacks. One was entirely filled by a jerry can of fuel for the generator. The other carried a miscellany of new torch batteries, camera equipment, tools, and food and water rations.

Paulo shouldered the fuel pack and stepped out of the hut. Nicholas followed, carrying the second pack by hand, and pulling the office door shut behind him. At that moment the satellite phone on Paulo's desk rang quietly, and an email was delivered to Nicholas's inbox, copied to Paulo.

Nicholas
Glimpse is extremely dangerous. Assume he is armed. His truck was funded through illegal channels. I am investigating. Interpol has arson and murder warrants in the name of Franz Blick. Don't go about alone. Stay in your station headquarters. Stay in large groups. Contact the police in Madregalo immediately. If you don't reply within one hour, I will do that myself.
Worse

'Hold on, Paulo. I forgot the sat.'

Nicholas re-entered the office, collected the phone and placed it in his pack. He didn't see the missed call alert.

At the cave entrance, they removed their backpacks and placed them on a natural rock shelf a few metres inside. Paulo took the jerry can and walked back to examine the generator. They had built a crude A-frame shelter over it for weather protection, and the last few days had provided their carpentry's severest test. Paulo tilted the structure onto one end.

'It looks fine,' he reported, as he unscrewed the fuel cap. Nicholas was standing behind him, just inside the entrance.

'Do you ever get the impression there's a very slight draught in the cave?' he asked.

'Why should there not be?'

'I don't mean into the cave. I mean from the inside,' said Nicholas.

Paulo looked up from pouring fuel into the generator's tank.

'That's interesting. I did say there might be other entrances somewhere, or chimneys. There could easily be airflow. That's good for us as we go deeper, in terms of air quality.'

Nicholas had been wondering how early people had installed the large josephites, which were over a metre in diameter, in the second chamber. It hardly seemed possible that they could have been carried from this entrance and then taken through the inside tunnel, particularly past the z-bend. He had reached a similar conclusion: there was probably another way into that chamber. But after his experience at the lake, he wasn't keen to go looking for it.

'I'll be relieved when Edvard gets a survey team here. They can do the exploration and things like air analysis, so we can concentrate on the linguistics.'

'I'm looking forward to that, too,' said Paulo. 'They'll also do a more professional job of the lighting.'

He started the engine and repositioned the shelter. 'Time for the clamber,' he said, as he joined Nicholas inside the cave.

Nicholas picked up his backpack and followed Paulo. About twenty metres in, where there was little light from the entrance, they had positioned a makeshift switchboard. Paulo flicked the main toggle to light the way ahead. The next section pitched quite steeply down, and they had learned from experience the best stepping route with some natural handholds along the way. When the team came, some of these more challenging parts would be made passable with boardwalks, ladders, and handrails.

Out of interest, Nicholas routinely noted the time it took to progress from the switch to the first chamber. He had set a private objective of thirty minutes but today, with his load, it required thirty-six. As they neared the end of this passage, the effort of descent, for Nicholas, was always alleviated by the imminent reward of seeing the great medallion wall.

Today, they planned to stay in the first chamber. Much of it had been photographed, but Tøssentern had sent a list of specific questions regarding exact disposition and dimensions, and he wanted a more comprehensive mapping. The information was needed in support of funding applications for a multidisciplinary research team, involving a dozen Cambridge departments, to explore and document the cave systematically and date its artefacts. To make the task easier, Tøssentern had sent a laser ruler from England. Paulo linked this mechanically and digitally to a tripod-mounted video camera such that the range measure was automatically recorded wherever the camera pointed. On the same platform, he attached a spotlight, powered from the generator.

It was Nicholas who would write the software to integrate their measurements into a stereo panorama, and Paulo consulted him about the best location for the tripod, which would thenceforth be their principal datum point for the whole exercise. Nicholas had already considered this, but still walked carefully over the cave floor, shining his torch at the wall. He chose a spot that was fairly central and level.

'Here, Paulo, I think.'

Paulo brought over the tripod, positioned it, and hammered

anchor pins attached to its feet into the rock floor. He tested its stability and declared it satisfactory.

He then brought a power board across. Nicholas opened a folding stool beside the tripod and placed a laptop computer on it. He connected this by cable to the camera. Another cable connected to the platform itself. When the platform, camera, ruler, spotlight and computer were all mains powered, there was an impressive tangle of cables and leads.

'I was thinking we might begin with footage of the largest fire remains, and then pull back so the viewer can see where it is in relation to the main cavern wall,' said Nicholas. 'Then start the systematic filming. Agreed?'

'Yes, good idea.'

Nicholas's first task was to zero and calibrate the accelerometers in the platform. As he peered closely at a spirit level, he asked of Paulo, 'Is that true, the forty-mile radius thing?'

'Not exactly. In fact, not approximately either. I decided it was how far I wanted him to go, at minimum.'

Nicholas smiled. He concentrated on his task for a few minutes before speaking again.

'Any news from Edvard on the carbon dating?'

Charcoal remnants from the main fire pit had been sent to Cambridge.

'Nothing yet,' said Paulo. He was adapting some light fittings to splice into the forward cable that they had laid on their last visit.

They worked quietly for the next hour, Nicholas at the computer, and Paulo reticulating more lights, including one about ten metres into the tunnel leading to the second chamber. He had just returned to fashion more electrics when their silence was broken.

'Don't you focking move, you two.'

It was loud and nasty, and Nicholas felt sudden, intense

fear. Despite the instruction, he switched off the spotlight, and subtly redirected the camera toward the voice as he turned himself.

Glimpse was just inside the chamber at the passage entry. His right hand was holding a rifle at waist level, pointed at them. In his left hand was a powerful torch, taken from their stock at the cave entrance. He shone it first at Paulo, muttered 'Focker', then at Nicholas.

'Vich vun Missingden?'

'Misgivingston,' said Nicholas. 'I am.'

Glimpse walked closer to Nicholas, keeping the torch on his face. Nicholas still had one hand on the camera toggle, and he angled it to stay on Glimpse, who either didn't notice or didn't care.

'You die,' he said.

The light moved back to Paulo.

'You die too. Too bad. Focker.'

Glimpse noticed the light coming from the inner tunnel.

'Vot's in dere?'

'It leads to another chamber,' said Paulo.

'Ve go dere, for you to die. Somevere you never be found. You first.' He pointed the rifle at Nicholas. 'Den you, den me.'

Nicholas led the way into the tunnel. Ten minutes later, they were beyond the range of Paulo's newly installed light, and Nicholas switched on his torch. His mind was racing to formulate an escape plan, but he couldn't confer with Paulo.

He thought of the z-bend. Immediately beyond the second hairpin, on the left, he remembered there was one of the side passages they had noted. Some were just alcoves but this was longer than most, though they hadn't explored it far. Maybe they could slip in while Glimpse was still behind the bend. If he went forward to find them, they could make a run for it back to the first chamber. On the other hand, if he followed them in they might be able to overpower him in the small entrance. He spoke in Ferent to Paulo.

'Keep close to me.'

'You be quiet, fockers.'

A minute later, Glimpse spoke again.

'Halt. Vot's dat sound?'

Nicholas and Paulo stopped to listen. Glimpse was right. There was a definite scraping sound ahead of them.

'Who's dere?' Glimpse asked. 'You got verkers dere?'

'There's no one else here,' said Paulo. Nicholas could sense a different fear in his voice. He felt it in himself as well.

'Keep going. All you fockers vill die.'

The tunnel floor was levelling out and Nicholas knew they were nearing the first hairpin. He held out one hand behind to urge Paulo to come closer, and increased his pace a little. The scratching sound was getting louder. More than ever, Nicholas was determined to get off the main tunnel path.

They reached the z-bend. Nicholas leapt forward around the first corner, jerking Paulo along behind him, then around the second. At the entrance to the side alley, he pushed Paulo inside.

Paulo instantly understood the plan and cooperated. In the moment before Nicholas switched off his torch to follow, he caught sight of something inexplicable. About four metres ahead there seemed to be a pale, pearlescent moving screen blocking the tunnel. He didn't linger, but dived into the alley before Glimpse could see him.

'Fockers,' they heard him say as he struggled to catch up without the benefit of Nicholas's torchlight ahead of him.

The scratching sound was louder. It seemed to be right outside their entrance.

'Fockers.'

Glimpse was rounding the second bend.

'Votzefock?' It was loud, and followed by a throttled scream ending mid-note, as if interrupted by a circuit breaker. There was a clatter of rifle hitting the rock floor. The dim light reaching them from Glimpse's torch was extinguished.

The scratching intensified.

Nicholas and Paulo were rigid with fear, trying to imagine what Glimpse had seen. They pushed up against the wall about two metres in—cold, uncomfortable, and in total darkness, straining to interpret what was happening outside. There were no more sounds from Glimpse. Perhaps he had fled from whatever was in the tunnel.

The scratching became louder.

Nicholas began to worry that it was coming from both directions, from deeper inside their refuge as well as out in the tunnel where Glimpse had been. He tried to dismiss the perception as an echo, unwilling to countenance being trapped between two encroaching, invisible dangers.

In the blackness, trying to breathe silently, unable to change posture in case their presence were betrayed, he was progressively deprived of orientation. It was impossible to judge time. Paulo, huddled up against him, was so still that Nicholas couldn't be sure that he was there.

The scratching stopped. Just when Nicholas thought it might be safe to move, it resumed. Now it was more a scraping sound, lower pitched, and louder. Louder or closer.

He felt Paulo start, and catch his breath; Nicholas feared that something might have brushed against him. Shortly after, he guessed the reason, when a drop of freezing water fell from the passage ceiling onto his own face. In his state of coiled terror and hypervigilance, isolated from the sensory world but for hard rock, threat and imagination, it felt like a sledgehammer out of the night.

The scraping became even louder, continuing for what might have been a half hour, when it abruptly softened, and seemed to recede. Nicholas hoped it was not in the direction of the first chamber. They waited to be certain of the silence before Paulo dared to speak.

'What was it?' Even in the whisper, there was tremulousness.

'I don't know.' Nicholas made no attempt to describe what he had seen earlier. He stood up, feeling above his head for the height of the cavern. They both knew instinctively their best course of action was to turn right in the tunnel and head back to the first chamber.

They switched on their torches and Nicholas led the way. In the tunnel, he first turned his light to the left and was relieved to find the previous apparition no longer there. He began moving to the right as he swung his torch around. Still in darkness, his face collided with something solid. He was seized by instantaneous, visceral fright, gasping as he fell back against Paulo.

Paulo staggered, then shone his own torch ahead of Nicholas. In the narrow beam, they first saw Glimpse's rifle and broken torch on the floor. Facing them, dangling half a metre above the ground, were two boots. Paulo raised his torch the full extent of Glimpse's body.

Glimpse's swollen head was close to the tunnel roof, supported there by a gigantic disarticulated crab claw clasped onto his neck, and itself wedged high up between the walls of the tunnel. The nearer of Glimpse's legs was still swinging like a pendulum from the impact with Nicholas.

The sight of a hanging man, magnified by torchlight and deep shadow into some grotesque expressionist artwork, was fascinating but profoundly frightening. Paulo moved his light away. On both walls, as high as the roof, they saw hundreds of scratch marks etched centimetres deep into the rock.

Nicholas was recovering from his shock, and used his torch to examine the monstrous claw. Paulo moved around Glimpse's legs, toward their escape. Before doing the same, Nicholas had the presence of mind to reach up and take a key ring from Glimpse's coat pocket.

He followed. Not until he could see the new ten-metre light beyond Paulo and the silhouette of his friend in front of him, did his thinking shift from the danger behind them to survival ahead.

They crossed the first chamber and headed directly for the exit, Paulo still in the lead. Getting out was always slower than coming in, due to the climb, and it felt like a long time before they stood at the cave entrance.

They hadn't spoken since whispering in the alley. Nicholas passed a bottle of water to Paulo, who was reaching under the engine shelter to switch off the generator. The silence, fresh air and natural light were almost intoxicating.

'I should report it from here,' said Paulo, taking the satellite phone from Nicholas's pack. He got through to police headquarters in Madregalo.

It was a difficult interaction. Paulo was describing the death by giant crab of a man named Glimpse who had been about to murder two foreign linguists deep underground but was now himself suspended by a crustacean claw from the roof of a cave that no one knew existed. Yes, the crab had got away. No, they hadn't actually seen it. Yes, the linguists were now safe. Yes, he would send all the information by email as soon as possible. Paulo's frustration was obvious.

They hiked in silence. Nicholas was trying to piece together the facts. Glimpse was grasped by the neck. The claw was jammed nearly three metres from the floor. Granted, it was clearly a monstrous creature—but that was very high. And those deep scratchings up to the roof: how could that happen?

Nicholas kept thinking about what he saw just before darting into the alley. It was like a pearlescent curtain filling the tunnel in front of him. He remembered in the moment seeing a curious movement, and its character now registered. It was shuffling.

Suddenly he understood what was happening, and what explained the other facts. The creature in the tunnel was certainly some kind of giant crab, but it was more than that. It had been *walking upright.*

Sustained **bipedal locomotion** in arthropods has not previously been observed in nature, though a highly specialized study by **Lord Enright**, *Depictions of Arachnid Bipedalism in Etruscan Art*, had given the concept a small place in academic discourse, albeit that of art history more than biology. The Etruscan imagery was taken to be fantastical or mythical with no basis in that people's experience, an assumption that must be re-examined in the light of the Joseph Plateau discovery.

Of course, it is possible that what Nicholas thought he witnessed is a highly localized adaptation to life in tunnels. Whether the Ferende cave crab is capable of a freestanding bipedal stance and ambulation (without the support of adjacent walls) is not yet known. Irrespective of issues of balance, however, the hindmost limbs must be suitably hypertrophied to perform in such a weight-bearing role. Anatomists speculate that coordination of gait is controlled by an enlarged caudal ganglion specialized for the purpose.

12 NUSERO'S MAP

Paulo crossed the clearing, heading straight for the administration hut. He slipped off his rucksack, which contained the empty jerry can, and dropped it by the door. Nicholas followed him inside to unload the equipment pack.

'Look at this, Nicholas.' Paulo was sitting at his computer. 'It's a message for you.'

Nicholas stood behind Paulo and read the email from Worse.

'The police might take things more seriously now we can give an Interpol warrant name,' he said.

Paulo wrote a short account of events, describing the difficulties and dangers police would face in retrieving Glimpse's body. He asked Nicholas for his opinion before sending it.

'Excellent, Paulo.'

'I think I should phone again.'

This time, he was put through to a senior officer who accessed the email as they were talking. Paulo was told that Madregalo police had received a high-level communication regarding Glimpse from an Inspector Spoiling in Australia, and preparations were underway to get officers out to the LDI station. They could expect a recovery team, mortuary specialist, coroner's officer and detectives to arrive late afternoon the next day. Paulo stressed that the body was deep underground and staff should be chosen who could cope with claustrophobia. They would need better lighting than LDI had available, a ladder, and a power saw to cut the victim down. Finally, they should have weapons in the event the crab returned while they were in the tunnel. And, by the way, there was no road access to the cave. They would need to hike their equipment for five kilometres.

When Paulo finished the call, he swivelled his chair to face Nicholas, who was sitting at his desk.

'They *believed* me,' he said.

It was the first moment in the day that Nicholas saw Paulo start to relax.

'Which bit?' said Nicholas. 'They believed a story about a monster crab squeezing to death an Interpol fugitive deep inside the Joseph Plateau and leaving him hanging from the cave ceiling? They will need a ladder to reach him? They should bring power tools to cut through a giant claw? They need to be armed in case they are attacked by a ten-foot-high crustacean running at them on two legs in the dark? Paulo, even I don't believe it. Do you think you were talking to the real police? Are you sure it's not an emergency psychiatric team that will be arriving tomorrow?'

Paulo was looking seriously at Nicholas. It was then that both realized the magnitude of what they had been through, and at last felt safe to connect with an intense relief. Simultaneously, they burst into laughter.

Early the next morning, Paulo and Nicholas went to Glimpse's truck. It was locked, and Paulo expressed admiration for Nicholas's foresight in obtaining the keys.

There was little of interest in the cab. They accessed the back through separate locked doors at the rear, which they left open for light. The inside at the cab end was set up like an RV, with bed, bathroom and kitchen facilities. The rest was workspace with benches along each side and an office chair that could be secured during travel. There was a library of geological references and a mineral sample collection.

Nicholas sat at a computer and activated the screen, pleased to find it not password protected. He examined email history and document files, setting up copy folders to send to his own machine. Paulo searched systematically starting from the rear. He untied the neck of a bulky sack under one bench, and felt inside.

'Look what we have here, Nicholas.'

He pulled out a small josephite. Nicholas leaned across and took it.

'It may just be quartz, but it does look like our specimen.' He got up and peered into the sack. 'I wonder where he found all these?'

Nicholas resumed his work at the computer. There was an office area with spring-back files and several papers organized with bulldog clips. Paulo flicked through them and stopped at a sheet headed 'Geode analysis'. There was a cover letter from Madregalo Analytical & Assay, with an attached physical description, crystallography report, and listing of chemical composition. Someone had circled Terencium, and underlined each terencium compound itemized below it. Paulo put it aside to keep, and continued his search.

He came last to the living space behind the cab. A small eating table was folded down, with some papers resting on it.

'Nicholas. Come here,' he said.

Nicholas pushed the office chair back and stepped forward to the kitchen. In front of Paulo was a hand-drawn map on an A4 sheet. A roughly circular region had a GPS reference written at its centre. An arrowhead indicated north. At the southern rim was a hatched area, labelled *Glitzernstein* to the side. From this, running south from the circle, was a line labelled *Vulkanstraße*. Below that a long arrow pointing east was annotated 'M 265'.

'Volcano Road. I don't know of any volcanoes in the Ferendes,' said Paulo. 'But supposing that M means Madregalo, it's between here and the capital.'

Nicholas took his smartphone from a pocket and searched

on the coordinates. He zoomed on a map of the Joseph Plateau, and showed Paulo.

'That position is north of the Madregalo road, deep in jungle. There are no roads indicated.'

'But we know that there are scattered logging tracks across the plateau. Maybe Glimpse got close with his truck then bushwhacked the rest.'

'He can't have bushwhacked very far carrying that sack of rocks,' said Nicholas. 'And if he got in with this rig, we should manage with one of our 4WDs.'

Paulo was still looking at the map.

'Volcano Street,' he said softly. 'It's a rather odd name to give, don't you think? As if there is some kind of road or track already there.'

'Glimpse was odd. We should keep the map, and the josephites,' said Nicholas, returning to his task at the computer.

The police arrived in two trucks at 6.00 pm, and set up a small work compound at the edge of the main clearing, near Glimpse's truck. The group was self-sufficient, but they accepted Paulo's invitation to join the station staff for dinner in the canteen. Paulo took the opportunity to address them all about conditions in the cave, what hardships to expect, and what safety rules to obey. He stated forcefully that while underground, he would be the person in charge regarding all but police operational matters.

After the meal, Paulo and Nicholas and two detectives walked over to the station office, where an informal interview was conducted. They were told that a joint statement would be prepared for them both to sign. If this accorded with findings the following day, the detectives considered that neither was likely to have to attend an inquest, as Glimpse's death was not actually witnessed and not itself suspicious in respect of foul play.

The whole team, with Nicholas and Paulo leading the way, set off for the caves at 6.00 am. Those in the police retinue, except for the senior detective, carried heavy equipment packs, and the walk was slower than usual.

They rested outside the cave entrance, where packs were reorganized, torches distributed, and Paulo held another briefing. The plan was to regroup in the first cavern and enter the tunnel with Paulo and two armed officers in front. This lead party would move beyond Glimpse, set up a torch battery, and take up position to look out for the crab. Because of the confined space and the awkwardness of Glimpse's location at the z-bend, sections of the team would come forward as needed, starting with the detectives and a police photographer, who would then withdraw to allow forensics in, who were also charged with custody of Glimpse's firearms. They would be followed by the recovery crew with ladder, power saw and two stretchers. Finally, a clean-up team would check the site. Glimpse was to be carried to the surface and bagged in daylight. Paulo requested minimal unnecessary noise in the tunnel so they could listen for the scratching sound. He emphasized that they had no idea how fast the crab was capable of moving using its unusual gait. When questions were dealt with, he started the generator, and climbed into the entrance. The police followed, with Nicholas at the rear.

They reached the first cavern without incident. Because they could not be sure if crabs ever ventured the whole tunnel length to this chamber, the forward party ran their torch beams around the space. When Nicholas caught up, Paulo was pointing out the tunnel entrance, and several powerful police torches were naturally directed at it. Nicholas had never seen that part of the cavern so well illuminated.

He had a fleeting impression, apparently missed by others present, that an enormous human shadow figure stood astride the tunnel opening. Within a moment, it was lost, as the torches moved away to light the ground for walking.

The party entered the tunnel in the order Paulo had planned. Nicholas stayed behind to examine his tripod-mounted survey camera, left there after their hurried escape. He disconnected the computer, which had video of Glimpse's first appearance in the cave, and placed it in his pack. Later he would provide a copy to the police, including the voice recording of Glimpse's plan to kill them. Then he crossed the chamber to join the others.

They were in the tunnel for an hour. First out was Glimpse on a stretcher, his puffy face unrecognizable. The cheliped had been sawn through, and the terminal pincer still clasped its victim's neck to the thickness of cervical vertebrae. The severed end projected sideways from the stretcher, making transport slightly difficult. Then came the rest of the claw, as large as Glimpse himself, bizarrely carried on a second stretcher like a human casualty. Last out of the tunnel were Paulo and the armed guards.

It was five o'clock when they arrived back at the station. Glimpse and the claw, each body-bagged and labelled, were placed in cool boxes on one of the trucks, and the expedition equipment repacked for the return journey.

The relief of having that gruesome task completed, and a physical and emotional exhaustion from the day, seemed to be shared by everybody, even those who had not made the arduous trek. For the station staff, this partly was the knowledge that Glimpse was finally to leave their presence.

Again, Paulo invited his guests to the canteen for dinner. Alcohol was rarely consumed at LDI, but tonight it flowed. Mostly, observed Nicholas, from a police cache somewhere in the body-bag truck. There were speeches and replies, and replies and replies, and Glimpse was rechristened, and the crab was promoted to honorary Sergeant, and then to Inspector, awarded a bravery honour, voted amputee of the year, and made Director-General of Interpol, and then the United Nations, issued a special nine-legged no-hands driver's licence and given the keys to Glimpse's truck, and finally auctioned *in absentia* for sushi, but still toasted all evening till the cache was drained. It was a night of the blackest humour.

The dark, heavy hessian sack containing Glimpse's sparkle stones was stored under Edvard's vacant desk in the office hut. Nicholas had chosen from it an especially nice example to place on his desk, as his previous find had been sent to Cambridge for identification.

This became for him a muse object that often brought to mind the avenue of josephites in the second cavern, and led him into elaborate fantasies of its ceremonial purpose. It was always a shock coming back to the sensory world of the actual, to accept that the ripples seen on the lake's surface were probably caused by the giant crab stirring, and that he was lucky not to have suffered the fate of Glimpse.

He wondered also about the shadow picture he had seen in the first cavern. Paulo had not noticed it, but without the lighting power that the police had provided they would be unlikely to re-visualize and define its outline. Increasingly, Nicholas felt frustrated that exploration of the cave was inadequately resourced, particularly regarding illumination.

Tøssentern, of course, was working hard in Cambridge to marshal those resources, not only financial, but intellectual. Every time he received a report from Paulo, there seemed to be need of a new and arcane expertise. The list had recently expanded to include a limnologist, archaeologist, dendrochronologist, mineralogist, analytical chemist, arthropod biologist, seismologist and now, of all things, a vulcanologist. What was expected to be a temporary visit to the station of some speleologists and an anthropologist was now looking like the establishment of a satellite natural history university.

Pending those developments, the cave soon took on a secondary priority for Paulo and Nicholas. This was partly because they knew it was unsafe to explore without better lighting and protection. But other work needed attention also. One of the main functions of LDI in the Ferendes was to provide schooling to children, and some adults, from dozens of regional villages. This generated a load of administration, which Paulo managed. For Nicholas, there was the ongoing linguistic analysis of Ferent dialects in pursuit of one of LDI's objectives, which was identification of their common precursor language.

Nicholas was a volunteer at the station, and had been so for some years. He derived his substantial income by consulting for global banking and insurance companies, developing their investment and risk-mitigation products. That work occupied him for some hours most mornings.

He was keen also to devote more time to his personal research interest of swint language, which was advancing rapidly in other centres. Finally, there was the volcano.

Glimpse's map was pinned to a corkboard above Nicholas's desk. When he wasn't concentrating on his computer screen, or contemplating the josephite, Nicholas would stare at the map.

He had purchased satellite photography of the region. Even knowing the exact location, it required imagination to discern any ring-shaped area differentiated from its surroundings either topographically or by vegetation.

Then Nicholas thought of something else. He accessed a meteorological earth monitoring service and ordered infrared imagery. The result was stunning. Centred on Glimpse's coordinates was a multi-kilometre diameter caldera with a thermal radiance several hundredfold that of the surrounding jungle.

They had found the volcano, and it didn't look extinct.

Those who deal occupationally with the macabre commonly seek emotional release through alcohol and humour, itself often morbid. Madregalo police bestowed upon Glimpse the Ferent name **Nusero Loosan**, which means hangman with crabs.

Under the extreme, pyroclastic conditions in which igneo-capsular condensation occurs, a josephite might be formed having lattice faults in its crystalline shell (effectively microfractures) through which the sulphide core, pressurized by dissolved argon, will slowly leak. The result is a hollow interior with an internal surface having a highly irregular deposition of residual terencium and other salts, the whole then resembling a transparent **geode**. Glimpse apparently discovered one of these, possibly already broken open, and had its internal composition analysed. By that means he came to realize that he was in possession of a novel, and commercially valuable, source of terencium concentrates.

13   THE INTUITION REMINDER

Richard Worse looked forward to Thursday evenings. Every week that both he and Sigrid were in town, they would meet for a conversation over an informal meal. Apart from his housekeeper's visiting, it was the single regularity in Worse's life, and had been so for many years.

Tonight they had chosen Indian, but the cuisine was never a priority; that was always the conversation. They would generally review the travails and amusements of their respective working weeks, talk about people, events, politics, psychiatry, art, illness, philosophy and language. Their friendship was deep, intellectual, and platonic. For Worse, in many ways, it served to restore the normative, as well as bring some lightness to a life that was often solitary, ruminative, and intensely focused on the criminal mentality of others.

On this particular evening, he did arrive ruminative. He had spent the afternoon studying a folder of documents from Thomas Worse, sent by secure email. It included a little about Thomas himself, a personal account of the Worse family in Dante, and a history of the disputation with a certain Mortiss family going back to the nineteenth century. As far as had been determined, it started in 1877 with a frontier-style gunfight between a Worse ancestor and an outlaw called Rigo Mortiss. A contemporary witness account of the incident was recorded in the town newspaper, and Thomas had scanned archival copy for Worse's benefit.

Ordinarily, Rigo Mortiss would have been forgotten along with his unmarked grave. But he had brothers, who seemed to have nothing more to occupy their time than to mount repeated revenge attacks on Thomas M Worse I, as he was now identified in family documents. Fortunately, these were routinely repelled.

Then something unexpected happened: the Mortiss brothers became rich. Starting with standover tactics in the licensed water storage and carriage trade, they next amassed a fortune in silver mines by expedient theft of title using the proven business model of forgery, extortion and murder. The following generation embezzled the family interests into railroads, ranching, and the nascent car industry, most of which survived in descendent businesses within the modern corporate empire still named Mortiss Bros.

Meanwhile, the Worse family had incarnated, over six generations, a Thomas M Worse, the First to the Sixth, in continuous incumbency of the office of sheriff, with oversight of the civil and legal protections of the citizens of Dante.

Worse described recent developments to Sigrid, beginning with the email from Anna Camenes, of whom Sigrid knew, though the two had never met. When he came to the part about the six incarnations of Thomas M Worse as sheriff of Dante, Sigrid gave a short laugh and said, 'Like the Dalai Lama,' at the very moment that a bowl of palak paneer was placed before her. The waiter gave her a curious look before disappearing.

'Thomas included a dossier on the current Mortiss business as well. He didn't say, of course, but some of the reports have a sophistication that suggests to me they run, or at least have in the past, a police intelligence operation on the family.'

'That's good,' said Sigrid.

Worse served food onto their plates, and Sigrid took up the discussion.

'The question for you seems to be whether the vendetta is going global, as Thomas suggests it might, and therefore whether they'll take an interest in you and your loved ones. From your distinctly dismissive tone, I take it that you don't view the possibility seriously.'

'I was avoiding that word,' he said. But he was thinking about 'loved ones'.

'Vendetta? You can avoid it. The whole dispute appears to be rather one-sided, though. More vendetta than feud. I think it's suitably descriptive.'

Worse acknowledged the point. Sigrid continued.

'What reason do you think Thomas might have for expressing that concern?'

'That's not really been made clear to me,' said Worse.

'Why might that be?' she asked.

'Maybe it's not clear to him.'

'Yes. An intuition perhaps, at this stage. If your cousin is anything like you, he would give value to intuition but want to establish the facts before arguing its case.' Sigrid looked up from her meal. 'Do you have any reason to suppose that Thomas is anything other than a competent, functioning law officer?'

'None at all,' said Worse.

He was beginning to see what Sigrid might be thinking.

'Then if he is a competent, functioning law officer, he is unlikely to hold an exaggerated or irrational view of what might be the case. In fact, such a person, by knowledge and training, would be among the least likely to err in that way.'

'Except, for Thomas this is personal. Professional norms might not apply in that circumstance.'

'Yes, that is true. But it's also personal for you, Richard, and you aren't developing a paranoia. Quite the opposite: you seem to be resisting ordinary caution, let alone paranoia. You are resisting a belief that is expressly tentative and doesn't even belong to you; it belongs to Thomas. But you are resisting also the possibility that his intuition might have foundation, and the necessary facts might in future be adduced to support his belief and that it could prove to be anything but paranoid.'

Worse felt himself being drawn reluctantly toward a shifted perspective by what seemed to be reasoning in a vacuum.

'What about my intuition? My intuition tells me there's absolutely nothing to worry about for me in Perth.'

It sounded defensive, and he knew he was in for some kind of logic storm.

'Richard. Your intuition is fine. It's not the point. Let's assume for a moment, in the absence of facts to the contrary, that you and Thomas have equivalent psychological health, identical skills of hypothesis formation, and don't differ in your powers of intuitive reasoning. Then we observe that Thomas knows far more, far more, than you do about the vendetta thing and the whole Mortiss story. Including the feasibility and likelihood of it becoming international. Whose hypothesis in the matter, formed intuitively, would you give greater notice to?'

Worse was going off his food.

'You've turned quite Bayesian in the time I have known you,' he said.

'I have you to thank for that, Richard. Now look at it from the other side, the Mortiss side. For all you know, there may be a heap of paranoia there. Or spite, or insanity, or extremist bigotry, or financial incentive, or coercion or anything else that might motivate attacks on the Worse family, as it evidently has in the past.'

Worse was deeply uncomfortable. He resisted the impulse to look at his watch. Sigrid's tone changed to something softer.

'Has anything odd been happening that you've noticed?' she asked.

'Nothing at all. I mean, why would they target me? How would they even know about me?'

'There are always possibilities. Thomas's email links you to him. It may have been intercepted. They may have business interests in Perth for which you are somehow a threat. You may be unaware there's a Mortiss connection to all sorts of matters.

Then there was Darian's book last year. Anyone who read that would find the Worse name and be able to piece together quite a lot about you. We tried to protect your identity, but he was very astute. Have you read it, Richard?'

'No.'

'You should. At the very least, for your personal risk management. There's a lot of detail.'

Worse could see a way of moving the subject in a different direction.

'What was he like, Darian?' he asked.

'Interesting. Charming. You're not going to want to hear this but he reminded me of you in some ways. Not physically. Intellectually. Read the book.'

Worse wasn't enjoying the digression any more than the safety lecture it was intended to evade. He adopted a defeated silence. Sigrid returned to lecturing.

'Richard, I have learned valuable things from you over the years, and it feels tonight as if I need to repeat some back to you. One is to trust intuition. Intuition is valid, you say. And I might point out that trust can extend to the intuition of others. There was also something about anticipating adversity; that it's better to deal with risk than realization.'

Worse was feeling exhausted. Sigrid seemed to be energized by concern for him. He hadn't expected her to take the subject so seriously. Dante, Arizona seemed a world away. Vendetta talk was archaic, or at least peculiarly foreign. He wanted the evening to move on. He wanted to regain his appetite for palak.

'Well, thanks for listening,' he said, thinking that really he should be thanked for that. He had hardly eaten at all, and reached for a papadum, though more for its name than nutrition.

He broke it in two and handed some to Sigrid.

'Now, what's been happening in your week?'

14   FRIDAY LATEST

Worse was meditative, and his walking slowed in step with the mood. The discussion with Sigrid had been disturbing. He knew from experience that her views were always well reasoned and presented with uncompromised directness. If Sigrid was not reassuring, it meant that she had determined there was insufficient reason to be.

He had brought to their dinner a family curiosity to share, a *divertimento*, and she had changed it into something quite different, something heavier and absurdly operatic in its threat.

Well, Sigrid alone hadn't. She was more the facilitator in a process of assisted discovery. Worse understood that such a change, some rehypothesized reality perhaps, falls naturally and often unpredictably from the dialectic of any serious conversation.

And Sigrid knew about realities. Distinguishing the sane from the not sane, the rational from the delusional, were tasks of daily clinical judgement. Worse trusted her unconditionally. But just now, tonight, he felt resistant to her analysis, and the weight of *Famille Oblige* that came with it.

He turned into a smaller, deserted cross-street for a quicker way home. The right side was a construction site for the entire block, and the adjacent pavement and road lane were closed to traffic and littered with machinery, building materials, security lighting and debris. Signs instructed pedestrians to use the opposite footpath, but Worse ignored them. He found places of industry fascinating, and was quite content to negotiate any obstacles in order to see what was there.

Then he heard the music. One bar repeated. A semiquaver of threnody, two bass *fortissimo*, closing with an outrageously intrusive audience cough. Every Seneca enthusiast, anywhere in the world, would recognize that sublime engine melody and wave the club sign. By tradition, every rider would return it and, whatever the urgency in their day, graciously pull over to display their machine and exchange motorcycle tales of the mythic.

Worse was walking on the road, and he straddled the temporary bollard fence into the closed lane to avoid being hit from behind. He was half aware that what he heard was somehow imperfect, not in proper keeping with its cause. When he looked back at the bike's headlight he realized what it was. Tempo. Even the meekest Seneca man or woman coming into that empty street would impulsively raise throttle uphill and to hell with it. Senecas were that type of machine.

Both riders stared at him under helmet visors as they passed. Worse made the badge wave. It wasn't returned. Worse now had two reasons to feel unsettled. Two ridiculously insignificant reasons, but they compounded on the agitation he felt since talking to Sigrid. *Intuition is valid.* He stayed inside the fence to watch them.

Fifty metres on, the bike slowed and turned. Worse was now in no doubt that he was in trouble. He couldn't imagine that they were coming back for some innocent chatter. *Hey, man. What was that with the weird hand thing? Like our bike?*

Out of habit, he had taken in his surroundings, noting defensive assets and escape lines. Across the road was glass-walled retail and office frontage. No protection. Ahead of him was a large refuse skip piled high with rubble. Not long before, he had passed a parked excavator. On his right was a wire-net security fence at the worksite boundary. The choice was uphill towards the approaching bike, or downhill away from it, and the merit of each depended on precisely how the others behaved. Better to be patient, read the enemy, and then make the optimal decision.

The bike came at him, headlight high, the music louder and the tempo faster. He saw them adopt a classic attack manoeuvre and it determined how he moved. Simultaneously, the steer man leaned to his left and the pillion man leaned to the right. The effect was to maintain the bike's balance while opening up a forward line of sight for the right-handed shooter at the rear.

Worse ran forward. In doing that, he frustrated their battle plan by putting the front man between himself and the shooter, who needed seconds to raise his right arm over the head of his accomplice. That action required communication and both to readjust their postures in unison. Four shots ricocheted from the edge of the steel as Worse disappeared between the refuse skip and the security fence. Keeping down, he reached the far end and slipped around its corner.

The bike stopped near where Worse had been standing just downhill from the skip. He could hear it idling and see lights reflected in the office building opposite. Worse anticipated their game plan. The steer man would stay with the bike, covering that escape. The other would walk up the road, jump the bollards, and force Worse to retreat along the security fence. What they might not be expecting was that the man in their pincer was armed.

The immediate threat was the pillion man. Worse followed the figure's distorted reflection in the window across the street, and had a very good idea of his location. In contrast, his stalker could only know that Worse was somewhere between the fence and the skip or at the forward end. In Worse's profession, this was referred to as a tactical asymmetry. Its effect was that when Worse suddenly stood up, he had the milliseconds advantage for targeting, enough to place a shot through the visor before the other could respond.

Worse stepped sideways as he panned to the man at the front, and fired. The visor shattered and a pistol jerked upwards, discharging into the air. The body collapsed sideways to the road with the bike gently reclining on top.

Still holding his weapon, Worse crossed over the bollard fence and checked the pockets of the pillion shooter. Then he walked down the road and searched the front man. He stood there for half a minute listening to the idling Seneca, wondering if he could ever love that sound again. When he touched his gun muzzle to an ignition short, the melody briefly surged, then stopped on the threnode.

15 MONSIGNOR PAPADUOMO

Dear Worse

You were right about Glimpse. He followed Paulo and me to the cave and surprised us. He was about to shoot us when we were saved by a big cave crab that came out of nowhere and attacked him. The police have been across from Madregalo to remove his body.

Paulo and I later had a look inside his truck. We found he had been collecting josephites. There was a hand-drawn map that suggests he found them in a volcano on the plateau. We've never heard of volcanoes here, but we think we will go exploring to look for it.

Well, thanks for the warning about him. He never told us why he planned to kill us, but I'm sure from the way he behaved that I was the one targeted and Paulo was just unlucky to be with me.

I hope you are doing well.
Regards
Nicholas

The next morning, Worse checked local radio and online news sources. There was one brief reference to an overnight motorcycle accident involving two deceased males, with no mention of gunshot wounds or the finding of firearms at the scene. Investigators had not ruled out alcohol and speed as factors.

Indeed. Zero speed. Had they not stopped to attempt murder, they would not be dead on the street. Worse smiled at the subterfuge: truth, but not the whole truth, allowing predictable human supposition to manufacture the desired false belief. Clearly, the police—Victor Spoiling, probably—had effectively concealed proceedings from press and public behind a cloak of the implicitly mundane.

Worse had spent some hours in the night examining two smartphones taken from his attackers. As he expected, they were prepaid with no contractual records identifying their owners. But they were informative. The stored number registers and call histories were dull, in that the two mostly phoned each other, except for two calls to the steer man from a silent US number. But the location data were valuable. Using dynamic mapping software, Worse could clock their movements over several days, compare the two profiles, and be reasonably confident that they both slept at the same location. Moreover, both phones had an integrated activity monitor that recorded in background mode the times of flights climbed, and these were correlated in place each evening.

At 6.00 am, Worse walked out on his level 33 balcony, holding a mug of coffee. He was about to make a call on his mobile, when it rang.

'Worse? Was that you?'

'Yes, Victor, this is Worse.'

'Worse. I am European. I once had an umlaut in my name. Plus a j. I do not mistake tenses. Was that you?'

'I apologize. Yes. I was about to phone you with a sensibly redacted confession. Why ever did you think of me?'

'Because whenever a person unknown vanishes intact leaving every perpetrator with a centred head shot, I am reminded of your preternatural skills in self-preservation. Tell me what happened, Worse.'

'It was unexpected. I was targeted. They did a U-turn for a look at me with the headlight. That gave me some time to react.'

'Who were they?'

'I've really no idea.'

'Well, who have you been annoying since we wrapped up that Humboldt matter, other than everyone who knows you?'

'No one. I've been nice.'

'Mm. You don't sound very changed. Worse, it's really very difficult when you thoroughly kill everybody. We're left with no one to interview.'

'It's elementary risk management, Victor. Plus it has proven counter-recidivism value. Your force should adopt it, like they have in other states.'

'Very droll, Worse.'

'What about the bodies?'

'Not yet identified. I've just left the coroner. Some interesting details that I will think about sharing with you. Did you see anything else?'

'No handler's car, no second bike. No loiterer on a mobile.'

'Did they speak to you?'

'Nothing. Professional. Did you recover two weapons?'

'More than two. There was a sawn-off in a pannier.'

'Really? No class after all. Have you traced them?'

'That is in progress. Worse, did you remove anything from the scene?'

'Two mobiles and a sentimental note. You're looking for a third floor accommodation in Fremantle, somewhere in the block bordered by these streets—Hold on.' Worse walked through to his workshop and read the names off a screen. 'That's the best resolution I can give you. Neighbours might have heard their arrivals and departures. Speaking of which, is there anything on the bike?'

'Not a scratch.'

'Victor. Anything on the bike?'

'Expensive. It was purchased new from a city showroom four days ago. The buyer was a male, almost certainly one of your two. We have CCTV. Paid for on a shell company account. We are investigating. Worse, what were you doing there at that time of night?'

'Walking home after a meal out with a friend. It's a regular beat on a Thursday evening.'

'Then be sure to vary your habits. I take it the friend was not with you when the attack happened?'

'No. She drove from the restaurant to her home, as usual. I have told her what happened in case her security is implicated. Also, she's a reliable source of sympathy in difficult times.'

'Sympathy? For you?' Spoiling paused. 'What did you do after the shooting?'

'Continued walking home. More briskly.'

'What is your friend's name?'

'Sigrid Blitt. She's a psychiatrist. Lapsed Freudian. She could help you. You are European.'

'Mm. I will have more information this afternoon. Come to my office at four o'clock. Bring the mobiles, please. You will need to make one of your usual brief and irritatingly guileless statements. Goodbye.'

'Victor. Wait. The Seneca sales people. Do they remember an accent?'

'Worse. You are holding something back. Yes.'

'American?'

'Four o'clock.'

'Hello, Worse. Close the door please.'

Worse complied, then sat down across from Spoiling, who omitted niceties.

'This is very unusual for Australia: an open street attack using a pillion shooter. More often, it is: find address, ring doorbell, and, surprise!'

'I don't have a doorbell for that reason,' said Worse.

Spoiling was seated behind his desk. Worse passed across his signed statement, completed in an outside office.

'And under what name do you masquerade on this occasion?' Spoiling asked, glancing at the signature before consigning the sheet to a document tray.

'Very amusing. Who will believe that a Monsignor would carry a weapon and dispose of two killers with such alacrity? You know, Worse, one day I will have to pull you in on the felony charge of mockery of convention.'

'And who else but you would be my companion on the scaffold, Victor?'

'Mm. Just when I was looking forward to a quiet working week to attend to more elevated business, you have to interrupt my train of thought.'

'What other business? Maybe I can help.'

'Thank you, but it's not in the specialty of justifiable homicide. An Academy lecture. On validity problems. Confession and denial, witness testimony, DNA match, application of precedent, that sort of thing.'

'Emphasize the fallacies; that would be my advice,' said Worse.

Spoiling looked at Worse, taking in the comment but staying with the matter in hand.

'This morning, we searched a short-term rental unit in Fremantle. Thank you for the address.'

He stopped talking, apparently deep in thought.

'Well?' said Worse.

'Travel documents, probably forgeries. Forensics has them. We have no record of either entering the country. They were living out of suitcases. Many hats, peculiarly.'

Again Spoiling fell silent.

'Well?' repeated Worse.

'There were three suitcases and three beds, Worse. Warm

coffee on the stove. Someone absconded, probably after hearing news of the motorcyclist deaths.'

'Made a haberdash for the exit, you might say. Male?'

'From the clothes, yes. We have prints, DNA, and a neighbour's description. Until we find him, you need to be extremely cautious, my friend.'

Spoiling gave Worse a look of genuine concern.

'So, we have an imported MO, probably imported operators, and international monies funding the bike.'

'American?' asked Worse.

'So far, everything's American. Now tell me why you ask.'

Worse gave an account of his communication with Thomas Worse in Arizona, and the American's concern that an historical vendetta was recrudescing badly with the threat of global reach. Not until the end did he state the name of interest: Mortiss.

'Ah. Then we have a connection, to the ultimate payment for the motorcycle,' said Spoiling.

'It was funded from a Mortiss entity, in Arizona?'

'So it seems. A shipping line.'

'In Arizona? In the desert?'

'You do cause me headaches, Worse.'

'I'm sorry.'

Worse was quiet for several seconds. When he spoke, he might have been in a different conversation.

'Let me help with the validity lecture, Victor. I could critique the proposition that intuition has validity. Let's name it "Premonition is Prediction".'

Spoiling stared at Worse.

'You seem to be more interested in philosophy than survival, Worse.'

'As is virtuous, Victor. It's Socratic. And it is European. What's the name of the shipping company?'

'Camelline Shipping,' said Spoiling, a little absently.

'Victor! Camel Line. Ship of the desert. It's a front!'

'Yes, of course. I was about to think that. You distracted me with Socrates.'

'This definitely warrants a covert expedition. I'll phone you tonight.'

'Mm. Actually, Worse, about my lecture. I would appreciate some discussions; perhaps your looking over a draft when I have written it.'

'Then may I see everything you have on the Americans, Victor? Socrates. Socrates.'

Spoiling's posture straightened. 'My dear Monsignor Papaduomo. This is a police investigation, conducted with scrupulous propriety, in which you are the principal witness. I cannot leave you sitting at my desk with all the files open and my office door shut while I go out on a time-consuming mission to find us coffees.' Spoiling stood up. 'Americano today, will it be?'

16 CAMELLINE SHIPPING

Thomas
A development here. Two shooters riding a Seneca came for me on a city street last night. Professional MO. The bike has been linked to a Mortiss company. Why the sudden heavy attention on me, I wonder?
Richard

Jeez, Richard. Are you all right? How did you beat them off?

Totengräber 9, Prussica sight. Every Worse should carry one.

Damn it, cousin. That's a very serious incident. Take care for God's sake. It looks like a hunch came true. All the same, what you're describing is major escalation. Nothing on that level has happened here for half a century. Maybe Regan's decided to go global, she could be that crazy. We might have to get alerts to the whole Worse family if that scenario takes shape. What do you do, by the way? Maybe that explains why they came for you. I've heard about the Prussica, but we can't get them here, at least not legally.

Not legally here, either. I live off income from the past. Nowadays, I assist the police in their enquiries, but in a good way. Generally related to financial crimes. Incidentally, would you mind if I look into your email security at the time we first corresponded? It's possible that a Mortiss was on the line. The bike attack is being handled here by Inspector Victor Spoiling. I would like to put you in touch informally, via secure mail. If the Arizona connection proves real, you can move to formal channels. Also, unless you have an objection I would like to make your Mortiss material available to Victor.

Worse was in his home IT workshop. He had been sitting before the screens for three hours without dinner and without a break. His first task was to examine Thomas's police email protection. The security was two years outdated in key patches, and Worse had no difficulty in accessing the sheriff's office accounts. Someone else had been there as well, and Worse sent an encrypted report to Thomas detailing the breach, advising on how to combat it, and providing the serial number and address of the machine that was implicated.

Then he turned his attention to Mortiss Bros and Camelline Shipping. It was just before 10.00 pm when he phoned Spoiling.

'Yes, Worse.'

'Victor. They don't own ships.'

'You are talking about Camelline Shipping.'

'Yes. No ships. No camels. They own casinos on ships, Victor. What does casino say to you?'

'Money laundering. Illicit transfers. Kitsch. False ceilings. Cigarette smoke. Body odour. Great sadness. Mm. Casinos. My staff had not informed me. Worse, I've been thinking. How would you like to work for me as my probationary sergeant? Public service rates, uniform allowance, police issue revolver, flexible work hours, paternity leave ...'

As Spoiling spoke, Worse stood in his kitchen, pouring tea.

'Victor. Nearly a thousand cruise ships in and out of hundreds of unsecured ports over seven seas. It's a dark pool, Victor, hiding under bright lights. Mortiss owns the floor in all of them. The counting house is in Chicago. I'm close to their accounts. When I'm in I will tell you the numbers. Just for now, I estimate there are two to three billion in bankable chips on the table on any given day. Chips, Victor. Easy to move on and off ships along with victuals and luggage and people.'

'What evidence do you have for illegality, Worse?'

'I'm looking, Victor. They could transfer millions across borders and it would wash through to the aggregated accounts. Physical transfers, if they wanted, port to port. Plus electronic transfer ship-to-ship, ship to corporations. Banks. Crime syndicates. Chicago. Those sums would be lost in the noise as far as regulators at the top were concerned.'

'Mm. I trust your methods of enquiry are legitimate, Worse.'

'You know my view that everything accessible to this ordinary member of the public is, self-evidently, available on the public record. The defence of the *ipso facto*, Victor.'

'Worse. The self-evident is moot. You need to consult more the hooligan on the Clapham omnibus to understand modern norms.'

There was a sigh. Modern norms were no more palatable to Spoiling than to Worse.

'Where does Camelline fit in structurally to the larger Mortiss empire?'

'I'm still figuring that out, Victor. There's information available, but I expect the reality is different. They're incorporated in Arizona, with financial control in Chicago.'

'I'm wondering why your Perth incident was linked to Camelline particularly, rather than any other Mortiss entity. Can you give me a complete list of specific ships that have Mortiss casinos?'

'Tomorrow. You are thinking about the Fremantle connection, Victor.'

'You may have to endure an ocean cruise, Worse, in a research capacity.'

'Would that be covered by my sergeant's expense allowance?'

'Good night, Worse.'

Worse was still in his kitchen when he finished the call to Spoiling, and the meaning of the space triggered awareness of hunger. He snacked unhealthily and carried his tea back to the workshop.

It looked as if Camelline was the clearing-house for the various front-end casino operations, such as Sea Dice, that were familiar to the public. It also seemed to serve as the administrating entity for Area Pi, as Worse found personnel records, budget data and requisitions in email traffic between the two. The odd thing was that even Camelline appeared to have little control of financial accounts. Income and expenditures were handled further up a company chain, Camelline acting as a conduit and a filter. It would not have surprised Worse if many casino employees were unaware of their connection to Mortiss Bros, or even Camelline.

Worse had decided that to understand the corporate architecture, and to find its financial control centre, he needed to enter at the top. As he sipped tea, he checked progress on another screen where he was running a classic password attack on the Chicago mainframe.

Meanwhile, there were other matters needing attention. Worse had the account details of the card used to pay for the Seneca, and it was easy to search on auto-teller withdrawals where the same card had been presented. Unsurprisingly, the most common location was in Fremantle. Using date and time information built into the transaction records, Worse could access bank security footage showing their wanted man withdrawing cash. He chose the best quality frames and forwarded them to Spoiling for use in police persons-sought bulletins. His message was headed 'Haberdash', Worse's code-name for their fugitive.

Worse checked the password program again. A new window had opened showing initial solutions by user name and password, and the list was growing rapidly. As he ran a cursor down the page, the identity and company role of each user was shown in a separate box. One stood out as likely to be the most valuable, and Worse chose it: he signed in as Arnold Tweisser, Chief Financial Officer.

It was immediately clear to Worse that he had struck the mother lode of Mortiss Bros financials. He was taken straight to a menu page for an entity called Unit Circle Fiduciary that had the hallmarks of being a private bank. It had several levels of secondary protection, all familiar to Worse. He found the financial trunk line to Camelline, and from Camelline the hundreds of connections radiating to shipping agents, casino suppliers, mainstream banks and, more interestingly, Area Pi. Worse followed it all, copying some files, and taking notes.

As he took advantage of Tweisser's access, and revisited some of his online history, something started to look unusual. At first, Worse was not greatly bothered by a few anomalies, but the further he explored, the more intrigued he became. He decided to run a specialist diagnostics package, and when it concluded, he could hardly believe what he was looking at. Someone before him had installed a mockingbird, a phantom account manager that could be concealed in the normally discarded decimal expansion registers of billions of real variable calculations. Worse was aware of very few individuals or security services that had the sophistication to design, install and operate such a tool. He had been planning to insert one into Mortiss Bros himself; to find a sleeper there already was extremely surprising.

The mockingbird had the potential to completely control the Mortiss enterprise, but only a minute fraction of its power had ever been utilized. There was a facility that monitored Unit Circle transactions involving Chinese entities, and there was a low-level siphon that Worse traced to a private account of the chief financial officer himself. Tweisser was stealing from the company.

The discovery altered Worse's plan. It was a far better option to use the mockingbird already in place than to install his own, which always carried a risk of detection. Worse's plan was to disrupt Mortiss Bros temporarily in order to study their security response and set off regulator alarms. He would cause exactly four hours of turmoil, and it would start the following morning, Chicago time.

Before finishing for the night, Worse turned his attention to Spoiling's question about cruise liners with Camelline casinos, and their schedule of visits to Fremantle. It did seem a reasonable possibility that Haberdash might be smuggled out of the country using company connections. He sent the information to Spoiling.

Worse himself was more interested in how Camelline operated as a shelf company, and particularly why it should be the administrative controller for Area Pi. He was also curious how a vast network of borderless casinos might function within a much larger criminal organization.

> Dear Sigrid
> You are cordially invited on an all-expenses-paid cruise to La Ferste, calling at Singapore, aboard *Princess Namok*, in the role of the mysterious, convalescing Mrs Worse, whose sole connubial duty will be provision of companionship, conversation,

and an inscrutably diverting casino presence in the course of routine enquiries. Embarkation Monday week. Fourteen nights at sea. Returning airfare included. Guaranteed reading, writing, and relaxing time in luxury conditions on calm seas.

Yours neptunically

Worse

Worse obtained **passwords** by making use of an input/output weakness common in mainframe services. When a large organization has many thousands of employees signing in over a short interval (such as the beginning of a regular workday schedule), user-password data will be queued in a secure ancillary cache in the event of overload. The password data enter the cache in random time order but, for service efficiency, they are accessed by the queue manager (the industry standard is *Q-Man*) in order of string length and alphanumeric homology. This strategy is designed to minimize switching frequency (and therefore queue service time). However, depending on the level of hacker penetration, this I/O regime can be exploited over multiple duty cycles using adaptive linear programming methods to solve for the simplest password, then the next simplest, and so on. The solution time can be dramatically reduced if the hacker submits indicial strings as (erroneous) passwords, but this increases the risk of detection. Paradoxically, one tactic deliberately promotes such detection in order to trigger a corporate-wide password reset. By utilizing the system's non-similarity settings, extra information is obtained using a sorting algorithm based on difference analysis.

17 MOCKINGBIRD

Arnold Tweisser sat in a windowless vestibule outside the boardroom, awaiting his summons. Saviccia had been in there an hour, on his own with Regan, and it wasn't sounding pleasant. Every few minutes Tweisser heard her raised voice, cursing and threatening. He didn't know if he could withstand that kind of scene.

But he didn't know how to avoid it either. He couldn't get away now. He could never tell Regan that he wanted out, that he was leaving Mortiss Bros. The company owned him, and she owned the company. From the time of its founding brothers, there were uniquely Mortiss traditions around managerial dissatisfaction, and Regan had relished their firm reinstatement. She would kill him.

He tried to work, to keep abreast of the turmoil in the Unit Circle accounts, but his mind was wandering. He closed his laptop and thought again about what was happening. In the last three hours they had been the target of an unbelievable attack. Although there was no evidence of theft, funds were oscillating between accounts so fast that balances didn't make sense and transactions were denied. Three hundred million dollars in creditor payments, including to the IRS, were blocked. Default notices were being issued. Auditor alerts and watchlisting had been triggered automatically. Secretive venture capital enterprises that banked with Unit Circle were pressuring for explanations. The more unsavoury client organizations and entrepreneurs were blatantly threatening.

The problem was spreading as they tried to understand it,

from Unit Circle to Camelline and every other business in the Mortiss Bros empire, as far away as the terencium operation that was supposed to be ultra secret. They were starting to lose their secure internal email channels as well. Area Pi was silent. Their own surveillance operations that had caught the Misgivingston–Worse contact were shut down. Here in the centre of downtown Chicago, they were progressively being isolated from the world outside.

Experts were on-site already. They weren't the best available because no one liked working for Mortiss Bros, and that was because no one liked Regan. The expectation was that the chaos would stabilize and they would soon receive a ransom demand offering to withdraw the attack. The business model was this: if the problem could be fixed internally first, and defences restored, the attackers got nothing. If not, the ransom would be paid on trust that services would be restored to normal. Expenditure of this nature was a recognized operational outgoing in the modern corporate world. It saved businesses and it saved people. The technology damage and the monetary demand would both be carefully calibrated to wound but not kill the company.

That was the strategic balance of the game. Enough poison to want to pay the witchdoctor, but not enough to render payment unfeasible. At this hour of the day, they were still awaiting contact. No one asked why, if an attacker could do this to them, he didn't simply raid their accounts for the fee he wanted. No one considered that the assault might be primarily malicious rather than extortionate. No one thought that the poison might keep coming, that its purpose truly was to kill off Mortiss Bros.

Tweisser heard more shouting. His pulse was racing and slowing crazily. He was sweating. He felt faint. Mortiss Bros may be in trouble, but so was he. A phantom account called a mockingbird, set up for him to supplement his wife's lifestyle, was not only exposed, it was front and centre of the attack.

Of all the possibilities, this had been chosen by the hacker as a central hub for the insanely fast traffic of funds in and out of subsidiaries. Not only had it been discovered and utilized, it was given special prominence by being labelled 'Mockingbird'. Regan couldn't fail to see it. She would ask why it was there. She was probably interrogating Saviccia about it. He would be saying he had never heard of it, and that would be the truth. When Tweisser was asked, he would say the same thing, but Regan would know he was lying.

On the other hand, she obviously liked him; she had practically undressed for him after the last meeting. She would want to believe in his innocence. And even if there remained doubts, she might be forgiving. The main thing was to recreate that tenderness they nearly had together. He felt better thinking about it, about the white lace and the lovely smile and being alone together. He had to let her know how important she was to him, and as long as his wife wasn't mentioned— that really did kill the mood last time—he could win her over and Mockingbird would become the last thing on her mind. He would shut down his link to it, stay with Mortiss Bros, and have assignations with Regan every working day. Now he was looking forward to seeing her.

The door opened and Saviccia appeared, looking shaken, and carrying a still-open laptop. He threw a dark look at Tweisser as he passed. Immediately, Tweisser's name was called. He entered the boardroom and closed the door.

'What the fuck is going on, Tweisser? What is Mockingbird?'

He wasn't invited to sit down, and stood beside the chair he normally occupied at board meetings.

'I hadn't heard of Mockingbird until this morning, Ms Mortiss. I assume the attacker set it up as a facility for this super-fast transfer activity. That appears to be its function.'

That was good. He was sure that he sounded calm.

'Wrong, Tweisser. Now we know what it looks like, we can see it in the archived transactions history. It's been there two years, Tweisser. It's an account. You're the accountant. Explain it to me.'

Regan was seated in the chairman's position, a laptop open before her. Her leather shoulder bag was on the table beside the computer.

'Well?' she said.

'I know nothing about that account, Ms Mortiss. I thought it was newly created.'

Regan reached out to her bag. Her grasp seemed much less caressing than last time. She removed a pistol and placed it on the table, sat back, and looked at him coldly.

'Tweisser. You're lying. Whatever damage our hacker is causing, he has done the company one service. He found irregularities, and he's told us about them. He tells us how much goes into Mockingbird and how much goes out. More importantly, where it goes when it leaves. Do you want to stop looking at my body and tell me where it goes, Tweisser?'

Tweisser felt weak. It wasn't turning out the way he wanted. He couldn't answer. He needed to tell her about his feelings. Regan filled the silence.

'You're a dumb-ass, Tweisser. It goes to a personal account in Oak Park. Where you live. The account has a number and a name. Your fucking name, Tweisser.'

She picked up the pistol and pointed it at him.

'Ms Mortiss. You know I ... I love ... I loved ...' he said.

'In that case you won't resent my little upsets,' she said.

Without getting up from her seat, she shot him through his pacing lead. Of course, that wasn't visible to her and not what she aimed for; it was a chance hit. The intention was a lazy chest shot—fatal, but indifferent to exact anatomy.

Tweisser stumbled, reached for his director's chair, and eased himself into it. He was staring down. From behind, he might have been the first to a board meeting, waiting thoughtfully for others to arrive. From the front, there was a bloody stain enlarging on his white business shirt.

'Regan ...'

For the first time, he dared to call her that. After all the fantasizing it was the most intimate moment he was ever to share with her.

'Don't over-dramatize it, for fuck's sake.'

She returned the pistol to her bag and crossed to a telephone intercom on a drinks cabinet.

'Tell Pastor Sendoff I want him here.'

Andrei Andreevich Sendoff entered the boardroom without knocking. Regan was seated before her laptop at the far end of the table, absorbed in the company crisis. Tweisser was still sitting halfway along, hunched forward and breathing stertorously, his hands clamped to the table edge for support. He managed to raise his eyes to look at Sendoff. Regan stood up.

'Console me, Andrei.'

Sendoff glanced at Tweisser as he crossed the room to embrace Regan.

'You have been bad, my little peasant undressant confessant.'

'I am penitent, Father.'

She pushed against his body and kissed him, then threw him back. Her voice turned businesslike.

'Get rid of him for me.'

Sendoff looked at Tweisser, who had managed to tilt his head slightly to observe their interaction.

'He doesn't seem quite ready. How long ...?'

'I know. He's dragging it out, the asshole. It's indecorous. Call the company removalists and we'll hope he's through in time,' she said.

Sendoff went to the telephone and made a call.

'Did you have a plan?' he said to Regan, when that was done.

'You're leaning on it,' she said.

Sendoff looked down at the drinks cabinet. If they emptied it of all the cocktail paraphernalia, they could easily conceal Tweisser and get him out of the building as a piece of furniture.

'Brilliant.'

He began moving bottles of liquor to the board table.

'Explain that we're refurbishing, and we want to install this one in the saloon on the cruiser. Then, go with William on a fishing trip and dump it in the lake. Pack in some bricks to sink it.'

Tweisser groaned objection, struggling to raise his head. Sendoff and Regan observed him.

'Isn't it all a little prolonged?' he asked.

'He's learning not to cheat on Mortiss Bros,' she said. 'The bigger the scam, the longer the lesson. Don't you usually do last rites or something?'

Sendoff looked uninterested, but dutifully seated himself across the table from Tweisser. He waved his arms around.

> 'Hoco poco witchimodo
> Presso squero sensu fu
> Ecce homo cum passis me
> Orla bestia yuta yu
> Orla bestia yu.'

He concluded with the sign of the cross, muttering what sounded like 'Limbo, Limbo'.

Tweisser's eyes were barely open, staring emptily at the ceremony.

'Sometimes I think you aren't a real pastor, Andrei,' said Regan.

'How hurtful you can be, my beautiful. That is the same Paleo-Romo-Moscovian prayer used by my father on the occasion of his fourth wife's spontaneous combustion. I shall be pleased to incant the conjugal version when I shortly hear your confession upon this table.'

Sendoff moved to stand behind Regan, his hands fondling her shoulders.

Tweisser stirred and groaned loudly, trying to turn toward her. He was the one who had wanted Regan on the table.

'Andrei, I've got a god-awful disaster unfolding here. Just get the damned cupboard ready and start dragging him over.'

Tweisser was now breathing rapidly and looking pale. Sendoff resumed the task of moving bottles.

'What will you say to the family. Do you know if he has a wife?' he asked.

Regan continued working for a few seconds before answering. She looked up when they heard a heavy thud as Tweisser's head finally rested itself on the table.

'I'll tell her the truth. We had a meeting. I will say he was most endearingly affected when we spoke of her. But I thought he didn't look well. When I last saw him, he was getting stuck into the liquor cabinet.'

It remains unclear, from the limited clinical description and in the absence of autopsy findings, precisely what injuries **Tweisser** sustained. It is possible that his underlying cardiac rhythm in the event of pacemaker disconnection was complete heart block. The slow, fixed rate would tend to reduce internal bleeding, accounting for his delayed deterioration, but also exclude a compensatory tachycardic response to progressive haemorrhagic shock. The agonal state was likely ventricular fibrillation, which might have been (at least temporarily) reversed if the cardioverter lead had not been shot through.

Though a competent chief financial officer, Tweisser lacked the expertise required to install and operate a mockingbird. Its provenance was subsequently revealed by Worse to a confidential enquiry. There have been persistent suggestions that it was planted by a federal agency in the course of a covert investigation, but this is denied. Typically in such situations, a suite of enticements would be directed to vetted individuals in order to establish compromise. Tweisser's theft account was undoubtedly set up and provided to him for that purpose.

18 HABERDASH

The *Princess Namok* docked early morning, and suite guests were allowed to embark from midday. Worse collected Sigrid by taxi and they were driven to the Fremantle shipping terminal.

When they were through passport and security checks and finally on board, they took an elevator to the Sky level and found their suite. As Worse was touching his key card to the stateroom door, a white-jacketed staff member appeared, seemingly from nowhere. He introduced himself as Hilario, and said he was their dedicated steward for the trip.

Hilario followed them into the suite to explain some of the services. Their luggage had already been delivered. Worse asked Hilario where he stayed.

'Just across the corridor, Mr Worse, but I do not sleep. You can call me at any time, day or night.' He demonstrated how he could be summoned through the ship's telephone.

Worse felt an instinctual trust of Hilario, and motioned him aside. He handed over a generous gratuity.

'We value our privacy. Very much,' emphasized Worse. Hilario nodded. 'Mrs Worse is recovering from an illness and will want no interruptions.' Hilario nodded again. Somehow the banknotes had disappeared from his hand without Worse seeing where they went. 'We will dine at the late sitting, table for two only, beside the window. No children within hearing.'

Hilario picked up a suitcase and Worse motioned toward one of the bedrooms, at the same time indicating that the other case should go to the second room. He was pleased to see that Hilario's face betrayed no sign of surprise or curiosity about this domestic arrangement.

When Hilario had left, Sigrid, who had followed her luggage into the first bedroom and begun to unpack, appeared at the doorway.

'And what illness might it be that Mrs Worse is recovering from?'

'You're a psychiatrist; make one up.'

Sigrid's look was unamused. She returned to unpacking. Worse stepped outside to survey the harbour from their balcony.

They weren't due to sail until the following morning, as the shipping line was hosting a gala charity event with many non-passenger guests. Worse and Sigrid had declined their invitation.

That evening, there was a small queue of passengers outside the restaurant waiting to be shown to their tables. As Worse and Sigrid joined the line, Hilario appeared.

'This way, Mr and Mrs Worse.'

He led them directly inside, politely positioned them before the mandated hand gel dispenser, then showed them to their table by a window. He introduced their waiter and sommelier before moving instantly out of sight.

'Are you forming the impression that Hilario can materialize at will within the space-time continuum?' asked Worse of Sigrid when they were alone.

Sigrid studied the menu.

'I have noticed that. Sometimes I wish I had that gift, especially the disappearing trick during trying consultations.'

Worse smiled.

'I am imagining being your patient: desperately unhappy, unloading my intimate, shameful secrets, verging on psychosis, and you suddenly dematerialize in your deep leather chair. How comforting would that be? What would that do to my tenuous grip on reality?'

Sigrid was unmoved.

'You would need to adjust your assumptions about the world,' she said. 'Which, by the way, is often the key to psychiatric healing in any case. So, you'd feel better and I'd feel better. Slipping in and out of the continuum might be the answer to patient–therapist mutual wellness.'

'Perhaps you should ask Hilario how he does it,' said Worse.

The waiter took their order.

'Speaking of disappearances,' said Sigrid, 'have you read Darian's book yet?'

Worse stored the segue for later enquiry.

'I have.'

'And?'

'Surprisingly good. Surprisingly accurate. How did he find out so much about what happened?'

'Observation and induction. Every question a hypothesis test. Every interview a discreetly controlled experiment. Researched the literature. The scientific method, no less. I said he was a lot like you.'

'Why did you link him to disappearance?' asked Worse.

'Oh, because he lacks an ordinary public persona. He's very private. No one even knows where he lives, though they say he's moved to Madregalo and possibly changed his name. One theory is that he's actually gone into hiding. He's Ferent-speaking, so he could easily blend in over there.'

'Why would he do that?'

'Well, he did offend a lot of people in that book. He's probably barricaded himself from academic and literary reprisals.'

'The very worst kind, I'm sure,' said Worse. 'I didn't see anything offensive, other than invasion of our privacy. My criticism would be that it was irritatingly factual.'

'Then you can look forward to more irritation, Richard.

The talk amongst my friends in the history department is that he's working on what publishers call an eagerly anticipated new work.'

Worse broke apart a bread roll.

'Well, I hope we're not in it.'

Back in their stateroom, Worse set up a work space. The ship's internet service was suboptimal, and he established his own satellite link. He offered Sigrid the use of it, and gave her a password. She puzzled over it, and looked at him enquiringly. Worse shrugged.

'Ask Darian,' he said.

Worse went to his room and re-emerged in a dark tracksuit and black sports shoes, carrying a backpack.

'You're up to something, Richard.'

'I thought it would be nice to look at the harbour for a few hours. I might be in quite late.'

'What's wrong with sitting on the balcony?'

'The view's too limited.'

Worse strongly suspected that Haberdash would be smuggled aboard to get him out of the country. Spoiling's people were checking all the comings and goings on the shore side. Worse would stake out the harbour side, but he had noted earlier that from their balcony the view of the waterline was obstructed by projecting balconies on lower levels. He placed some packaged fruit and nuts in his pack.

'See you in the morning.'

Worse opened their stateroom door and slipped into the empty corridor.

From an earlier reconnaissance during their lifeboat drill, Worse had determined that his best outlook was from the lifeboat deck, which was below the balcony levels. It was also the sporting deck, where passengers could walk or run the ship circuit for exercise. He would not be out of place in a tracksuit, though his choice of timing might seem odd.

He took the elevator down and stepped through a foyer door onto the outside teak decking. There was no one in sight, but the dim safety lighting made his presence obvious. He moved several metres aft to a point where there was least illumination, and looked upwards. Modern lifeboats were very big and stowed very high, he decided.

Worse grasped a steel column and climbed onto the deck rail. From there he could reach up to a crossbeam. Holding that, he walked up the vertical column until he was able to wrap his legs around the beam, then shimmy along to the davit. Once close, he pulled his weight around, stood up, then shuffled sideways to a point where the lifeboat appeared to have a flat upper section. Here, he placed one foot in a lifeline and pulled himself up.

He felt for the most comfortable place to lie down, positioning himself with his head outwards. Looking down, he had an uninterrupted view of the side of the hull to the waterline. Several decks below, close to the stern, there was a large open sea bay that cast yellow light far out onto the water. He checked the time: nearly midnight.

Worse took a scarf from his pack and wrapped it around his neck. He also removed a pair of night vision–recording binoculars and set their focus in day mode on the light from the sea bay. Then he waited.

Lights from other ships across the harbour were progressively extinguished. The sea bay below him went dark. The water was black, and there was no small craft traffic to capture his interest.

At about 3.30 he saw the sea bay light up. Though only momentary, it caught Worse's attention. He raised the binoculars and scanned the river. A small motor launch was heading downstream toward them, with no navigation lights showing. From mid-harbour, it turned toward the ship, heading to the sea bay. When it came alongside, Worse saw a rope ladder dropped to the water line. A man reached out to grasp it and threw his weight across. As he began to climb, he turned his face in Worse's direction while he waved off his boatman.

Worse filmed him until he disappeared into the ship. Then he moved the glasses to focus on the launch, following it until it was out of sight. Satisfied that the action was over, he packed away the equipment and prepared himself for the hazardous descent to deck level. Still lying down, he put on the backpack and turned himself around to look over the inside gunwale and ensure the deck was clear. He was very surprised at what he saw.

Extending from the deck to the hull of the lifeboat just below him, and looped within a lifeline at the top to secure it, was an extension ladder. Worse studied the situation for a full minute. No one was in view. He decided that the sensible thing to do was use it. When he reached the deck he set off for the door leading to the elevators. Before going in, he glanced back. The ladder was gone.

In the elevator, he phoned Spoiling. It was nearly 4.30 but the call was answered on the first ring.

'You're awake, Victor.'

'This lecture, Worse. This lecture. Do you know what a difficult subject is validity?'

Worse briefly sympathized before telling Spoiling of the secret embarkation, and asking if police could intercept the motor launch heading upriver.

'I will send you the video within an hour, Victor. Get some sleep.'

When Worse reached his stateroom, Hilario was in the corridor, impeccably dressed in a starched white jacket.

'Is there anything I can get for you, Mr Worse?'

The door to Sigrid's bedroom was closed. Worse sat at his office desk and downloaded his night vision from the binoculars. He studied the raw footage, then reprocessed a copy through edge-enhancement software. Several frames showed the boarding man's face in sufficient detail to identify him, and it matched the image from the auto-teller in Fremantle. He was Haberdash. Worse sent the material to Spoiling.

There was a soft knock on the stateroom door, and Worse rose to open it. Hilario entered with a tray of tea and fresh sandwiches. He began to set his wares neatly on the breakfast table, but Worse interrupted.

'Thank you very much. I can do that.'

Worse turned to his computer screen with its portrait of Haberdash in eerie green. He motioned Hilario to look at it.

'If you see this man on board, please let me know.'

'Of course, Mr Worse.'

They were due to leave port at 7.00 that morning, bound for La Ferste via Singapore. At 6.00 am the ship's captain broke the silence with an announcement that shore police had determined a need to search the ship, and that all passengers should remain in their cabins with IDs available for inspection. Their sailing time would be later than scheduled.

Worse and Sigrid were perfectly happy to stay in their suite. Hilario served them breakfast on the balcony. As he was leaving, Worse spoke.

'Hilario. Do you know people who work in the casino?'

'The casino people are not part of the shipping line, Mr Worse. They are a different company. They have their own quarters and dining room. They do not mix with our staff. Even the casino bar waiters and cleaners are not ours.'

'Thank you, Hilario.'

When Hilario had gone, Worse looked across at the shipping on the other side of the harbour.

'For an ocean cruise, we haven't gone very far.'

Sigrid didn't mind. She was absorbed in writing a conference paper. Worse went inside to collect his laptop, returning to the balcony to work over breakfast. They didn't notice the next two hours passing, until there was a knock on their door. Worse opened it.

'Victor!' he said. 'Come in. Have you made an arrest?'

'Thank you, Worse.' Spoiling stepped inside. 'Worse, I have seventy officers searching this ship and we have not found him. I feel a headache coming on.'

Worse gestured Spoiling across the suite.

'Come and meet my travel companion.'

They walked out onto the balcony.

'Sigrid, let me introduce Victor Spoiling. Victor, Sigrid Blitt.'

The two shook hands. Worse indicated to Spoiling that he should sit down on a third chair. Without asking, he poured some orange juice and placed it before his friend.

'Thank you, Worse. It is infuriating that we know he is on board and we cannot apprehend him.'

'What do you want me to do if I find him after we've sailed?' asked Worse.

'It's very messy. Detaining him at the captain's discretion. We will need an international warrant, extradition proceedings, escort detail. Very messy.'

'Simpler if I interrogate him then toss him overboard?' said Worse.

Spoiling looked at Worse to judge his seriousness. Then he turned to Sigrid, leaning forward.

'Do you have a strong interest in the matter of validity, Dr Blitt?'

The inexplicable manifestations of their steward noted by Worse and Sigrid almost certainly place Hilario in the rare company of **Erscheinenvolk**. The term was coined by von Steppenbert in 1919 to describe those (one in fifty thousand, approximately) individuals who are notable in the way they appear and disappear in social situations with what would commonly be viewed as unexpected, often arresting, suddenness. Early studies excluded motivated deception and conjuring techniques as explanations; indeed, Erscheinenvolk typically lack insight into their behaviour until made aware by the distress of those around them, for example in the workplace or within intimate relationships. For much of the twentieth century the phenomenon was marginalized to the paranormal, but it is now attracting mainstream scientific attention. The best recent review is by Anna Camenes in *Psi Quarterly*.

Sigrid Blitt's invited conference lecture was entitled *Symptoms Verbalized: The Ekphrastic Challenge of Psychiatric Description*. Also executive editor of the diagnostic manual *Fifteen Valid Moods in Adolescence*, she demonstrably has a 'strong interest' in the subject of Spoiling's question.

19 HIGH ROLLERS

Once aboard, it is not difficult to stow away on a large cruise ship, particularly with the assistance of conspirators. The manhunt was deemed unsuccessful, the police team withdrawn, and the ship allowed to sail at 11.00 am. Worse and Sigrid stood with a group of other passengers on a starboard observation deck, just forward and below the bridge, to watch their departure.

They still didn't know the identity of Haberdash. Finger-prints and DNA from the Fremantle accommodation were nowhere on record, and facial recognition databases using Worse's images proved unhelpful.

Given the connection to Camelline, Worse thought it was likely that Haberdash had been moved through the ship to the casino staff quarters. He had conveyed this idea to Spoiling, who promised that their search of that section was especially thorough.

Thinking about this, Worse messaged Spoiling to ask whether Haberdash was a smoker. Yes, he was; his DNA was on butts recovered in the flat. The only places aboard where smoking would not set off alarms were the outside decks. Sooner or later, reasoned Worse, Haberdash would risk exposure.

The deck surface on this level was dimpled steel plate, but grip was compromised by a glossy paint coating. It also sloped seaward for drainage. Worse walked to the edge and looked over. All that protected him from a long fall to the water were two strands of stainless steel wire tensioned between steel posts topped by a varnished timber handrail. No wonder a sign inside the door declared this deck off limits to passengers during bad weather, with compliance encouraged by clearly evident security camera monitoring.

The casino, inauspiciously situated on level 13, was closed while in port. The public-access section was designed to be a thoroughfare to capture impetuous souls walking through the ship, seduced by the sparkle of gaming machines.

Worse found no enjoyment in gambling, and detested card games especially. When he and Sigrid entered, the dozens of colourful slot machines were alight with flashy promise, and a few blackjack tables were staffed by croupiers awaiting custom. At one end, below the sign *Bank* in gold antique script, were two cashier windows with curlicue grilles. Beside this was a door guarded by a casino employee. Hilario had described this as the entry to the private room reserved for high-stakes gamblers. He thought there were also management offices there, connected to the bank.

They passed through the area slowly, headed for the next aft elevator lobby, and returned to their stateroom. Worse poured glasses of mineral water, handed one to Sigrid, and toasted.

'Underway at last.'

'Underway at least,' she responded.

Worse picked up a telephone extension to request lunch, but before he had pressed for service there was a knock on the door. It was Hilario with menus. When he had left with their orders, Worse followed Sigrid out to the balcony.

'It's unsettling, you know. No sooner do I think of calling him than he appears. It can't all be explained by coincidence.'

'Yes it can,' said Sigrid definitely.

Worse looked at her doubtfully.

'And another thing,' he added. 'Have you ever seen him laugh, or even smile? For a man named Hilario, it's out of character.'

'You're obviously not amusing enough. Try to be more witty,

Richard. I could be better entertained as well.'

'Then I shall do my best to make him smile at least once on this cruise,' said Worse.

After a short silence, Sigrid asked, 'You do trust him?'

'Oh yes. Very much so,' said Worse.

After lunch, Sigrid left to explore the library. Worse investigated the ship's security system. He could easily access the CCTV feed, and he set up a multi-panel display from those cameras covering exits to outer deck areas. To this he added a screen-based movement detector with an alarm, which he planned to switch on only at night. Police had shown their wanted person's photograph to all passengers and crew; if Haberdash decided to emerge from hiding for a cigarette, or to assuage claustrophobia, he would choose a time when most people were in bed. Worse also studied the ship's deck plan. The closest, most easily accessible fresh air to the casino was the observation deck where he and Sigrid had watched their departure from Fremantle.

The next day was rougher, with the threat of a storm. It was a formal night in the restaurant, and Worse reluctantly wore a tuxedo.

After dinner, he led Sigrid to the casino. There, he went straight to the cashier and showed his passenger ID to purchase five thousand dollars of chips. As he turned away, the doorman at the private entrance said, 'Sir, Madam,' and used a key card to open the door for them.

Inside, there were five tables. A door to their right appeared to lead to the bank area, and probably private offices. Next to it was a large mirror that Worse suspected was one-way glass. If there were a staircase to the catwalk used for surveillance of the tables, it was probably in the office. There seemed to be no other doorway; apparently, access to the casino staff quarters was also through the office. The deck map had not been sufficiently detailed to reveal this, and he decided that he needed to access the original naval architect's plan.

Worse led Sigrid to a roulette table at the far end of the room. There were four empty seats, but he chose to stand. Those gambling were being served lavish quantities of champagne and spirits, and he felt sorry for them. In a game of chance, the only control players retained was how much to lose—whether to start and when to stop; alcohol stole even that from them.

He watched the wheel and the chip placements for about fifteen minutes, when the croupier spoke to him.

'Placing bets, Mr Worse?'

'Observing the balance, for now,' replied Worse. A few minutes later, he and Sigrid moved to a blackjack table, watched the game briefly, then made their exit. At the bank, he cashed in the chips.

'Not lucky today, Mr Worse?'

'I wouldn't say that,' Worse replied. 'The swell is a little strong for the wheel, I thought.'

'We hope to see you back when the weather calms. Good night, Mr Worse.'

But the weather didn't calm. Worse sat at his computer and studied the ship's plans. There was a service elevator accessed from the casino office area adjacent to the private room. This would connect to level 4, where Hilario had said the casino employees were quartered.

The key drawings were those detailing the ship's services. Worse estimated that the ceiling space above the gaming tables was more than two metres in height, accommodating air conditioning, power, communications, drainage and sprinkler system ducts. There was no indication of access for casino security, but a catwalk could easily have been a *post hoc* modification during the fit-out. If so, Spoiling's search team, using the ship's plans, would likely have missed it. Worse wanted to get into the casino office and see for himself. He suspected the way up might be via a folding attic ladder concealed above a disguised roof panel. It was possible that Haberdash was secreted there.

By midnight the storm had hit. The ship was tossing wildly, the wind flipping between whine and roar, and rain pelted almost horizontally against their balcony door. Despite its weather seal, Worse could feel a cold draught from outside.

A warm drink would be nice. He decided on an experiment: he thought to himself *I would like some hot cocoa*, and reached for the phone. As he did so, he heard a knock on the door. There was Hilario with a mug of hot chocolate on a small tray.

'Good evening, Mr Worse. I hoped this might be calming, given the conditions.'

Worse stared at him, starting to wonder about telepathy. He was tempted to wake up Sigrid and report the result.

'Thank you, Hilario. I should have thought of that myself.'

'If there's nothing else, good night, sir.'

Worse settled into an armchair to enjoy his drink. He thought about their fugitive, cramped somewhere in his hiding place, feeling the wildness of the sea, wanting a cigarette, trying to sleep.

It was 2.30 in the morning when Worse's motion detector awakened him. He leaped from his chair to look at the computer screen, in time to see a dark figure passing through an observation deck door. Still in his crumpled tuxedo, and oblivious to the temper of the Indian Ocean, Worse left the stateroom and took an elevator to the starboard deck where he and Sigrid had stood the previous day.

Worse pushed opened the outside door against the wind with great difficulty. Despite his effort to be surreptitious, it slammed shut behind him. Rain was beating down faster than the deck could drain it. There was hardly enough light to see, the wind was stinging his eyes, and he was cold. He stayed close to the wall, edging around its curved section to the bow aspect with little to grip for support. There was no one there, and it occurred to him that not even the most desperate nicotine addict in history, or in fiction for that matter, would bring himself out here for a cigarette.

He turned back towards the door, beginning to worry whether he would be able to open it and get inside. The ship crashed into a trough and shuddered, sea spray soaking him in saltwater that seemed even colder than the rain. Worse clung to a public address speaker high on the wall, waiting for any small lull that might allow him to return to the door. He would rather be holding its outer handle for safety than this rusty fitting engineered to support no more than the weight of a loudspeaker. The ship rolled to port, and Worse thought he would make a run for it while gravity held him against the wall. When he let go of his flimsy anchorage, he felt adrift, and alone in the world.

But he wasn't alone. Halfway to the door, Worse suddenly found himself enclosed in a bear-hug from behind. It took him a second to realize what was happening, it was such an insanely risky manoeuvre for anyone to try under these conditions.

Despite the cold, and the improbability of his plight, Worse's reflexes were intact. His assailant made the common tactical error of enclosing a victim's arms within the embrace. Before it had fully tightened around him, Worse abducted his arms violently, at the same time bending his knees and dropping his weight a metre to the deck. He reached between his legs, grasped the soaked trouser cuffs of the man behind, and pushed himself backwards. Unable to rescue his balance, the attacker fell heavily to the deck with Worse on top.

Worse rolled onto his stomach towards the wall, and got to his knees. He might have made his escape, but above the wind he heard a loud semiconscious groan that informed him the other man was badly stunned. Worse leaned over to examine his face; even in the darkness, he recognized Haberdash. He searched his pockets, taking a mobile and a wallet, then snapped a lanyard carrying a key card from Haberdash's neck. Worse stuffed these into his own pocket.

There was another loud obstructed inspiration from Haberdash, and Worse decided that he couldn't abandon him there. He dragged the comatose man toward the door but the ship was beginning its cyclic roll to starboard. Worse reached out with his left arm to hold onto a wall-mounted lifebuoy, his right hand grasping Haberdash by his saturated coat. As the roll advanced, Haberdash became heavier, and Worse wondered for how much longer he could hold on. Both hands were frozen numb, and either might give way first. It could be Haberdash alone who rolled to the precarious barrier at the edge, or both of them in an ironic and unwilling embrace.

Worse guessed the roll angle reached forty-five degrees before it stopped. When the ship righted he let go of the lifebuoy and dragged Haberdash along the deck. They were now rolling to port, the rain wash collecting so rapidly against the wall that Worse realized he had to prevent Haberdash from drowning.

Worse used both hands to try to open the door. Even the wind pressure alone would make it difficult. Now the effort was also uphill against the roll of the ship, and his arms had little strength in the cold. If he waited until the next starboard roll, when the weight of the door might assist its opening, he would also be trying to stop Haberdash from sliding overboard.

He had no choice but to wait, and the inevitable roll began. Worse tried to lever the handle down while pulling on the door, as well as grasping Haberdash as the incline worsened. He couldn't manage. At the full roll, all his strength was taken in holding on, to the handle and to Haberdash.

He wondered about getting back to the lifebuoy and devising some method of securing them both. His mobile phone was useless, but he thought about using its camera flash to get the attention of the bridge; he knew that would be futile in this density of rain. In the end he considered it best to stay where he was and hold on. Each time the ship righted and he could briefly let go of Haberdash, he pulled on the door with both arms. But whenever he managed to open it a crack, the wind seemed to surge in order to defeat him. Then, either the roll to port would weight the door closed or the roll to starboard would require he grasp Haberdash.

Worse counted five full rolls in attempting this exercise. During the tilt to port he found himself sitting down between the door and Haberdash, too exhausted to care about the freezing rush of rainwater that washed back across the deck to be dammed against the wall. His thinking was already blunted by the cold. He knew that he risked perishing from hypothermia, even if he managed to save himself from hurtling across the deck and through the flimsy wire rail at its edge. He needed a better plan.

Worse's tuxedo trousers came with no leather belt, but Haberdash was wearing one. If it had sufficient length, Worse could loosen it and restrain Haberdash during a starboard roll by looping a foot within it while he used both hands on the door.

From time to time, Worse had been checking as best he could whether Haberdash was still breathing. Under the conditions this was almost impossible, and he had adopted an old medical device of knuckling the man's sternum and noting the arousal response. It wasn't improving, and at one point Worse wondered, rather incongruously given their predicament, if cruise ships carried CT scanners.

He reached over Haberdash to loosen the belt. Its wearer stirred, and Worse interrupted the task to lean forward and give him a sharp slap on the side of the face. Haberdash opened bloodshot eyes, focused on Worse. He lifted his head slightly from the deck, and brought his hands up to his face. Worse was relieved. At last, he might have the assistance of a second man to get them to safety.

The ship was starting its starboard heel, and Worse needed to grip the door handle. As he reached up with his left hand, he shouted at Haberdash.

'Hold on to me.'

Haberdash's idea of holding on was to grasp Worse around the throat with two icy hands, thumbs pressed on his larynx. Worse attempted to pull them off but they were fixed like the jaws of a steel vice. The ship's lean was picking up, and Worse felt himself and Haberdash starting to slide. He knew he had only seconds of strength and consciousness in which to act, and his tactic was both desperate and definitive. He grabbed Haberdash by the hair, pulled his head up from the deck, and thrust it down as hard as his enfeebled state could manage. Haberdash released his grip.

Worse gasped for breath. He was well out of reach of the door lever and had only Haberdash to hold onto. They began to roll, locked together, over and over, accelerating down the deck as it approached a forty-five degree incline.

It was Haberdash who took the full impact against a stanchion post, cushioning Worse from injury. Freezing water poured down the deck upon them, and for several seconds Worse had nothing to grasp but the other man. At last his hand found the cold smooth steel of the upright. He locked his fingers around it, and struggled to his knees.

At that moment the ship troughed, still at full heel, stressing the hull and superstructure with forces they were never designed to withstand. Worse felt a buckle wave passing through the steel deck, followed by an explosion as the deformation ruptured a major weld close by. The steel plate beneath him began ringing, causing a strange sensation in

Worse's legs that was almost warming. Now there was a new noise, louder than the wind, of steel grinding against ragged steel.

Worse looked up to where he knew the bridge should be, but it was in total darkness. Then somewhere over the sea behind him, sheet lightning held for a few seconds. In that light the bridge windows looked black and lifeless. He began to fear that the ship was breaking up, or a weld had sprung below the waterline. He wondered whether over the whole deafening chaos he was hearing the general alarm, if there had been an order to abandon ship. He thought about Sigrid in her cabin. He wanted to see her, to help her, to get her to a lifeboat.

The stanchion Worse was holding suddenly vibrated like a tuning fork. Even though numbed with cold, he felt a sharp knock on his arm. It was a wire tensioner whipping around as the lower railing wire snapped. Haberdash, who had been wedged up against it, went half over the side. Worse had been looking down under the handrail, poised directly over the blackness of the sea. When he understood what had happened to Haberdash he instinctively reached out, managing to grab a trouser cuff.

The ship seemed to stay at maximum heel for longer than before, and Worse thought it might be cusped there in some maritime hesitation rite before capsizing.

He tried to pull Haberdash back to the deck, but lacked the strength. A moment later he felt the strain abruptly give. Haberdash, belt loosened, had slipped into the sea leaving Worse holding a pair of trousers.

The rain was still blinding, but Worse had an impression there was more light on the deck. It didn't last, and it occurred to him that it had been the classic near-death hallucination. That thought forced his will back to survival. He pulled the soaking trousers towards him, grateful for any detritus that might be useful.

The ship slowly began to right itself. When it was nearly

level, Worse tried to stand up, determined to return to the door rather than be reliant on the broken railing. If he couldn't open it, he would lash himself to the handle using the trousers or the belt.

He found his legs were too weak to take the steps, and he fell back to the deck, rolling uncontrollably towards the door as the port heel increased, his eyes shut against the hurt of the rain. He thought he would have the strength at least to reach for the handle, and once on it, not let go until he was rescued or succumbed to the cold.

But when he stopped rolling he couldn't feel the handle. His arm flailed, searching blindly for one small item of physical security in his terrible isolation. What he felt instead was no rain, a little warmth, and the texture of wet carpet. It took a second to realize that somehow he had rolled from the edge of the ship straight through the open door that was now slammed shut behind him.

Worse was aware of a blanket wrapped over him, and thought he could smell hot cocoa. He opened his eyes, and even in his state of confusion and exhaustion, even *in extremis*, he laughed.

Hovering over him was Hilario, soaking wet, and he was grinning.

By reference to the familiar physics of a pendulum, the reader will appreciate the special invidiousness of Worse's plight. The ideal condition for his being able to open the door outwards and not simultaneously be required to restrain Haberdash was a level deck. But at the point in the ship's roll (ignoring other degrees of freedom) when the deck was level, its angular velocity was at maximum, affording Worse the very briefest of opportunity.

20 CORE TEMPERATURE

Hilario helped Worse to the stateroom, ran a warm spa, and excused himself. Worse emptied his pockets, placing Haberdash's possessions on a table within reach of the bath, and discarded his soaked tuxedo on the tiled floor.

He lay in the warmth for an hour, periodically restoring it with hot water, and studying the harmonic oscillation of its level with the movement of the ship. When he closed his eyes he experienced visceral flashbacks to the struggle with Haberdash, to the terrifying high-speed roll to the edge of the deck, and to the sense of impending hopelessness that he felt when he couldn't open the door. It made him wonder about his trying to save Haberdash, why he had risked so much for the man who wanted him murdered. Humanity was a complex, contradictory thing.

Worse glanced at the items on the table. There was only one piece of information that he wanted for now, and he had saved up the gratification of learning it. He opened the soggy wallet. Inside was an Illinois driver's licence with the name Benjamin James Mortiss. Worse looked at the date of birth and his mouth stretched a grim millimetre. The Piscean had returned to his element.

At about 6.00 am, he heard Sigrid stir. She looked into the bathroom.

'You're up early,' she said.

She glanced at the wet tuxedo crumpled on the floor and entered, appearing concerned for him. The ship was still rolling uncomfortably, and she sat on the edge of the bath at Worse's feet. She was dressed in her monogrammed bathrobe provided with the suite.

'What happened to you?' she asked.

Worse recounted his ordeal with Haberdash. It helped him to talk about it. He shared his reflections about human nature, about trying to save his attacker.

'I'm not surprised in the least,' said Sigrid. 'After all, you have an acquaintance with Hippocratic ideals.'

'Things change.' Worse looked down.

'Richard! I believe you're navel-gazing. Essential goodness doesn't change. And you have saved many more lives than you will ever persuade to a conclusion.'

It was a logician's attempt at lightness. Worse didn't reply. Sigrid stood up.

'You look as if you might stay in the bath all day. Do you mind if I share the facilities and have a shower?'

'Not at all, Mrs Worse. I shall watch over you most protectively.'

Sigrid slipped out of her bathrobe. 'I can see your core temperature is recovering.'

Worse reached for a tap to replenish the heat. After a few minutes, Sigrid asked from the shower space, 'Did you report "Man Overboard", or whatever is meant to happen?'

'He wasn't recoverable in those conditions, Sigrid. I'll make a report to Victor. He's the one who needs to know. I suspect the shipping line doesn't even believe they had an illegal passenger.'

Sigrid returned to showering. When she emerged and picked up a towel, Worse spoke.

'It seems that I continue to call him Haberdash, but it turns out he was a Mortiss.'

'There's trouble for you,' said Sigrid, resting a foot on the bath's rim, to dry her leg. Worse switched on the spa pump, covering himself with foaming suds.

At 7.00 am the captain announced that during the night the ship had turned back to run from the freak storm, which was the worst in his experience. A freighter thirty nautical miles to their north had lost dozens of cargo containers overboard. He assured passengers that the *Princess Namok* was perfectly seaworthy, but its stabilizers were malfunctioning and one propeller shaft had a vibration issue that meant it could not be run at full speed. They would return to Fremantle for a damage survey and repairs. He spoke about the priority of safety, apologized on behalf of the shipping line, and gave an estimated time of docking. Passengers bound for Singapore and La Ferste would be flown to their destinations. Meanwhile, for their own comfort, guests were encouraged to remain in their staterooms until the seas were calmer. The formal restaurants were closed temporarily.

'No Ferende adventure, then,' said Sigrid.

'I'm over luxury cruising, anyway,' said Worse. After a brief silence, he added, 'We're not running from the storm, we're limping.' He suspected that the ship's damage was more serious than the company was admitting.

A minute later, the captain made another announcement, advising of a crew-only lifeboat drill scheduled later in the morning. Passengers would not be participating and were not to be concerned.

'Which goes to suggest,' observed Sigrid, 'the company plans to save the crew and abandon passengers with the ship.'

Worse was studying the security vision recorded from the observation deck exit. He saw Haberdash go out, followed by himself. Then came Hilario, who left but reappeared with blankets and a bag. He fought hard to open the door, and shortly after he succeeded Worse saw himself body-rolling in at high speed. Hilario, obviously using all his strength, had managed to clear the way for Worse, braked his roll, and assisted him safely through the gap before the door shut.

They ordered breakfast. Sigrid opened the door to let Hilario bring in a dining trolley. When its wheels were locked, Worse stood up and walked over, holding out his arms for an embrace.

'Thank you, Hilario,' he said quietly. Sigrid saw her friend's emotion and looked away.

Worse slept for much of the day, and went without lunch. Sigrid answered a call for any doctors on board to assist in the ship's infirmary, given the numbers of fractures and sprains. She quite enjoyed revisiting her house job days of reading radiographs, sculpting plaster casts, folding slings, and dispensing analgesics. There was even some psychiatry required, mostly managing anxiety.

By evening, the ship was more stable, and the restaurant had reopened. It was a night of casual dress code, but many tables were unoccupied. Sigrid surmised that motion sickness as well as injury had taken its toll.

'By the way, I did some online research on the subject of disappearing people,' she said.

Worse looked sceptical.

'Seriously. I thought I had read about them somewhere. They're a special group, very rare. First reported by a Viennese physician a century ago.'

Worse raised an eyebrow.

'Don't imagine that they dematerialize, anything like that. They're individuals who can be continuously present in some social situation but characteristically not noticed, even un-consciously, by other people. It's thought to be a reactive phenomenon, an altered subjectivity and sort of social blindness induced in the group; they simply fail to register the so-called appearance person's comings and goings.'

Sigrid was clearly intrigued by her reading, and the possibility that they may have discovered an instance in Hilario. She continued.

'There's a social construct theory based on the idea of projected object persistence—these are people whose existence is validated somehow only in the present. In the unconscious of others, for whatever reason, they are deprived of inferred extension into the past or future.'

'Condemned to life in the hesitant tense,' said Worse.

'What?'

'Nothing. Are you saying that they are conspired against, in some way?'

'I don't think so. Early on, there were some interesting "Who was in the room?" studies where typically no one remembered them. They used independent subjects to eliminate collusion.'

'Like the scissors on the tray,' said Worse. 'Something must be special about them; they are the phenomenon's cause, surely. How can they affect subjectivity in those around them?' He was reflecting on his own experience when in the presence of Hilario.

'Yes. Well. That's the question. They seem normal in all respects but one. In every case recently studied, the subject scored zero on measures of self-consciousness. That's rare, you know. Most people transact self-consciousness one way or another more than they converse. Between strangers, it's very apparent. It shows in their behaviours.'

'Embarrassment is the currency of the agora? I've always thought that,' said Worse.

'Very amusing. You could put it that way. More its contrived minimization. Superfluous acts, redundant speech, inappropriateness, concealment, withdrawal, pretence of concentration, shifting glance. They're the signals you attune to, and in that way you notice the person. Anyway, that's the current theory. There's some work out of the Compton in Cambridge. Anna Camenes has written a reappraisal of it.'

'What about empathy, say, social skills otherwise?' asked Worse.

'Intact, it seems.'

Worse gave Sigrid a suspicious look. 'I really believe you would like to capture Hilario and study him in a behavioural science lab.'

Sigrid looked around the restaurant. 'He's already in one, don't you think?'

Their meals were served. Worse and Sigrid exchanged looks, both studying the waiter's actions like keen researchers. They were interrupted again by the sommelier, whom Worse judged to be greatly endowed with self-consciousness. When he had too conspicuously taken his leave, Worse changed the subject.

'How is the lecture writing going? It's a plenary session, isn't it?'

'Yes it is. I think I'm pleased with it. I've worked out how to introduce the ideas, using that Satroit poem about the self-portrait. It almost seems written as a metaphor of psychiatric observation.'

'The one where in the end the artist stops painting and the poet stops writing?' asked Worse.

'Yes. A little bleak, I know. But I'm using it to illustrate the complexity of interacting forms of description when they are non-commensurable in some way. That will lead into the equivalent problems of interpretation across the therapeutic space; basically how meaning is lost when the subjective is verbalized.'

Worse always found these conversations with Sigrid fascinating. He had stopped eating to listen. Sigrid had stopped eating to talk.

'Of course,' she continued, 'our ordinary mental world does not by nature present to us linguistically. It doesn't come perfectly expressed in words. What we experience, and try to describe, is essentially a symptomatology, normal or otherwise. The problem is that the psychiatric formulation of illness, our clinical notes, our referrals, our whole corpus of research, and our psychotherapy in turn, are explicitly verbal. Hence the idea of ekphrastic translation, and error.'

'Some patients express their mental world visually, rather than verbally, don't they? Richard Dadd, famously, for instance?'

'Oh yes. But we still come back to Satroit's painter. The problem hasn't gone away.'

'You know, the reason I remember that poem is that our English teacher at school asked us to think about whether the madness, or violence or whatever, rested with the painter or the poet.'

'And you thought?'

'I thought about the butterfly dreamer.'

'I could almost have guessed that.'

'Those were the days when ambiguity was prized. Literature teachers were attracted to the unknowable. Genuine complexity was valued. There's a lesson for psychiatry in that, I submit.'

Sigrid smiled. 'Very perspicacious, counsellor.'

A waiter filled their water glasses.

'It's interesting, Sigrid,' said Worse. 'I'm really pleased for you.' He raised his glass. 'Here's to your session's deserved success.'

It seemed to close off the subject, but suddenly Worse expressed an afterthought.

'Was he mad, actually? Satroit?'

Sigrid looked surprised.

'No. Well, I don't know that he was. Why do you ask?'

'I ask that of everyone. I thought you did too.'

Sigrid realized that she should find out the answer before invoking his poetry to an audience of eminent colleagues as a metaphor, even a loose one, for the psychiatric interview. She was grateful.

'He was reclusive, nihilistic perhaps. The artistic temperament, I suppose. I will find out more.'

'Yes. Must minimize embarrassment in the agora of ideas,' said Worse.

Worse decided he had eaten enough, and placed his knife and fork together.

'Actually, I've been reading poetry too, as it happens.'

'What are you reading, Richard?'

'A book recommended by Anna after she had been to Dante, and heard that I might be going. It's by someone called Monica Moreish.' Worse hesitated. 'They're limericks.'

'Limericks? Richard!'

'I knew you would find that amusing. They're actually serious. It's a Dante thing, apparently. The Moreish ones are themed around Virgil in the underworld.'

'The *Inferno* has been translated into limericks?' Sigrid put a slow, dramatized emphasis on the last word. Combined with interrogative inflection, the effect was devastating parody.

'Not translated. A new account. Some of them are quite good. They say you'll never fit in over there unless you understand their tradition.'

Worse was a little annoyed at finding himself defensive.

'Well, maybe not fitting in would be preferable.'

'Perhaps I should read some to you. I might even write one when I perfect the technique. On ambiguity in the therapeutic space. You could use it in your lecture.'

'Thank you, Richard. I'm sure Satroit will be quite sufficient.'

Worse was still curious about where Haberdash had been hiding, and he knew that Victor would also be. At 3.00 am, he dressed and headed for level 13.

As he expected, the casino was deserted. Haberdash's key card gave him access to both the private gaming room and the inside office. There were dim lights on in both areas, and

Worse noted that his surmise about the one-way mirror was correct. Within the office, a door with another electronic lock led to the cashier's counter. At the far end of the office was an elevator entry. There were several desks, one holding a dozen flat-screen security monitors.

Worse studied the panelled roof. There were lights, sprinklers, air-conditioning vents, a smoke alarm, a speaker and a camera, all the usual services that intrude on the aesthetic of a ceiling. Near one end, a bunch of party balloons was tied to an eyebolt. They seemed inappropriate in a business office, and Worse guessed their purpose. He looked under the main desk and found a two-metre wooden pole with a brass hook ferruled to one end. Taking it, he grasped the eyebolt and pulled down a folding attic ladder. He ascended the steps, detaching the pole to carry it with him. When he stepped onto the catwalk the spring-action ladder retracted into the roof space.

Worse used a torch to explore the grid of catwalks. At the far end, over the public section of the casino and half hidden behind a duct, he found a rough camp bed made from blankets and a sleeping bag. There was an assortment of clothes, magazines, and food wrappers. He collected a beret, compressed it into a plastic bag, and put it in a pocket. Spoiling would match DNA from hair to that found in Fremantle to link definitively the fugitive Haberdash to the stowaway Mortiss.

He was heading back to the ladder when he heard voices. A light was switched on below him. Through the grid, Worse could easily see down into the office. Two men had appeared from the elevator, and one's voice was raised.

'Well, where could he have gone?'

The other, whom Worse identified as the doorman from the entrance to the private casino, was silent. The first man continued.

'Have you checked again?'

'Sam. I've been up six times today and nothing's changed. He's not there.'

'What on earth am I going to say to Regan? The whole reason she's calling is to talk to Ben Jay.'

'Yeah. Well. You'll just have to apologize.'

'There's no such thing as an apology with Regan. Particularly with money and family. And this is both. Jeez.'

'What'll she do?'

'She'll kill us, for heaven's sake. And the more we apologize, the quicker she'll do it. I've heard about it.' He sat down. 'Check up there again. She'll be calling in a few minutes.'

The doorman shrugged, went to a desk, and reached under. Then he bent to look under.

'The hook's not here.'

He looked toward the balloons.

'Well, where did you put it?'

'Back, of course. Back where it should be. Under the desk. Who would take the hook?'

'What am I going to say to Regan? The whole La Ferste operation is messed up, and now we can't even find Ben Jay.'

'Look. Don't say we can't find him. Say he was meant to be here for the call and he hasn't shown up. Say he's not in his place. Put the blame on him.'

'Good idea. I'll put her on speaker so you can hear, but stay quiet.'

The desk phone rang.

'How're you doing, Ms Mortiss?'

'Put Ben Jay on.'

'Ben Jay's not here, Ms Mortiss. He's, ah, not here.'

There was a long silence.

'I'll call back in five minutes. Have Ben Jay pick up. I don't want to talk to you.'

Worse heard the call disconnect.

'Jeez. What am I going to do?' He replaced the handset and sank back in his chair. The doorman had no suggestions. After a few seconds, his manager reached some resolve and sat forward.

'I won't pick up. I just won't answer. She wants Ben Jay to pick up. He's not here. So, no pick up. That's it.'

Worse didn't want to stay hiding in the roof indefinitely, and decided he had heard enough. He picked up the hook-pole and stepped onto the ladder.

From inside the office, the effect was dramatic. In one action, a ceiling panel hinged down, the attic steps swung into view and unfolded to the floor, and Worse appeared in a flurry of party balloons, descending with the aplomb of someone who was meant to be there. The manager and the doorman stared at him; neither moved. Worse carried the pull-down pole rather like a spear.

'Pardon the intrusion, gentlemen. I set out exploring and seem to have lost my way in all the ducting.'

He walked to the door and turned.

'If you do decide to pick up, you might entertain Regan with a shanty from the southern seas:

Once there was a Tweisser
Inside the Mortiss walls;
Tweisser was a oncer
But Mockingbird still calls, still calls.
Mockingbird still calls.'

Worse whistled its metre as he left, closing the door behind him.

Most liberally educated readers will know the **Erico Satroit** poem referred to by Sigrid Blitt from translations deemed suitable for school and college study. This author admits to a longstanding interest in the problem of **ekphrasis**, and was disappointed to revisit standard sophomore texts and realize that taught versions of 'Poet Regarding Artist' suppress elements of a very deliberate harshness quite uncompromised in the original. A new translation is offered with approval of the trustee of his literary estate, Libraire Satroit à Istanbul. It is argued that the tone and ambiguity of Satroit's language have been rendered here more honestly in order to convey the disharmony and oppressing counterpoint that was surely intended.

> Mirror, palette, canvas, mirror.
> Reflected restless eyes return
> while in the hand an articulate blade
> scrapes oils to elegy, or exclamation
> or some eloquent phrase
> more suddenly seen than I can speak

> then pastes a wintry depth on worsened flesh
> that is his face. Yet, by airy sable touch there comes
> a nuance to the lips and resignation to the pose
> and greater knowing in the analytic gaze
> that rests ungrateful on this violent man
> rebuilt in mineral pigments with a solvent smell.

> The master in the wilderness steps back.
> His brush is hesitant and I am quiet.
> We are stopped before the crossing fears
> that words were better made in paint
> and paint in words.

We can be confident of Satroit's intention because the theme is discussed elsewhere (see, for example, his memoir *Damascene*, and the preface to the collection *Black Levant*). For him, the problem of ekphrasis is simply expressed: the descriptive is interpretive is paralysing. (The first equivalence because description is inevitably analogizing, the second because the arrogance implicit in this erodes artistic confidence.) In consequence, Satroit's ideal poet is one who comes to observe everything and state nothing—which might explain a spareness in all his work. Whatever its ugliness, our sympathy must turn to the object of ekphrastic intrusion, be it the art, its maker or the process; if not, we are complicit in a fatal indecision where art is stopped in time. Actually, Satroit demands even more of us: to accept that for the artist his mental wilderness is properly ineffable, and never more so than within the pain and introspection that is a self-portrait. Here is a place in which to be creatively lost, and not for visiting by outsiders.

But for the poet, too, there is a wilderness. The symmetry of doubt in the closing lines dissolves both privilege and any belief that *the one regards the other.* When the artist looks to the mirror, he sees his visitor reflected. And so the poet enters the portrait, just as the portrait enters the poem. This is the problem of ekphrastic translation; within it is contained an infecting dialectic that is mutually subverting. Satroit's response is a form of silence.

(Indeed, the spareness noted above is a poetry of the missing—replete, we can assume, in substance and sentiment, and safe in the privacy of observant withdrawal. The contemporary British poet **Vissy Mofo**, whose philosophical sympathies with Satroit have been argued by **Alison Pilcrow** in the encyclopaedic *TWF Compendium* (UITA Press), has interpreted this aspect of Satroit psychoanalytically as a symptom of exhaustion. It is this rather than fear, according to Vissy Mofo, that is the instrument of failure in evidence at the end of the work above. Others hold that the key to Satroit's poetic reticence, and reclusion, is pessimism—see note to Chapter 23, Appendix A.)

Satroit asks (in *Damascene*): What is the universe of the poet? And answers: The poet alone. This is read existentially, but he is saying more. In regarding the world, he regards himself. The act is deeply self-indulgent, because the poem and the portrait are together corrupted into something new. In consequence, as others have pointed out, not only is the ekphrastic enterprise wilfully damaging, it is theft. This surely explains why, for Satroit, there were many words in the wilderness left unwritten.

Readers familiar with the concept might note that ekphrastic translation is a **Thortelmann equivalence**. Furthermore, all ekphrastic writings are themselves Thortelmann equivalent. Because of transitivity, every artefact so translated thereby enters an equivalence class. This is the most powerful theoretical argument establishing the maleficence of poetry in the visual arts. It is left to the reader to apportion reprimand regarding other forms, such as gallery notes and curatorial essays, whilst in mitigation accounting for intention, consent and public interest.

In respect of Blitt's thesis, the parallels between Satroit's observation of a subject portraying himself in paint and the mental state examination are too obvious to labour, except to point out that a thoughtful psychiatrist, like a thoughtful poet, is a largely silent one.

Incidentally, the identity of **Satroit's painter** was never revealed, though there are said to be clues in an interview given for *La Tortuga*. When the poem first appeared in English, a catalogue of fashionable artists denied being the study. After Satroit's fame was established and the poetic subject re-beautified with postmodern illusionism, the same catalogue clamoured for recognition, including artists incapable of producing a human likeness of themselves or anyone else.

21 RETURNS POLICY

Two hundred kilometres off Fremantle, the *Princess Namok* was taken in tow. There were repeated assurances from the captain that this was no cause for concern, and the development was solely for the comfort of passengers.

That would be the comfort of passengers who might otherwise be clambering into lifeboats, thought Worse. The ship had taken on a perceptible list to port, and it was obvious that power supply to nonessential services was being rationed. Internal lighting was dimmed, nightly live entertainment was cancelled, and there was an unnatural preponderance of cold foods in the buffet dining room. It seemed to Worse that the only part of the ship unaffected was the casino.

Despite the general austerities, Hilario managed to look after Sigrid and Worse with the usual level of perfection. In the twenty-four hours before the tugboats arrived, the engine noise within the ship had changed in pitch following a distinct shudder and a momentary blackout. It became a slightly nauseating low-frequency vibration that was difficult to ignore, and was most uncomfortable when they lay down to attempt sleep. At one point, when Hilario was in their suite, Worse asked what he thought of the state of the ship.

'We are to say that everything is satisfactory,' was the reply.

'Do you think everything is satisfactory, Hilario?'

'I must be loyal to my ship. But I cannot lie, too.'

Worse did not want to force the dilemma, but he asked, 'Are you frightened at all, Hilario?'

'I am a little frightened, Mr Worse.'

Worse left the subject there.

Once under tow, the mood of passengers improved. Sigrid suggested that the novelty of the experience now exceeded the anxiety it had caused. Worse thought it had more to do with an engine shutdown that ridded the ship of its uncomfortable vibration. He failed to see how anyone would find relief from anxiety when the captain had ordered another lifeboat drill, this time with the whole ship's company and passengers directed to the port side only.

At least now electrical power seemed to be fully restored, which brought a slightly irrational sense of celebration. The camaraderie was compounded by the captain's announcement that the shipping line would refund fares, and all alcohol was now complimentary. People were eating more, drinking more, and socializing more.

Gambling more, too. Worse noticed this as he made his way through the casino to a forward observation deck. He would suggest to Sigrid that anxiety was not suppressed by novelty, but buried under exuberance. On a cruise ship, profligacy banished mortality, at least until the punter died.

Worse went outside to watch the tugs over the bow. Although the sea was now relatively calm and there were patches of blue sky, the wind was bitterly cold. He pulled his collar up and walked over to the rail, where half a dozen other passengers were standing.

He was absorbed for several minutes watching the interference patterns of the two tugboat wakes, and didn't notice immediately that the person to his right had turned his head toward him. Worse looked around and recognized the casino manager, who continued to stare at him. Worse decided to share what he was thinking.

'You know, Sam, if one of those tow lines parted and

whiplashed, we would all be decapitated, quite probably.'

'Seven heads and seven tails. I don't think so.'

Worse was impressed by the humour, and the fact he knew the body count without looking. Perhaps he had trained as a croupier, and was an inveterate counter of things. Worse was also, for other reasons.

'I'm pleased to find you here,' said Worse. 'I was going to visit your office later for a chat, but this saves me from the odious closeness of gamblers.'

'You don't enjoy games of chance?'

'Perhaps if I owned the vigorish,' said Worse.

The manager turned to look forward.

'Here is where that chat starts,' said Worse. 'What happened when Regan rang back?'

'Who are you?'

'I'm Worse.'

'Worse?'

'It's a name. What happened when Regan rang back?'

'That's private business. Why would I tell you that?'

'Because,' said Worse, 'I am willing to help you. But my patience is limited.'

The manager turned back to face Worse, but stayed silent. Worse spoke as if they were just starting an idle conversation.

'This ship is a wreck, you know. Its single remaining resemblance to a cruise liner is that it's floating on the sea. For now. My guess is they'll decide to tow it to La Ferste and scrap it.'

'You think so?'

'That means you will lose your casino,' said Worse.

'The company's big. I'll be moved. We're always being posted to new ships.'

'You won't be free to move. You'll be in prison.'

The manager looked shocked. 'Why are you saying that?'

'We are returning to the jurisdiction of the Australian police.

You harboured a criminal. That makes you an accessory to his crimes.'

'Wait. Wait. What crimes? What did Ben Jay do?'

'Crimes including attempted murder. I know because I was the target.'

'Wait—I don't know anything about that.'

'Inspector Spoiling will not be happy that you concealed a fugitive in the casino roof space during his very expensive search of the ship. When I say not happy, it means angry. Emotional. Inspector Spoiling is European.'

'But I knew nothing about what Ben Jay's done.' The tone of earnestness shifted to dismay. 'That moron disappears and leaves me with this.'

'We all are burdened with the wrongs of others,' said Worse.

The manager was staring at him, looking almost tearful.

'But if I talk to you about Regan, she'll kill me. Everyone knows the rules. Mortiss has power all over.'

'She won't kill you,' said Worse. 'She is about to lose everything. Mortiss Bros will shortly be destroyed.'

'How do you know that?'

'Because I am the one who will destroy it.'

The manager turned again to look forward. So did Worse, watching the pitch and yaw of the tugs straining under the load of their deadweight hulk. After a full minute of silence, the manager spoke.

'It's freezing out here.'

'Mr Worse?'

Worse turned around to find Hilario holding a silver tray with two mugs of hot cocoa. Worse handed one to the manager, taking the other for himself. Hilario vanished.

'Why would you do that, destroy the company?'

'They shipped me assassins. The merchandise, as it were, was unsatisfactory and I'm returning it. Seeking a refund, you might say. Plus punitive damages.'

The manager sipped his drink and continued to look into the mug as he spoke.

'How can you help me?'

'I know Spoiling.'

There was another long stare into the mug.

'What do you want me to tell you?'

'Let's start with something easy,' said Worse. 'Did Regan enjoy the sea shanty?' It served as a simple honesty test.

'I didn't say it to her. No way could I do something like that.'

'What did you mean when you spoke to the doorman about the La Ferste operation?'

Docking in Fremantle was a slow operation, but an impressive display of old-fashioned pilotage. Their ship had clearly lost power to its thrusters, and was fully reliant on tugs to be brought alongside. In the calm of the harbour, and against the perpendiculars of land structures, the list of the ship was now obvious.

When gangplanks had been attached, no one was allowed to disembark until Spoiling and a small forensic team boarded. A ship's officer escorted them to the casino, where they met Worse. The manager and his doorman had been told to wait in the office. When Worse identified them as the two persons of interest and pointed out the eyebolt attaching the roof ladder, Spoiling spoke to the officer.

'My compliments to the captain. You may proceed with disembarkation.' He turned to Worse. 'You may go as well, Worse. I will be in touch. Please give my regards to Doctor Blitt. I hope the luxury cruise has not been too arduous for you both. I have a car for you. A sergeant will meet you outside the immigration hall.'

Worse returned to his stateroom, where Sigrid was using the delay to work on her paper. Hilario was there, rechecking the identity tags on their luggage. Worse motioned him out onto the balcony, closed the door, and invited him to sit down. They spoke for ten minutes. Sigrid concentrated on her writing, but she did notice when they both stood and shook hands. As they re-entered the suite, Hilario spoke to Sigrid.

'Is there anything more I can do for you, Doctor Blitt?'

'I don't think so. Everything's fine. Thank you again, Hilario.' She offered her hand.

'Then I will have your bags collected in five minutes. Thank you, Doctor Blitt.'

When he had left the room, she spoke to Worse.

'I see I am no longer Mrs Worse. That was a brief and bliss-less state of matrimony.'

'I wanted to part with no lies,' said Worse.

'I know.'

She didn't ask about the conversation on the balcony.

Spoiling's sergeant drove them first to Sigrid's house, where Worse helped carry her bags inside. They hugged as he left. At Grosvenor Apartments, where Worse lived, he was dropped off next to an elevator in the underground car park. When he entered the apartment, his housekeeper was there.

'Did you have a wonderful time, Dr Worse?'

She had no idea of the life Worse led.

'I did, Mrs Brackedger. A very interesting time, thank you. You are well, I hope?'

He opened his backpack and passed a small gift to her.

'Open it now, if you like.'

It was a silk scarf from one of the ship's boutiques, and she was delighted by it. Worse felt he needed time to himself, and suggested she might like to leave early, given that the place hadn't been lived in for days and the cleaning requirement was minimal. He saw her to the door.

He had a lot of affection for Mrs Brackedger. She had been with him for years, but recently confided the demands of her husband's illness and her own increasing tiredness from work. Reluctantly, she had decided to retire, and reluctantly, Worse had engaged a recruitment agency to find a replacement. Today was her third last visit, and Worse was sad to see her off.

After she had gone, he checked the apartment security. Then he lay on his bed to think. When he closed his eyes, the motion of the sea replayed, and he was soon asleep.

22   ENGLISH IN PERTH

Dear Worse

My plans for taking up the fellowship in Perth are
starting to come together. I expect to arrive in mid-
September for an October start, and was hoping that
I could take up the offer of staying in your second
apartment for a few weeks until I find somewhere of
my own close to the university. Please say if this is no
longer convenient. I also need to buy a car, or I was
thinking maybe a motorbike, for the year.

Rodney Thwistle sends his regards. He and I have
been working on a paper looking at error distributions in certain divisibility problems (inspired by
swints, you will be unsurprised to learn). The general
case gives rise to some nice results that I think you
will find interesting. I assume you have read Tertia
Thurdleigh's paper in *J. Numerical Ornith.*, which
started it all? She gave a Lindenblüten lecture at
Nazarene a few weeks ago. Very impressive. Some
of us thought it would be nice to take her and May
Ball on a drive to the Broads for some birdwatching.
I think TT enjoyed the day but it turns out she can't
see birds, let alone count them, because her eyesight
is so poor. May Ball, on the other hand, can see a
mosquito at ten metres.

I spoke to Anna yesterday, at a college function with Edvard. They are well, and still looking forward to a holiday in Perth. They are thinking, if they do visit, of returning via the Ferendes to spend some time at the LDI station. The tentative plan is to incorporate an ocean cruise on the Perth–La Ferste sector, for some much needed relaxation.

Nicholas is working hard, as usual. We were so relieved that he wasn't hurt in that awful man's attack inside the cave. My brother does seem to get himself into situations, as you well know. Who would have thought mathematical linguistics so dangerous an occupation? I suppose he's told you about the amazing quartz-like stones they've found. They flew one to Cambridge for analysis and it turned out to have a liquid core of terencium sulphide, which apparently is extremely poisonous. I think I will never stop worrying about Nicholas. *Famille Oblige.*

Well, that's the Misgivingston news from Cambridge for now. I hope you have been getting the peace and quiet you need for your work.
Best wishes
Millie

It was early evening when Worse was awakened by a call from Spoiling. He would interview the casino manager the following morning, and Worse was invited to be present.

When the call was finished, Worse walked around his apartment. There were signs everywhere of Mrs Brackedger's presence; cleaning and tidying habits that had once irritated him now formed part of his sense of home. He unpacked his bags from the cruise, sorted laundry, and returned various items to where they belonged, mostly in his workshop. Then he sat at his kitchen table checking flight schedules online.

When Worse entered the interview room, the casino manager was seated across a table from Spoiling and a sergeant.

'Good morning, Worse. We've been through the formalities with Mr Burlinger. I trust you are recovering from your prodigal days of luxury cruising.'

'I doubt that I will ever recover, Victor. And my hostess *Princess Namok* certainly won't.'

Worse nodded at the sergeant, then smiled at Burlinger.

'Sam.'

He seated himself to one side, away from the table and from where he could see all three. Spoiling got straight to the point.

'The main charge you are facing is harbouring a criminal. From that will follow hindering a police investigation, interfering with the course of justice, and other charges. What have you to say?'

'I didn't know Ben Jay had done anything wrong. He said it was a mix-up, that it wasn't him the police were looking for.'

'But it was unquestionably him for whom we were looking. That was clear from the photograph we circulated throughout the ship. Were you shown the photograph of the wanted person during the police operation?'

'Yes.'

'Did you recognize Ben Jay?'

'Yes.'

'Why did you continue to harbour him?'

'Because I believed what Ben Jay had said. And I was frightened.'

'Frightened?'

'Frightened of Regan, his sister. She was the one who said I had to take care of him.'

'That is Regan Mortiss, of the company Mortiss Bros?'

'Yes.'

'Explain to me why you should be so frightened of Regan Mortiss that you would not comply with Australian law, that you would fail to assist police in their enquiries when it was clearly in your capacity to do so.'

'Regan would kill me. Since she took over, we all know how the rules work. If you harm the family, or lose money for the company, she sends a messenger. Or kills you herself, they say.'

Spoiling looked at Worse, who nodded almost imperceptibly. He moved on.

'You were overheard to be talking about a certain La Ferste operation. What did you mean by that?'

'When we docked, I was to take on board a special consignment with the usual stores. I had a contact number of someone in the chandler's office who would sort it all. After La Ferste, we were on-sailing to San Diego for a new casino fit-out, and the load was something to do with that. Big crystals for an artist to make a feature sculpture in the gaming room, they said. I told Mr Worse about it on the ship.'

'Big crystals?'

'Yes. Quartz, I think. Valuable, fragile, and obviously important to the company.'

'Had you ever done that before?'

'No. But I had heard from other managers that it had happened. Only when a ship was headed to the San Diego base, I think.'

'Why would the company smuggle them, rather than import them legally?'

'I didn't know they were being smuggled. I thought it was just a convenience thing for the company.'

Spoiling sat back, and looked at Worse.

'Worse?'

Worse didn't alter his posture, but looked at Burlinger for several seconds before speaking.

'Did you know that you would be transporting terencium into the United States?'

'What's terencium?'

'An element. As in the periodic table.'

'No. I've never heard of terencium. It was quartz.'

'Have you ever met Regan Mortiss?'

'No. I've only talked to her on the phone.'

'Why have you not met her?'

'Why? I'm no way senior enough, that's why. If she came near me I would know I was in trouble.'

'Has Camelline been in touch about what they want you to do, now the *Princess Namok* is bound for scrapping?'

'Yes. They want to fly me to San Diego. Then, I guess, it will be another ship.'

'Do you have a family, Sam?'

'Yes, in San Diego.'

Worse looked at Spoiling, indicating that he had no more questions.

'Excuse us for a few minutes, Mr Burlinger,' said Spoiling.

He and Worse left the room. They spoke in the corridor.

'What do you think, Worse?'

'He's unfortunate. I would get a full statement and contact details, issue a warning, and let him go.'

Worse walked home from police headquarters. On the way, he stopped off in a city lunch bar for a fresh sandwich. It was a change for the ordinary after the sophistication and fussiness of cruise ship meals. He looked around at other customers, sitting alone or in pairs, reading financial papers or speaking on mobiles as they ate in their work breaks. It was a strange business, other lives; the thought made him pleased for Sam Burlinger, returning to his family.

As he left, Worse bought another sandwich, to have later for his dinner.

Dear Worse

Please forgive me for not writing sooner.

I was sorry to hear about your La Ferste cruise disaster. That was really bad luck. Paulo and I were looking forward to having you come west to LDI and spending some time with us.

Obviously the Glimpse business was a huge shock to everyone here, but at least there seems to be nothing sinister happening at the moment. We have had to abandon mapping and recording the cave pictograms for now. Paulo considers it too dangerous until we know more about where that big crab hangs out. (The zoologists in Madregalo have labelled it the Shuffler crab until they sort out its species. They haven't got very far with the DNA.) We also need much better lighting in there, not just for the project but for our own safety. It's a pity because during our last visit with the police I think I saw an impressively large shadow picture of a human figure on one wall, and I'm keen to have a look at that. Then there is the processional (as I think of it) avenue of big josephites in the second chamber that I told you about. That needs an expert survey, but it's too risky to go that far in for now. It's where the Shuffler came from. I get a bit queasy whenever I think that I was exploring in there with nothing but a torch.

At least all that has left me more time for the birdsong research, which is coming along quite well. We've always known that swints can count, or at least subitize, (because of thricing) and I am hopeful that by the end of the year I will have sorted out their low integer vocab. It appears almost certain that they effectively count mod 3 and have, you will be amazed to learn, a designator for zero (in the sense $3 \equiv 0$). From the language-theoretic point of view, I suspect we will need to generalize Edvard's n-grammars to the mod n case, but we will see.

One of the difficulties I'm discovering is that number element identification is complicated by regional accents, which seem to alter subtly during migration as well (just as their blood does: I take it you know about that). I'm not aware of what other people working in the field are finding with this, but it hasn't been mentioned as an issue in the literature. The funny thing is, accents might account for discrepancies I've noticed between some of my findings and those of our US colleagues working with American swints.

Naturally, my concern is that the problem may turn out to be much bigger than one of just accents. If swints actually have more than one distinct language, we're up against real challenges. I'm thinking we may have to use Parsan gap analysis just to separate language groups in the first place, and that's never been tried in birdsong. Ideally, of course, we would find some polyglots to study, a Rosetta thrice one might say. The difficulty there is that if swints are interpreting, they will inevitably introduce translation errors. I expect these would show as verbal response or behavioural inconsistencies.

The other big news I've already told you about is the possibility of a volcano somewhere on the plateau, if Glimpse's map is to be believed. His annotation suggests that josephites are found there, and he seems to have been collecting them, as we found a sackful in his truck. It would be amazing if the Neolithic peoples transported the large ones that I saw any great distance to the cave.

Anyway, while the cave project is on hold, Paulo and I are planning an expedition to find Glimpse's volcano. I will let you know how successful we are.
Regards
Nicholas

Nicholas
I will come to La Ferste in the next few days and visit LDI by charter flight. Arrival details will follow when finalized. I would like to accompany you and Paulo on the volcano trip. If I can assist with bringing supplies from Madregalo, please let me know. From the Ferendes I will go direct to US on the Dante matter.
Worse

It is impossible to overstate the significance of Nicholas's speculations, based soundly as they are on research in progress, regarding an arithmetic faculty in swints. In order to count **modulo 3**, they must possess signifiers for 0, 1 and 2. Given the discovery of so many linguistic elements already, identifying three more would not, in itself, be remarkable. What are remarkable are the conceptual implications of this, such as an awareness of cardinality, but most particularly the occurrence of **zero**. The invention of this notion (and symbol) is considered a triumph in the history of human numerate thinking, and it occurred relatively recently. To discover that zero might have existed in avian calculation for millions of years is humbling in the extreme.

The reader familiar with modular arithmetic will appreciate the special suitability and efficiency for swints of counting mod 3, given its primary purpose is presumably in the maintenance of thricing. Suffice it to point out that the numerical size of any flock (known as a *tidings* in the case of swints) is divisible by three with a remainder of 0, 1 or 2. It is important not to forget that enumeration in practice carries a chance of error; for example, determining a remainder to be 2 when the true value is 0 (signifying an erroneous surfeit of 2 or a deficit of 1, or any congruent magnitudes, being 5, 8, ... ; and -4, -7, ...). These errors have probability distributions, which are the subject of a generalized study mentioned by Millie. Incidentally, the Thurdleigh paper referred to, 'Prime factorization of avian flock counts', is the classic in the field, and a recommended starting point for the student setting out.

It is obvious that one method of reducing such error is to repeat the count, preferably multiple times. (This is equivalent to repetition in critical messaging, or the redundancy structured into grammar discussed in Appendix A, note to Chapter 7, where the concern is accuracy of information content, rather than of number specifically.) Thurdleigh has suggested that the phenomenon of **murmuration**, spectacular to us as a display, is really an exercise in census taking in which constant re-checking is occurring. If swints truly do use repetition as a strategy in error reduction, it would be evidence of a capacity for mathematical abstraction well in excess of counting.

Of course, we should remember that varieties of intelligence might not be uniformly distributed; roles may be specialized, as in human culture. For example, there may be theologian swints or mathematician swints (and interpreters, if Nicholas's multilingual concern is proven), each dedicated to discrete tasks. For researchers in avian linguistics, this possibility raises important considerations of sampling. Though potentially complicating, some comfort can be drawn from the fact that basic methodological principles and their theoretical underpinning apply universally; these include randomization, sample size adequacy, repeated sampling, and the central limit theorem.

Interestingly, modular arithmetic and language have been intimately linked before. Darian describes devastating linguistic weapons deployed by the **Romans** in their defeat of the **Syllabines**, one of which was the iterated negative (another was the amnestically long question), easily evaluated mod 2 but desperately confusing otherwise.

The reference to **Parsan gap** requires explanation. Misgivingston (in *Stochastic Signatures of the Parsan Gap*) and others have demonstrated that human languages can be distinguished solely by statistical properties of the brief silences (Parsan gaps) that occur naturally in speech. It will be quite revolutionary if this technique, which is very recent, finds application in the taxonomic separation of swint languages.

An elementary treatment of the subject is given in Pilcrow's *TWF Compendium*, from which the following is abstracted with permission.

> Nicholas Misgivingston's discovery that every language is identifiable from the stochastic properties of its Parsan gaps is fundamental. The direction of research now is to determine whether these gaps carry information not only about the language they belong to, but also the sense communicated by the speech of which they are an integral part.
>
> This latest hypothesis is that the gaps, which are very rich statistically, do encode meaning essentially equivalent to that more obviously conveyed by the words they apparently serve to separate. Indeed, there is a suggestion that in Ferent languages the bandwidth of gaps exceeds, in theory, the capacity of vocabulary, and is already exploited subliminally by native speakers. (Perhaps this explains why that language group was thought to be at risk of extinction, when in fact it was simply a case of silence becoming more functionally dominant.)
>
> Human hearing has a sensitivity, in frequency and interval terms, in the upper microsecond range. This is more than sufficient, with properly directed learning, to detect, analyse and interpret the fine-structure statistics of gaps. (Those with a musically trained ear are likely to acquire this skill more readily.) Misgivingston envisages a universal language (his term is *lingua Parsa*) that exploits this semantic content in the silence. Then, spoken words, foreign or otherwise, will come to be seen as arbitrary tokens of partitioning that serve exclusively to define gaps.

Nicholas's comment about **swint blood** changing during migration will hold no mystery for ornithologists or swint fanciers generally. For those not wishing to access academic sources, a reasonable account of the physiology is given in Darian.

23 VOLCANO STREET

Worse didn't care for La Ferste, where he had stayed for a few nights the previous year. His disaffection wasn't lessened on seeing from the air an enormous plume of pollution spreading many tens of kilometres into the South China Sea from the Peril River delta.

Nevertheless, there were some things he needed to do there before moving on to the smaller and very beautiful capital of Madregalo.

He had organized ahead a car and driver, and was met at the airport arrivals hall. Worse gave an address, correct in street but wrong in number. He was duly delivered to premises at No 337, where he loitered before walking back across an intersection. When he opened the door of No 303, the philatelist shop-owner smiled in recognition. He was an unlicensed gunsmith whom Worse had met through Spoiling. They shook hands.

'You are well, I ... trust?' he asked.

'Yes, thank you. I hope all is well with you,' said Worse.

'Things are well with me. As is your ... collection. Wait.'

He left through a door at the rear of the shop and returned a minute later, holding a parcel out to Worse.

'As before,' he smiled.

It was Worse's Totengräber 9 purchased previously, and stored with its supplier. 'As before' signified a single ammunition clip.

Worse placed the parcel in his backpack, thanked him, and shook hands again before leaving. Even now, neither knew the other's name.

Worse had the address of a ship chandler who looked after Camelline interests in La Ferste. Their office was right down on the wharves close to where cruise liners berthed. After a rapid interaction in Ferent ending in laughter, the driver persuaded security guards to let the car through to the harbour frontage. Worse wondered what had been said about him. Out of sight of the driver, he transferred the T-9 from the pack to his jacket.

It wasn't a salubrious place of business. The office was a lean-to attached to a large warehouse, and had a front-facing door with a dirty window at the side. There was no one there when Worse entered. The rear wall was fully open to the storage facility, and he could see shipping containers, baskets, boxes on pallets, and several loose items. Worse was interested in the baskets. These were what the casino manager had been told to expect when delivered aboard, and he had been given rough dimensions ahead of time so that he could plan their storage.

There was nobody in sight, and Worse decided to help himself to an inspection. It took just a moment to conclude that all baskets with 'Winnings' labels had a special yellow streak for quick identification by handlers. He tested the weight of several by a tilting force. The first heavy one he found was taped shut, but had not yet been steel banded like some of the others. He cut the tape with a pocketknife and lifted the lid. The interior was black-plastic lined, and all he could see were polystyrene beads. He reached through and felt something hard, shelled his hand around it, and brought it into view.

It was as Nicholas had described, like a great crystal of quartz, about twenty centimetres in diameter. Worse drew it up to the light to appreciate its clarity.

'Hey. What are you up to, mister?'

A large red-haired man stood up from behind a forklift tractor.

'I'm inspecting for quality,' said Worse, holding up the crystal again and feigning the critical study of minor officialdom.

It seemed to work for a few seconds. He knew he was a

failed imposter when the other man bent to pick up a length of pipe and came towards him.

'That needs to be kept out of the light. You know shit quality if you don't know that.'

Taken literally, it seemed a convoluted argument, but Worse put down the josephite. He pointed to the weapon.

'That must make quite a sound when you hit someone,' he said.

'You don't worry about the sound, mister. You worry about the pain.'

'Not worried,' said Worse. 'Got pipe too, makes a sound.'

It was a warning, but the redhead's thinking lacked the metonymic. He came at Worse with the pipe raised.

To the attacker's surprise, Worse didn't retreat but suddenly moved in closer. The next thing the storeman felt was a T-9 muzzle pressed hard into his red-locked forehead.

'Want to feel the pain mine makes, mister?' said Worse.

Worse had never seen a man shrink so visibly. The threatened sound became the redhead's steel pipe half bouncing on the concrete floor.

'Don't move. Just talk. Where were these going?' said Worse, tilting his head toward the josephite basket.

'For the *Princess Namok*, going to San Diego. Something happened to the ship.'

'Your dumb boss fell off it. How many are there?'

'Seven baskets.'

'Have you shipped others before?'

'Every few months for about a year.'

'Always crystals?'

'It started off some kind of ore, like black sand, in plastic bags.'

'How does it get to you?'

'I only know him as the prospector. He brings the stuff in on his truck.'

'Why did you say to keep it out of the light?'

'I don't know why. The prospector just said it was important.'

'Listen carefully,' said Worse. 'Now I am going to step back and you are going to move slowly. Come and take me through some business records in the office.'

Fifteen minutes later, Worse had nearly finished his search. The storeman apparently used the time in some redemptive search of his own.

'I wasn't really going to hit you, mister,' he said.

Worse was absorbed in a document and ignored him.

'With the pipe.'

'Mm.' Worse was still reading.

'You weren't really going to shoot me, mister, were you?'

'Mm? Yes.'

'Madregalo,' said Worse.

The driver nodded and started the engine. Worse settled into his seat in the rear, placing an appropriated josephite into his pack. He was tired after the flight but resisted sleeping. The Ferendes was a place of surprises, and he had no reason to trust the driver.

The roadworks on the intercity motorway seemed hardly advanced on the previous year. There were still detours and passing lanes and red lights and rough surfaces. Worse watched the activities with fascination. His driver made a few attempts at conversation, beginning with 'Have you been to the Ferendes before, sir?' Worse was polite but not expansive. The forty-kilometre journey took ninety minutes, and eventually Worse was delivered to his hotel on the Kardia, the historic main square of Madregalo.

After checking in and seeing his bags to his room, Worse walked out to the famous weaver fish fountain in the centre of the Kardia. It was cast in glass, using a special lamination process that even when explained in detail seemed not to account for the miraculous result. Worse had been introduced to it by Nicholas and, in turn, he had shown it to Millie on the day they released the swints.

Otavio Fitrina's masterpiece was one of those rare sights in tourist travel that belong in the album of archetypes. Worse was drawn back to it, and the magic and beauty in its making were immediately familiar to him. He sat on one of the surrounding glass benches for half an hour, studying the sculptural form, its refractive subtleties, and the interplay of glass and water. Eventually he stood up, returning to the hotel with no greater understanding of its impossible geometry than when he walked away the last time.

The next morning, Worse took the tram down Ahorte, the main north–south boulevard of Madregalo, to the bay. Felicity's was still there, by the jetty, and he chose an outdoor table.

As he waited for his breakfast order, he thought about events of the previous year. They were sitting here when Prince Nefari was taken, in full view of huge crowds gathered to see a signing ceremony with the Chinese envoy, Admiral Feng. That compact fell through and a revolution started. In the pandemonium of the first hour, he and Millie had found a way into the deserted palace and released the swints kept cruelly caged by the prince.

He thought more about Millie. He admired her courage and adventurousness. He especially appreciated her intellect. It would be good if they could spend time together while she did her research year in Perth.

Worse looked around. There was no sign of the café's owner, Mr Felicity, but the business seemed to be prospering. No doubt its fame as a forward observation post for the prince's fate and the weaver fish visitation attracted many who liked their excitement vicarious, served safely subsequent, and with coffee on the side.

Worse had booked a helicopter charter to the LDI station

at midday. The fee included a limousine pick up from town. He had also arranged to take some lighting gear that Nicholas purchased, which was to be delivered to the heliport further along the bay. Before leaving Felicity's to return to the hotel, he phoned the charter office to confirm they had the freight.

Paulo and Nicholas heard the helicopter's approach, and were waiting at the edge of the clearing as the pilot put down. Nicholas introduced Worse to Paulo, and the three carried Worse's bags and the equipment boxes over to the canteen. They were followed by the pilot, who had been invited for a coffee. One of the teachers needed to attend an antenatal appointment in Madregalo, and she and her husband, a cleaner in the school, were flying back with him.

When they had left, Worse was shown to his accommodation by Nicholas. Worse swung his backpack onto the bed, opened it, and held out the josephite.

'Where did you get that?' asked Nicholas, surprised.

'I found it in a shipment at the La Ferste docks, bound for the US,' said Worse. 'Your friend Glimpse had a little export trade happening. For the terencium in them. I'll explain.'

They crossed the clearing to the administration hut where Paulo was working. There, Nicholas and Paulo briefed Worse on events at the station, finishing with an outline of their plans for the time Worse was to be with them. First, there would be an expedition to find the volcano. Second, they would show Worse the first chamber of the cave and ask his help to install the new lighting.

Worse then told them about his researches into Mortiss Bros and Area Pi, and how the key to everything seemed to be terencium taken from the Ferendes. He had brought the josephite across from his unit, and now held it up.

'I see there's one on your desk,' he said to Nicholas. 'What do either of you know about its behaviour in light?'

Paulo and Nicholas looked blank.

'It's just that Glimpse told the chandler in La Ferste to keep the stock in the dark. I wondered if apart from the sonoluminescence you described there was something photochemical going on.'

Nicholas reached for the josephite that had been on his desk for several days. He held it up.

'You know, Worse, I think it has turned slightly dark, slightly brown.'

'Do you have information on what its chemical composition is, exactly?' asked Worse.

'Not completely. Terencium sulphide in some of them, at least. We're still waiting on a comprehensive report from Cambridge,' said Nicholas.

'Hold on,' said Paulo. 'We have Glimpse's assay.'

He shuffled papers on his desk, and handed some stapled sheets to Worse.

'Glimpse seems to have found a leaked-out specimen, a geode, and had the internal precipitates analysed,' explained Nicholas.

Worse studied the report.

'There's a lot of chemistry here,' he said, and passed it to Nicholas. 'Notice the silver halides. They might account for it.'

After dinner in the canteen, Worse retired to his hut. It was the one used by Edvard and Anna, but also by other visitors. A shelf under the window displayed magazines and books donated or abandoned by previous occupants. Worse found such accidental microlibraries fascinating, like an archaeological record of a past civilization. He examined it, not for something to read, but as an historian of the room.

He already had something to read. Before leaving Perth, Sigrid rather forcefully placed in his care her copy of *Black Levant*, with the instruction that he should neutralize the limerick with something more cerebral. Worse undressed for bed and lay down to look at it. He remembered there was a piece somewhere that was vaguely about chemistry, and the halide discussion earlier had put the subject in mind. He was pleased to see it listed in the contents, and went to the page. Sigrid's bookmark, a purple ribbon, was already there. He read and reread, until he fell asleep.

You say the art is lost.
I say, art embraces loss for absolution.
Some good remains in brilliant fragments
awaiting resurrection.

The artist-consort in this consummation
—perceiving emptiness—
will comprehend anew her servitude and struggle.

While you and I explore
the flawed topography of wishful senses
for meaning-shards and weaving-threads
and buried kicking-stones of loss disfigurement.
So making text of ancient purpose
effort, chance and willing subjugation.
So recreating genius and the long passion
that ends in shocking intimacy.

You say the resurrection is unreal,
our slim volume of refutations
will disallow returning.

I say, my universe is generous. I would be
entertained as well by different speculations
were that chemistry never read
murex left on the wine sea bed
or mother indigo yet unwed.

They set out in two Land Rovers, Nicholas driving one, with Worse as navigator, and Paulo driving the second. As he always did, Nicholas had loaded special sound equipment he used for recording birdsong in the wild. There had been sightings of large swint flocks over parts of the plateau.

The previous evening had been spent planning. High-resolution satellite images gave some indication of old logging tracks, but most would be overgrown. They reasoned that if Glimpse had got through, the recent disturbance from his truck should show, even if sporadically. On that basis, they plotted a route from the Madregalo road to the volcano.

About ninety minutes east they reached the point where Nicholas believed Glimpse had gone in. He slowed while he and Worse scanned the forest border. When they saw the track, both vehicles stopped, and all three walked into the forest for fifty or so metres. Even after rains, it was clear that tyre ruts were recent. They returned to their vehicles, confident they had found the route. Worse recorded their position.

'Here we go,' said Nicholas, turning into the mud.

Progress was slow. On several occasions, they lost sight of a track, and needed to walk the ground to find it. Worse attempted to document their course using GPS, and periodic-ally attached reflective tape to tree branches to assist their return navigation.

'Perhaps we should have used the charter pilot to get us in,' said Nicholas at one stage.

'Except that all of Madregalo would then know about the volcano,' said Worse. 'I'm sure Glimpse kept it quiet, given we think it was his private terencium quarry.'

Three hours in, Worse commented that they were gradually gaining elevation. The forest floor drained a little better here, and they had good sightings of Glimpse's tracks. At four hours, they came to a clearing where the tyre ruts indicated that a vehicle had been turned. They stopped and explored.

'Either we are close, or we've followed Glimpse to a dead end where he had to find another way, in which case so will we,' said Nicholas.

Worse was walking across the clearing. He kicked the dirt.

'I think he camped here,' he said. 'This has been a fire.'

The others came over to look.

'By my reckoning,' said Worse, 'we're only a few kilometres from the edge. I vote we eat and then hike it from here.'

Worse plotted a compass course, but it wasn't difficult to follow Glimpse's trail. At intervals they could see drag marks as if something had been pulled along the ground. That would probably be a sack of josephites, headed for the truck, suggested Paulo.

The ground was still rising. At one point the path seemed to become clearer. Paulo commented on the fact, and they stopped to examine it. The demarcation from surrounding forest was subtle but definite.

'You know, Nicholas,' said Paulo. 'If the big josephites you saw in the second chamber came from the volcano, how did those people get them there?'

Nicholas had considered this.

'A lot of labour. Sleds of some kind. What are you thinking, Paulo?'

'I wonder if we are on Glimpse's Volcano Road, and he discovered traces of an ancient path between here and the caves.'

'Are you meaning Neolithic, that sort of ancient?' asked Worse.

'Possibly,' said Paulo.

'Neolithic roads have been identified,' said Nicholas. 'Quite a number in Europe. Some in the UK. I went on a school excursion to see one.'

They all looked at the ground.

'Poor Edvard. Now he'll need to find the right archaeologists for an excavation out here,' said Paulo. He was smiling.

The incline became noticeably steeper, which they took as indicating that their objective was close. Nicholas was leading the way when he suddenly stopped, raising a hand.

'Listen,' he said.

The others stopped, but could hear nothing unusual.

'That's swint song,' said Nicholas, 'but quite unlike anything I've heard before. It's ...' He hesitated, concentrating. 'I think it's *terza rima*. My God.'

He was urgently removing recording equipment from his pack, and set off holding a microphone high in the air while he adjusted an amplifier in his other hand. Paulo and Worse looked at each other, and followed him, staying back to minimize noise.

Nicholas was about twenty metres ahead of them when he stopped again, still holding up the microphone. He turned and beckoned. Paulo was the first to reach him. Worse held back a little, recording their position.

When Worse climbed the final few metres to the rim of the caldera, he had just a few moments to take in the scene before an extraordinary thing happened.

As one, millions of swints rose from the forest in front of them, blackening the sky across the volcanic plain. Nicholas stopped recording; that sound would not be analysable.

'I think some have recognized you as their saviour at the palace, Worse,' he said, 'and they're letting the others know.'

Worse stayed focused on their project.

'See if you can pick up Glimpse's tracks from here.'

A short distance to their left they found drag marks similar to those seen before, and followed the trail into the caldera. The swints were gradually resettling, and seemed unperturbed when the three men passed close to large groups feasting on seki fruit. Nicholas began recording again.

'We seem to have discovered the secret food bowl of our swints,' whispered Paulo to Worse. 'The seki here may have higher levels of gold—volcanic gold. Swints need that for their blood.'

Glimpse's track was easily followed. Two hundred metres in, they reached a small clearing where the vegetation was cut back and the ground had obviously been disturbed. Without exchanging words, they all knew that here was Glimpse's mine site.

Worse detached a long sound from the back of Paulo's pack. He tested the ground near the centre of the previous excavation, moving outwards to the edge. His expectation was that any readily accessible josephites would have been taken, but pristine samples might be found at the perimeter of the dig.

And it was there, at the boundary of the turned-over soil, where the sound struck stone at half a metre. Paulo came over with a spade and set about digging. Within a few minutes he lifted to the surface a twenty-centimetre-diameter clear josephite and held it up, brushing peat-like earth from its surface. Worse quickly supplied a black plastic bag to protect it from the light.

All this time, no words passed between them. Nicholas, wearing bulky headphones, had watched the exercise as he held a boom microphone high into the vines, capturing the chatter of inquisitive swints.

The **seki** vine is known to concentrate gold from alluvial soils, and Paulo surmised that this might occur even more so in volcanic strata. Seki fruit is the main source of this essential element for swints, whose yellow blood cells seasonally utilize a gold-heteroglobin for oxygen transport, in place of iron-containing haemoglobin (see note to previous chapter).

The presumed acclamation of the swints, attributed by Nicholas to recognition of their saviour from the palace, might have a different explanation. In being the third to appear on the caldera rim, Worse completed a human thrice. Avian psychologists suspect that sums to 1 or 2 (mod 3) cause population anxiety in swints.

Nicholas soon came to realize that the changeable **infrared** radiance he had studied was not due to subsurface volcanic activity, but explained by the thermal mass of enormous swint roosts. In subsequent weeks he obtained high-resolution radar imaging and gravity mapping of the region. These reveal a rising elevation at the centre of the plain, many kilometres from where they had explored. When informed of the findings, Tøssentern, whose imagination can have a leaping, consternating character, immediately suggested that in the past the caldera accommodated a lake with a central island, evoking once more the Circular Sea and Rep'husela's throne. He would need yet another team of specialists to test that hypothesis.

24 SIMILE OF THE CAVE

When they returned to their vehicles, it was too late in the day for safe navigation back to the Madregalo road. This had been anticipated and they were well prepared for a night camping. Worse raked dry fuel away from the remains of Glimpse's camp oven, dug it out, and started a fire. All three knew it wasn't necessary for warmth, light, cooking or protection from beasts, but it was indefinably comforting. Paulo set out folding chairs, and Worse chose to sit with his back to the forest, the fire between him and the Land Rovers.

It was still light, and Worse offered to make proper tea. The others wondered what an Australian might mean by that in the remoteness of a forest, and were curious when he produced a billy requisitioned from the LDI canteen storeroom. Worse filled it with water, supporting it over the fire on a rig fashioned from the steel sound and two makeshift uprights.

They talked about the day's events, and discussed how the discovery of the volcano should be handled. Paulo had researched the subject and found no references to their occurrence in the Ferendes, which had never been considered as volcanic in origin. It was decided he should refer the question to Edvard, who would inform the appropriate ministries and propose research policies.

Night fell quickly. Worse noticed that Nicholas had been unusually quiet.

'The swint song has stopped,' said Worse.

Nicholas looked up from the fire.

'We think that they still sing very softly at this time of day, just within the thrice.'

'As in vespers, perhaps?' asked Worse.

'We shall shortly know, I believe.'

By virtue of his schooling, Worse had once been well read in talmudic, biblical and koranic legend, but for many years his atheistic interest had been narrowed to the exquisite *Second Letter to the Syllabines* (its precursor is lost) and the first-century *Gospel of St Ignorius*, or more particularly the fragmentary writings of its Renaissance interpreter, Leonardo di Boccardo. Fundamentally ethical and free of mendacious provenance, these were more agreeably humanist, with a worldliness and occasional irony that Worse found suited to modern life.

Naturally, he was very interested in Nicholas's programme of birdsong decipherment, particularly any elucidation of the swint's counting ability. Solving those challenges would be a monumental achievement of experimental design, applied acoustics and computational analysis, quite apart from its existential significance to human civilization. He was, with others, unimpressed that certain combatants in the Chirping Wars had chosen skirmish over civil engagement, voicing prejudgement in the popular press. Worse had no such concerns with Nicholas, whom he knew to be a scrupulously unbiased thinker. That last answer he gave, ending in 'I believe', had nothing religious about it. It just sounded enormously respectful.

'If the mythology is proven, that swints really are the true Prophet and Apostles of God, how imperilled will they be?'

Worse was looking at the fire, but Nicholas knew the question was to him. He was shocked at the thought.

'They will be revered, Worse. They will be properly revered.'

'Not by all, Nicholas.'

It was quick, definite and blunt. Nicholas was dismayed.

'Are you thinking of some kind of slaughter of the innocents?' asked Paulo. His spectacles reflected red flame light.

The barbarity imaged in the softly spoken question might reposition some in their thinking, but Worse was already there. He was still watching the fire.

'Well, that never really came to an end, did it? The dogs bark, but the caravan of tyrannies moves on.'

Paulo and Nicholas stayed silent. Worse was not finished.

'The charlatan saint is a many-layered fiend.'

It was a line from Monica Moreish, spoken by Virgil in the underworld. Worse omitted the canto's unpeeling vileness, and its 'core of kneeling lust' conclusion.

Nicholas was clearly upset. He summoned his mathematician's idealism.

'It's a matter of education, Worse. If they prove to be what you say, the swint gospel, as it were, will speak for itself. Surely.'

Ah yes, thought Worse. *Listen to the thriced.* But in the matter of learning, Leonardo had also written

> Reason turns a Devil's spell:
> The remedied to good,
> But not the infidel.

It made Worse depressed, and he offered no reply to Nicholas.

Every so often, Paulo or Nicholas would stand up to do a chore, and Worse could see their dramatically enlarged shadows projected on the Land Rover sides. Fire, cave, shadow, prayer, treachery, and walking the path of ancient peoples carrying supernatural crystals—if we know and hold the human condition by inheritance, then these were surely in its altar-burse of passing-pieces.

With a pennyweight of melancholy as well. Worse looked upwards to the earliest stars, then back at his two friends across the fire. It was the remorseless hour, when the compass of inconsequential mortal being becomes those small infinities of night.

He thought again about the swints, and for the first time felt drawn to one preferred truth: out here, in the forest, lost in wonder, he hoped their holiness would be proved. That made him depressed again.

On the trek back to the campsite, Worse had collected some foliage that he found interesting. To lighten his mood he now retrieved a handful from where it was dumped near the front vehicle. As he walked around the fire, a new shadow took form, alive, fleeting, and not identifiably his.

He returned to his seat, tearing leaves into thin strips that he piled on his lap. Nicholas and Paulo watched in silence, concerned that Worse's idea of proper tea was to brew these suspect pickings of the forest trail. There was also a palpable quiet left over from the swint conversation.

Quite unexpectedly for the others, Worse leaned forward and threw the strips not into the billy, but directly onto the fire. There was a sudden, loud whoosh, and a flare of brilliant blue-white light that died within a second. Paulo and Nicholas recoiled instinctively. Even Worse was surprised at the result of his experiment.

'What was that, Worse?' asked Nicholas, with undisguised reproach.

'The leaves reminded me of a tree from my childhood,' said Worse. 'A similar terebinth smell, I thought. Rich in volatiles, obviously. Interesting.'

Alarming, more than interesting, the others were thinking.

'It's boiling,' reported Paulo. He hadn't spoken since the Herod reference.

Worse stood up and threw black tea leaves into the water. He watched the turbulence for a minute before lifting the sound off the fire, carrying the billy with it.

'Watch carefully,' he said.

Worse grasped the lidless billy's wire handle, using green forest leaves for insulation. He stood back from the fire, and began to swing the billy like a pendulum. Suddenly, from a forward under-swing, it went full circle at high speed, revolving around and around at arm's length, the boiling tea retained by nothing but centrifugal force. He stopped the exercise by running forward as it slowed.

'Settles the tea leaves. Not for use indoors.'

Nicholas and Paulo, scientists as they were, still looked disbelieving. Worse walked around the fire to them.

'Hold out your mugs. This is genuine outback billy tea, for which we can thank physics.'

The next afternoon, Nicholas took Worse for a walk to see the Edge. This is the southern escarpment of the Joseph Plateau, high over the plain that extends to the Bergamot Sea. Their path ended at a clearing that had functioned as the anchor station for Tøssentern's research balloon *Abel*, which was lost in a storm the previous year. LDI kept a few shelters and storage facilities there, but it mostly served as a constitutional retreat for staff, particularly in the evenings.

Nicholas unfolded two canvas chairs and set them up overlooking the sea. For those fortunate to have explored outside the main population centres of the Ferendes, this was one of the most beautiful views in the whole country. Nicholas had something on his mind.

'Are you looking forward to having Millie come to Perth?'

Worse turned to look at him.

'Of course. Very much so.'

Nicholas continued looking into the distance. It was as if he had felt the need to raise a subject only to find he had nothing to say. Worse was slightly discomforted. He spoke unnecessarily.

'I've offered that she stay in the spare apartment, until she can organize exactly what she wants,' he said.

Nicholas didn't speak for several seconds.

'You know, this is a special place for us. When Edvard was missing, we would spend a lot of time here, looking out. Especially Anna. I think we all hoped that *Abel* would float into view, come into dock, and Edvard would walk over and sit beside us with some amazing adventure story to explain his disappearance.'

'I can imagine how hard that time must have been,' said Worse.

'Now, I gather Edvard is thinking this would be a good place to site offices and labs for all the teams he's putting together, archaeologists and the rest,' continued Nicholas. 'They will need accommodation as well, seminar rooms, dining hall, and so on. Very likely, there will be graduate students out here too. Placing everything at the Edge will be Edvard's way of protecting the LDI educational and language functions from disruption by all the new cave and volcano studies.'

'So, a Ferende campus of Cambridge, effectively?' said Worse, looking around the clearing.

'Something like that,' said Nicholas.

'How do you feel about all that change coming?'

'I think it will be fantastic.'

'There's no talk of a replacement for *Abel*?' asked Worse.

'None at all. Edvard's done that. He's seen weaver fish.'

Mention of *Abel* set Nicholas staring out to sea again. Worse relaxed in his chair. They stayed like that for several minutes, until Nicholas spoke.

'I've been thinking over the things you said last night. About swints.'

Worse waited. Nicholas continued.

'It brings up that old science–ethics dilemma. Should one— should I—do research that foreseeably could have social or other harm as a consequence?'

Worse remained quiet.

'It's not a question that mathematicians need to ask normally,' said Nicholas.

Worse didn't speak. He hadn't been asked to.

'I would value your opinion, Worse,' said Nicholas a minute later.

Worse spoke slowly, still looking at the sea.

'In the case of your swint studies, my view would be that you are entitled to continue with a clear conscience,' he said. 'More than entitled. Obligated.'

Nicholas waited. Worse resumed speaking, softly.

> 'We are servants of the lighthouse
> —all of us,
> carrying wood to the fire,
> making light.
> Making shadows.'

'Satroit?' asked Nicholas after a moment.

'It's about Pharos of Alexandria, but I think he's saying we are all responsible for a truthful world.' Worse looked at his friend. 'Light falls guiltless even on the tyrant, Nicholas. Meaning, the evil in a shadow is not of light's making.'

They were quiet again for some minutes. Worse was the first to speak.

'Nicholas. As I understand it, you have in mind that in the near future you will be able to interpret swint speech, synthesize it, then presumably hold conversations, interrogate them, perhaps.'

'Yes.'

'What will be the first thing you say?'

Nicholas smiled. 'Hello. My name is Nicholas. Tell me everything you know.' He stood up. 'Perhaps we should get back to Paulo.' As he folded the chairs for storage, he said, 'You know, Worse, Millie likes you.' He met Worse's eye in a way that added to the words without repeating them.

They walked back to the station in silence.

The office door was open, with Paulo sitting at his desk. Worse followed Paulo in, and glanced at an image on Paulo's screen as he crossed to Edvard's desk.

'Who's that?' he asked.

Paulo turned around, wondering whom Worse could be addressing. He found Worse looking at him and pointing to the image. He looked back at the screen himself.

'Do you see a face?' he asked.

Worse came closer to study it.

'I did fleetingly. Now I'm not certain. What is it?'

'It's a blotching from the wall in the first cavern. There are thousands of them. Hieroglyphs of some kind, we assume. We are hoping to get better pictures with the lighting you brought in.'

Worse nodded and sat at his desk to work on aspects of the Mortiss connection to the Ferendes gleaned from the documents in La Ferste. He found himself not concentrating, and after a few minutes interrupted the silence.

'Paulo, sorry. What program did you have that blotching open in?'

Paulo turned around.

'Pel-Lucida.'

'Would you mind bringing the same one up again and showing me its negative?'

Paulo looked puzzled before turning back to the screen and reloading the image. Nicholas leaned over from his desk to see. It was a simple matter for Paulo to digitally reverse the contrast, but the effect was dramatic.

'My God,' said Nicholas. 'It is a face. Isn't it?'

'Possibly,' said Worse, more reserved.

Paulo was looking at the screen, smiling broadly. He loaded multiple others, doing the same transform. None was unequivocally a human face, but all looked vaguely as if they might be. This potentially changed the significance of the cave discovery completely.

'What colour is the cave rock?' asked Worse. 'Pale, I take it?'

'Yes,' said Nicholas. 'The blotchings are generally dark markings on an almost white surface. A marble, we think.'

'And the large silhouette figure? Pale with dark edges?'

'As far as I could see, yes,' said Nicholas.

Paulo turned toward Worse and Nicholas.

'What are you suggesting, Worse?'

Worse sat back, staring at a reversed blotching on Paulo's screen, trying to recapture that instant of complete confidence when he first looked as he entered the room.

You say the art is lost.

He was struggling to assimilate ideas, and only managed to form an argument as he spoke, beginning tentatively, then with increasing cogency.

'We have a coincidence of findings here that we can form into a ridiculous hypothesis.'

Nicholas and Paulo leaned forward expectantly.

'These people, these Neolithic people, had a giant darkroom in the form of the cave. They had a source of silver halides within their josephites. We know that they valued that mineral because they troubled to mine it, and were sufficiently observant of its properties to use it for scintillation lighting, so you believe. That strongly suggests they would also have noted that josephites darken in sunlight. In fact, they must have known that, in order to prevent it happening during transport to the cave, where according to Nicholas the specimens are pristinely transparent. They potentially had flash illumination as you saw with that almost explosive terebinth flare. And we can suppose they probably had primitive natural lenses in the form of fortuitously biconvex josephites.'

'You're saying they had photography? Flash photography? You're saying these blotchings are photographs?' said Nicholas.

'That's the ridiculous hypothesis,' said Worse. 'They would be negatives, of course. The remaining question is the chemistry: what did they use to develop and fix the images?

You said that you thought seki juice was used to stain the rock, that blotchings were painted in some way. Maybe the seki wasn't a stain but part of the photographic process. The other thing we don't know much about is terencium. As the rarest of rare earths and the most recently discovered, it's the least understood. Maybe terencium halides are also photo-reactive and behave differently from silver salts on that particular rock surface. And, for all we know they might be sensitive to wavelengths more exactly suited to terebinth light.'

Worse stopped to let the others speak.

'That is fantastic,' said Nicholas. He was already thinking of the next step. 'We need to lift one off *en bloc* and get the whole surface analysed.'

'I think you're on to something, Worse,' said Paulo.

'Actually, that might be too destructive. But we should try to reproduce their methods, to establish feasibility,' continued Nicholas.

'Well, it's a circumstantial mix for now,' said Worse, replying to Paulo.

'... using only materials that were available to them,' said Nicholas to the room generally.

'It is that very circumstantial mix that was, in fact, available to them,' said Paulo quietly to Worse.

'Then we need to decode the blotchings numerically and establish that they are irregularly focused images,' said Nicholas.

Worse and Paulo smiled to each other. Nicholas was way ahead with planning a research programme.

'Photography! I love ridiculous.' Nicholas was typing rapidly as he spoke. 'Who remembers anything about Zernike polynomials?'

'Paulo, can I have a copy of the blotchings album?' said Worse.

'And Edvard,' said Nicholas. 'Edvard will have to get some specialist chemists involved in this. Some old-school photography scientists as well. And spectroscopists. And more computing. And more maths.'

The campus at the Edge had just enlarged by several buildings.

There had been no further visits to the cave since the police operation to recover Glimpse. Paulo considered it too hazardous for the two of them alone, and suspended the survey until an expert team was organized by Tøssentern, or at least they had devised suitable measures against the Shuffler crab danger. Having Worse with them altered the balance. He was keen to see the cave, and he would assist in the task of transporting and installing the improved lighting brought in from Madregalo.

There was extra motivation now, too. The photographic theory of the medallions made Paulo and Nicholas anxious to examine them anew, and to seek Worse's views on their appearance *in situ*. The expedition was set for the following day, and they spent some of the evening planning, packing kit, and briefing Worse.

They started out at 6.00 am, heavily laden with generator fuel, batteries, rope, camera gear, and the new lighting system. It was hard trekking, and they needed frequent rests. During one of these, Paulo shared his thoughts.

'You know, Nicholas. This isn't going to work when the team arrives. Not everyone will be fit enough for what we're doing. We need to be able to get vehicles in for equipment anyway, or for emergencies. For one thing, we'll have to replace the generator with something much bigger, and that means transporting diesel in by tanker, not backpacks.'

'You'll have to ask Edvard for a road survey and a bulldozer crew,' said Nicholas. 'At least all that can be sourced from Madregalo.'

'From everything you two have described, you've discovered a world heritage site,' said Worse. 'I would have thought that means high-level authorization, environmental impact studies, international best practice assets management. Will Edvard fix all that?'

Paulo exchanged looks with Nicholas.

'If you want to see a typical Ferende environmental impact statement, Nicholas and I will take you to the northern plain. Until last year, the Chinese were destroying hundreds of square kilometres of forest for milling, followed by ripping up the subsoil for rare-earth mining. Luckily the attack on Feng generated enough superstition to close it down.'

'Let's hope the standards improve,' said Worse, shouldering his pack. 'I don't think I told you that before he hit on josephites, Glimpse was scavenging those abandoned mine stocks for terencium ore and smuggling it to the States.'

At the entrance to the cave, Nicholas and Paulo repeated their well-practised routine of fuelling the generator, reorganizing loads for the descent, and checking torches. Paulo reiterated for Worse the climb hazards of the first section, and advised how he would call them at each point, and how Worse should acknowledge.

The hazard not discussed was the Shuffler. Paulo was hopeful that given the creature's size, the z-bend in the tunnel would present a natural impediment, if not a complete barrier. What wasn't known was whether there were smaller relatives able to get through, yet still large, upright and agile enough to be a danger. Also, they didn't know at this stage whether there were other routes into the first chamber. But the key to safety, as Paulo had consistently argued, was good lighting, and the main purpose of today's expedition was to install more wattage while they had Worse's assistance.

Nicholas, while conscious of the risks, was more driven by his excitement in the science and human history. In the chamber, when he threw the switch on a new floodlight, it was pointed toward the tunnel access. There was the great pale shadow picture, ten metres high, legs splayed and arms wide, dominating the entrance like a giant fertility goddess.

'To paint their emulsion that far up, they would have needed ladders, or some kind of demountable scaffold,' said Nicholas.

'It would be the same for these,' said Paulo, redirecting the flood to the main blotching wall. It was Worse's first clear sight of them. He walked across to where Nicholas had left a camping stool beside the camera tripod, sat down, and stared at the enormous medallion matrix illuminated before him. It was beautiful art, more visible to human eyes than ever in its history.

'*Sunt lacrimae rerum,*' he said softly.

Paulo and Nicholas came over. Both sensed Worse's emotion about what he saw, and hesitated to speak. Eventually, Nicholas could no longer restrain himself.

'What do you think?'

Worse took time to answer.

'I can understand why you thought they were elements of language,' he said. 'They do look palaeographic, I imagine. Similar to each other, but sufficiently different. You would need to determine repetition rates, obviously, and identify a classification. I presume you are looking at that. You're the experts.'

'Yes, yes,' said Nicholas impatiently. 'But what do you think, Worse? What are you seeing?'

'Well. They don't strike me as human faces in any obvious way. Otherwise, you would both have had that thought already. All the same, what I see here, and I'm not sure why, are people. I think you have discovered a kind of national portrait gallery.'

Paulo and Nicholas were looking intently at Worse as he spoke. Both shifted their gaze to the blotching wall when he had finished.

Worse wanted time to be alone with his thoughts, and with the incredible document of unknowable human experience displayed before him. He stood up and moved away from the other two.

Fire and shadow and night: certainly. But this was a passing-piece more intimate, perhaps more sacred, than any other. Worse faced the wall, absorbed in its meaning. These people had devised a language of identity, recording who they were, not how they lived. Each medallion was a form of signature, asserting to posterity its owner's life. And here was left their written being, defiant and intensely personal, kept in darkness for the ages.

> *Some good remains in brilliant fragments, awaiting resurrection.*

Worse felt grieved, and honoured to be reading it. This was the *trace humaine* made visible. For his ability to see, and for his understanding, he was thankful to interpreters, who are the poets of art and loss.

25 LATENT IMAGE

Welcome to Dante where the local time
Is Paradise Now! and the weather Divine.
Feast on twicing
Doubled in icing
Sing Dante *ti amiamo* in triple the rhyme.

Worse flew direct La Ferste–Los Angeles, overnighted to make the best Air Asphodel connection, and arrived in Dante early Tuesday afternoon. He was collected at the airport by Thomas in a police vehicle. Their meeting was warm but not effusive. On the ride to the BHEH, Thomas pointed out a few sights of interest, but neither was talkative. In town, he drove Worse along the historic Main Street, which was closed to normal traffic, and pulled over outside a building on the north side, lowering the driver's window.

'That's where the session will be on Thursday. It's walking distance from your hotel.'

Worse looked across, in front of Thomas, but said nothing. Thomas resumed driving, keeping the car at crawling speed as Main Street functioned as a pedestrian mall.

'You prepared, Richard? For Thursday?'

'I'm prepared. There's one idea I'd like to follow up. I'll charter a helicopter tomorrow. I want to take a look with a metal detector at the exact location where the drone was recovered. I know the coordinates from military surveillance.'

'You don't need a charter, cousin. That comes under official police business. I'll take you out in Sheriff Bird. Would first thing in the morning suit?'

At the BHEH, Thomas left the patrol car on the concourse and walked inside with Worse. He sat in the lobby lounge making phone calls while Worse checked in and carried his bags to his room. When Worse rejoined him, Thomas was looking at the bar menu.

'I take it they didn't serve a meal on your flight, Richard?'

'No, they didn't.'

Thomas handed the menu to Worse.

'The steak sandwich is best. Can I get you one?'

Thomas called a waiter over, and ordered for them both. That done, they chatted for several minutes on matters ranging from Arizona geography to email security. Worse brought the subject back to the safety board meeting.

'When does Walter get in, do you know, Thomas?'

'He's on a tight schedule. Arrives tomorrow afternoon, evidence Thursday morning, and leaves on adjournment. You've never met Walter?'

'No. But he's close to people I'm close to,' said Worse.

'You'll like him. But you do know Anna?'

'We met last year in the Ferendes. Anna and Edvard.'

'She's a very nice person, Anna. I'm sorry she can't be here for this second hearing. She had a lot of interest in Walter's situation.'

'Anna's been helpful to me,' said Worse, 'filling in about the board proceedings last time, and a little about Dante, where to stay and so on. If she hadn't told me about the limerick custom, I would have been rather mystified at the cabin crew announcement when we landed. I've also been reading the book by Monica Moreish, on Anna's recommendation, for homework.'

Thomas smiled. 'People don't refer to them as limericks here; they just say them. It can be a sensitive issue with some folk. Best advice is take it all seriously and save up any guffaws for the privacy of your hotel room.'

Their meals were served on a coffee table in front of them. Worse was surprised at the elegance of the presentation. Thomas insisted on signing the tab.

'Speaking of hotel room, what's your number?' asked Thomas.

'Five-one-two.'

'I chose that; I hope you don't mind,' said Thomas. 'There's a lot of interest in the mystery stranger come to give evidence, and not all of it will be welcoming. That room is a little easier to keep secure. If you have no objection, I would like to place a twenty-four-hour guard outside.'

'No objection, Thomas. I'll keep the guffaw volume low.'

Worse was looking around as he ate. 'Who is that party?' He tilted his head toward the other end of the lobby, and across the lounge space from where they sat. He had an idea already.

'I've seen them. That party,' said Thomas, stressing the words, 'will be waiting for the presidential suite to clear. That's Regan Mortiss, brother William on her left, and the man about to stand up is the most errant confessor in Chicago. His name is Sendoff. He and Regan spend time together. Night-time.'

'I've followed Sendoff's curriculum vitae, so to speak, online. He needs to be investigated as an accessory to murder. So does the brother.'

'Jeez, Richard. How do you know?'

'I'll pass you an evidence file on Friday. The victim was a corrupt accountant named Tweisser. I suspect he's deep in Lake Michigan. She's the killer.'

Worse looked again at the others. Sendoff had walked to the reception desk. 'How could you tell he was about to stand up?'

'Body language. He's Regan's personal bellhop, and I read feminine imperative in the pointed finger.'

Now Regan also stood, walking slowly toward Sendoff while taking a call. She was tall, slim and beautifully dressed. Despite the subdued interior lighting, she had on sunglasses. Thomas noticed Worse watching her.

'Be careful with her, Richard. She never moves without a shoulder bag and we know what's in it. She can relieve you of half an earlobe at thirty paces.'

'She's really that good?'

'She certainly used to be.'

They had finished eating, and Worse shifted in his chair to put the Mortiss party behind him.

'How often does she get to Dante?' he asked.

'Infrequently, now. The family owns a lot of property but they don't like the place. The connection to Area Pi was a complete surprise to us, I regret to say.'

Worse nodded. He was reprocessing the conversation as he listened.

'What did you mean by "used to be"?'

Thomas showed no surprise at Worse's delayed question.

'She was once our junior state pistol champion. By her mid-twenties, her scores were falling off and she gave away competition.'

'Do you have an opinion as to why that might have been?'

Thomas smiled. 'You are persistent, cousin. Rumour has it there's a vision problem in the family. Retinitis maybe. We haven't had just cause to examine their medical records.'

Their plates were cleared. Thomas excused himself to make a short call.

'I want to introduce you to someone. He'll be along in a minute,' he said when finished. 'What are your plans? Can I give you a lift anywhere?'

'Thanks, Thomas. I'm good for now. I'll go for a walk, then be in my room.'

'And tonight? If you are free, my wife and I were hoping you might come over for dinner. My son won't be home but I would like the two of you to meet later in the week.'

'That would be delightful, Thomas. Thank you.'

'We're on a ranch thirty minutes out. I'll collect you, seven thirty.'

They stood up and shook hands, just as a uniformed deputy approached from the main entrance.

'Richard. This is Deputy Frank. He'll be taking first watch and coordinating the rest. Deputy, meet your charge, Dr Worse.' They also shook hands. 'Deputy, room five-one-two is confirmed. Thank you.'

Deputy Frank excused himself, heading to the lift station. Thomas gave Worse his business card, and also left.

Worse sat down for a few minutes before following Thomas through the main entrance and out to the concourse. He had an address to find and a parcel to collect, organized by Spoiling.

Five-one-two was an end room, and Deputy Frank had set up a small office space in the hallway, with a good view of the elevators. He turned down the volume of a radio programme when he saw Worse.

> ... *was for Beatrice from Duran who says, 'Come back, baby ...'*

Worse greeted him as he unlocked his door.

Once inside, he opened Spoiling's parcel. Then he unpacked his bags, removing a business suit from its carrier and hanging it in the room closet. Worse disliked formality, but accepted that he needed to conform on occasions, and this occasion was Walter's.

There were still several hours before he was to be collected for dinner, and Worse felt an overwhelming need for thinking time. This was always best spent lying down. He set a clock alarm in case he fell asleep, leaving time for a shower before being ready by 7.30.

Worse was confident of giving satisfactory testimony at the hearing; he had names, communications and surveillance. But he hadn't comprehensively solved the science, the technology, going on at Area Pi. Terencium was important, but he didn't know why, and the incompleteness of his understanding was troubling. He fell asleep worrying about it. When the alarm wakened him, he was dreaming about the medallion gallery in the Joseph Plateau cave.

Early the next morning, Thomas again collected Worse in the lobby to drive to the police department sector at the airport.

'Thank you both again for last night, Thomas,' said Worse when they were in the car. 'I enjoyed it very much. It was lovely to see your place, how you live, and to meet Rebecca.'

'It was our pleasure, Richard.'

Thomas manoeuvred between vehicles congested at the hotel entry.

'It seems busy today,' said Worse.

'The action's picking up for tomorrow. Walter Reckles has a national profile, air safety always gets reported, and putting the mysterious Area Pi into the mix gives you a guaranteed segment on the news. And, as I say, some will have heard about a surprise witness. They'll be very curious about you.'

'Area Pi is a mysterious entity,' said Worse, removing himself from the subject line. 'But only because they're secretive. When it's uncovered, we'll just find science and criminality, I'm sure.'

He fell silent, not for thinking about Area Pi, but about the previous evening at Thomas's ranch. To have been invited into his family life was a privilege for Worse. Every so often, after an experience like that, he confronted what was lacking in his own world. He looked at Thomas and admired his good fortune.

Thomas introduced Worse to their pilot, Bernice Brales, at the dispatch desk. Worse provided their destination coordinates. They had deliberately left filing a flight plan till the last moment in case informants alerted Area Pi security.

Worse's expectation was that the recovery mission for the downed drone would have prioritized speed over thoroughness, on the basis that detection of the search party was a far higher risk than discovery of any missed fragments so distant from the Condor crash site. If the drone search went unobserved, investigators would have no idea where to concentrate their effort, and that is exactly how events transpired. What Mortiss couldn't have foreseen was that Worse would discover, to within half a metre, where to bring that search.

Bernie landed forty metres off point, and powered down. She passed water bottles to Worse and Thomas, and the three alighted. The Bleacher was still sandy here but a little more stony, with some withered grasses that were burnt near the primary crash site.

Thomas unloaded two metal detectors from the stowage bay, and handed one to Worse. They had planned a concentric grid search centred on the impact point and using their aircraft as a reference. Bernie was lookout; they didn't want to be surprised by any response from Area Pi.

Worse and Thomas walked the site systematically for an hour before taking a break, sitting out of the sun in the helicopter.

'Either there was no fragmentation, or they checked the ground very thoroughly indeed,' said Thomas, drinking from his water bottle.

Worse was staring at the search centre when he abruptly reached for his laptop and opened a file, copying some data into his smartphone.

'I've got an idea,' he announced as he stepped to the ground, picked up his metal detector, and walked across the site while looking at his phone.

Thomas followed with the other detector. Worse stopped at

a point some way beyond their earlier search perimeter.

'Here,' he said, waving his arm around. 'The one place they might not have looked was under their aircraft, and this is exactly where it put down.'

Worse had read the location from a satellite image.

Thomas smiled. Two minutes later, Worse had a find. He bent down and brushed aside sand, picking up a twenty-by-two-centimetre strip with fine rivet holes. One surface was raw metal, the other had a slightly iridescent black coating. Thomas held out an evidence bag.

'What would you say it is?' he asked, sealing the top.

'A cowling tie, something like that,' said Worse. 'It was probably covered by their sand blow when they landed.'

Worse returned to the BHEH at 11.00, acknowledging the deputy on duty as he entered his room. While out, he had received some emails but delayed opening them until now.

> Dear Dr Worse
> Re: Position of Housekeeper (Ref 3589)
> We are pleased to inform you that we have identified five suitable candidates for the above position. All are able to commence on or before the date you have specified. Interviews will be held in our offices as indicated in the attached schedule. Please inform us if you intend to be present at these or elect to have a representative attend in your place. Following selection at interview we will call up references and, if they are satisfactory, implement a contract of engagement. As agreed, this will be for a probationary term of three months in the first instance.
> Assuring you of our most diligent attention at all times,
> Ralph Plinco-Brown, for RPB Personnel Search

Dear Mr Plinco-Brown
Thank you for your letter. I will not be in Perth on
the day of interviews; nor will I have a representative
present. I look forward to learning the outcome.
Yours sincerely
R Worse

A message from Nicholas was far more interesting.

Dear Worse
I tried the old SNR trick of averaging out noise. This
image is 25 superpositions aligned and scaled on
my best estimates of pupillary centres. What do you
think?
Nicholas

Worse opened the attachment. His screen filled with a mono-
chrome portrait, unmistakeably a human face. It was not, of
course, that of an individual, but a composite of twenty-five.
Nevertheless, it was a likeness of their people, and Worse
felt moved to be seeing it. He studied it for a long time before
replying to Nicholas.

Worse lay on his bed, looking at the portrait until the screen
shut down. He was thinking about Area Pi again. Somehow,
they had found a way to fully absorb radar energy and dissipate
it, probably as heat. From their materials orders, he knew that
graphene was important. So too, it appeared, was terencium.
Perhaps it served as a dopant in some novel silicon–graphene
semiconductor physics. He returned to his comment made
to Nicholas and Paulo: *We don't know much about terencium.*
Either he needed to go back in electronically and do a thorough
clean-out of their research records, or he had to work it out for
himself. He fell asleep thinking about it.

He was woken by a call from Thomas saying that he and Walter were in the lobby. Worse went downstairs. He wanted to meet Walter but not particularly interact with him before the hearing. After introductions and a mention that they both knew Edvard and Anna and the LDI team, Worse asked what Walter thought was expected of him the following day.

'They want me on in the morning,' Walter replied. 'Basically to confirm the evidence I gave last time, as I understand it.'

'Has anything changed in that respect?'

Worse wanted no surprises before giving his own testimony.

'No.'

'Are you still convinced you caught sight of a drone?' asked Worse.

'Absolutely.'

'What colour do you think it was?'

'You know, it's funny. They didn't ask me that at the hearing. They were so convinced it didn't exist.'

'What colour was it?'

'It was black, Worse. Black as Hades.'

Worse had dozed off thinking about the radar problem, and woken up still thinking about it. Even while talking to Walter, it was foremost in his mind. By the time he returned to his room, he had grasped the notion of what technologists at Area Pi had achieved.

And he knew whom to thank for the idea. Satroit, for colour latency and *brilliant fragments*. And someone else: Worse opened Nicholas's composite medallion portrait and looked at it admiringly. Neolithic they might be, but modern too. Ridiculously modern.

Worse guessed that the Mortiss enterprise had discovered a new photochemical transduction method based on reduction of terencium in halides at radar energies, rather as occurs with silver salts in the visible and ultraviolet spectrum. Almost certainly, they had developed a silicon–graphene wafer substrate to optimize electromagnetic absorption, dissipate heat, and facilitate high-frequency terencium ion regeneration using a suitably modulated EMF.

26 AMICUS CURIAE

[Chair] Your name is Dr Richard M Worse. Your permanent address is in Perth, Western Australia. You appear before this enquiry voluntarily in the role of amicus curiae. You declare yourself a disinterested party in relation to the Flight Control Corporation, any associated business entity, any product of that Corporation including the FC100 airplane, and any director, owner or employee of that Corporation including Dr Walter Reckles. Is all that correct?

[Richard M Worse] All that is correct.

[Chair] Are you represented by counsel?

[Worse] I am not, Mr Chairman.

[Chair] Are you willing to answer questions under oath at the conclusion of your testimony?

[Worse] I am, Mr Chairman.

[Chair] Please state for the board your purpose in summary.

[Worse] My purpose is to provide information to this investigation that would not otherwise be available for your consideration.

I am confident that this information will materially affect

the board's determination of the cause of the FC100 Condor crash.

I am further confident that the information to be provided will be seen to constitute evidence of criminal wrongdoing, in respect of which at least one responsible person is now present in this room.

[Uproar. Chair calls for order]

[Chair] I remind those present that this sitting of the board has the legal standing of a grand jury. I will not tolerate interruptions. I will not hesitate to apply sanctions or to employ the bailiffs. I will not hesitate to clear the gallery. You have been warned. Proceed, Dr Worse. Perhaps less tendentiously, if you find that possible.

[Worse] Thank you, Mr Chairman. The issue to resolve is the cause of the Condor crash. The proposition is that the Condor collided with an unmanned aerial vehicle, or drone, that was not legitimately in that airspace. The evidence in support is that the pilot, Dr Walter Reckles, briefly sighted the drone in the moment before impact, and that traces of foreign material, stated to be exotic to the Condor's composition, were detected on Condor parts salvaged from the crash site. Under this proposition, the said foreign material is taken as belonging to a drone that was not otherwise recovered in wreckage, and is *prima facie* evidence of the drone's existence and its party to a collision. I foreshadow to the board that the nature of that foreign material is significant.

The counterproposition, most forcefully advanced by the member of the board to your left, Mr Chairman, is that there was no collision with a drone. I note for your interest that the line of argument in this case is curiously neglectful of determining the actual cause of the crash, instead being concerned with persuading the board that a drone was not part of that cause and, indeed, that no drone exists.

The facts put forward as evidence that no drone exists include the lack of a regulation-mandated transponder signal, the lack of a radar presence in either the Condor system or the Dante tracking sector records from that date, and the lack of wreckage of a drone, all notwithstanding the contradicting facts in support of the original proposition, namely that the drone was sighted and that foreign material was obtained from the Condor wreckage.

I will shortly remind the board of an interesting truth, that a given set of facts may be judged evidence in support of many different hypotheses, and sometimes two such hypotheses are mutually contradictory on other grounds. The facts to examine here relate to the transponder, radar, and wreckage, and I will deal with all. The board will be convinced that the very same facts, transponder, radar and wreckage, are consistent with, and evidence of, an alternative hypothesis. And the board will be convinced that this alternative hypothesis is the very same proposition first advanced, that the cause of the Condor crash was collision with a drone.

[Chair] Dr Worse. Could you please indicate to the board how long your submission will take?

[Worse] I expect twenty minutes, Mr Chairman.

[Chair] Continue, Dr Worse.

[Worse] This alternative hypothesis is that some seventy-five minutes prior to the Condor entering Dante Control airspace, an experimental jet-engined drone was illegally launched from a facility northwest of Dante. This drone was guided to an altitude of thirty-five thousand feet while certain tests were conducted, then instructed to return to its point of launch, during which descent it collided with the Condor.

Its transponder was inactive for the very reason that the flight was illegal and part of an extensive, secret research program.

Now I come to the absence of a radar signal. There are several explanations for this. One is that there was no drone, as enthusiastically put, Mr Chairman, by the member of the board to your left. Another is that there was a malfunction of radar systems, or failure of operator performance. The requirement of a joint failure, that is, both within Dante Control and in the Condor, makes this highly improbable. A third possibility is that the illegal drone was blind to radar. Indeed, the hypothesis posits that the illegal drone was undergoing trials to prove that very capability, its invisibility to Dante radar.

What is the state of science pertaining to low radar reflectance of objects in flight? Of course, this technology is closely guarded and shrouded in government and defence contractor secrecy. But it is known that four factors obtain: evasion—as in terrain-hugging navigation, electronic countermeasures, aircraft shape, and surface. Here, we are concerned with surface. And what more serendipitous sampling of this surface radar-absorbing coating could we engineer than a scraping deposited on another aircraft in the course of an accidental midair collision? So we return to the nature of the foreign material recovered from the Condor wreckage.

I now invite members of the board to view their screens.

[Excision 1. Appendix A]

Where did this hypothetical drone take off, and where did it go? Let me re-familiarize members of the board with a curious facility in the northwest neighbourhood of Dante. It has long been known to Dante residents as Area Pi. The reason for this designation is not reliably recorded, and I will not speculate, except to draw attention to the mathematical fact that the area of a unit circle, that is a circle of radius one unit, is pi square units.

Area Pi is a very mysterious place. In fact its mystery, its isolation, is virtually celebrated by the people of Dante in the manner of a horror folkloric tradition. But how can one visit Area Pi? How can one find out what happens there? There are three ways. First, visit in person. That won't get you in, because of an intensely patrolled security perimeter. Second, electronically, via internet portals. And third, by aerial or space-based reconnaissance.

Page four on your screens is an image obtained from a low Earth orbit commercial satellite service. You can see several buildings and a runway. I point out that this runway is only twenty nautical miles from the Condor crash site. Note the rail structure running for about one thousand yards along its west side. I am now moving the cursor over a number of aircraft parked at the southern end of the runway. These two are large transport helicopters. The building is a hangar. I will next show a video of the area obtained by a United States military reconnaissance satellite. The date and approximate time are those of the Condor crash. You will see considerable activity on the ground, but the resolution is not sufficient to interpret events with certainty.

[Video. 1 min]

I must now inform members of the board, particularly those with a connection to the military of this country, that sadly there exists a reconnaissance resource superior to that belonging to the United States. It is perhaps not surprising that a foreign power should look down on the US with greater scrutiny than the US looks at itself. We might expect the converse to apply over that nation.

The following ultra-high-resolution images were obtained from Chinese military satellites codenamed Mìmì 117, 48, and 59C. The first video is of Area Pi, beginning at 0847.11.13 MDT on the day of the crash. In the interests of the board's time I have speeded the frame rate. You will clearly see an aerial object being launched from a specialized vehicle on the runway rail. The object gains speed and altitude very quickly.

[Video. 30 sec]

The Condor was lost to radar at approximately 1002.29. The following video shows two helicopters scrambled from Area Pi at 1005.17. At 1009.16 a large desert-capable vehicle also leaves the site. All are heading into the Bleacher.

[Video. 2.25 min]

The next footage from Mìmì 59C shows a helicopter landed in the desert and several personnel recovering a dark object, loading it into the cargo bay, and the aircraft taking off. Again, it is speeded up for your convenience.

[Video. 1.45 min]

Further surveillance confirms that this helicopter returned to Area Pi. We can surmise that a non-standard transponder was activated remotely to expedite this location and recovery operation.

We return to the initial fact that no drone wreckage was found by the investigating team. The member to your left, Mr Chairman, who appears to be tirelessly texting below the bench, is strongly of the view that this fact constitutes evidence that no drone exists. On the contrary, what we see is that this fact is explained by, and indeed is evidence for, drone wreckage having been clandestinely located and removed from the Bleacher before the safety board team could find it. And, as even the member to your left must concede, if there was drone wreckage, there was a drone.

[Excision 2. Appendix A]

Members of the board: as promised, I have now dealt with the three original facts, transponder, radar and wreckage. The facts support the first proposition that the Condor crash was caused by collision with an illegally launched drone.

I would now like to move your attention to Area Pi. We have examined this site from space-based reconnaissance. The next feasible method is via electronic penetration. I will present two lines of evidence, the first related to financials and the second to that operation's ordering system, which is conducted through secure email channels.

In the course of a separate investigation originating in Australia, I discovered a financial connection between outgoings at Area Pi and a shell company called Camelline Shipping which, though incorporated in the state of Arizona, has all its financial operations centred in Chicago. It is part of a vast underworld of shell and sleeping-partner companies that are used to conceal and illicitly transfer monies across states and across national borders. Camelline Shipping is the covert parent entity to a worldwide seaboard casino enterprise trading under the public names of Winnings, Sea Dice and Neptune's Treasure.

[Loud murmuring in court. Chair calls Order]

Camelline Shipping is itself a subsidiary of a Chicago-based company called Unit Circle Fiduciary. I emphasize the name. Unit Circle Fiduciary seems to operate as a private bank, and is the centre of the whole web of secret companies to which I have alluded. Only one entity sits above Unit Circle, and I will return to that fact in a moment. It will not surprise members of the board to learn that there is an intimate connection, other than the mentioned geometric one, between Unit Circle and Area Pi. All financial transactions related to Area Pi are conducted through the Chicago entities via Camelline. These include payments for materials and labour costs arising from activities at Area Pi.

I have stressed the significance of the foreign material found on the Condor wreckage. Analysis of this material informs us that it belongs to a class of very advanced radar-absorbing alloys that can be applied as a surface skin to aircraft. The frontier science in this research area is focusing on graphene laminations sandwiched between alloy layers. In the United States at present, there is only one specialist company that can supply lambda-graphene in commercial quantities. If you would look again at your screens, I am showing you a requisition sent from Area Pi to Camelline Shipping for the purchase of a large quantity of lambda-graphene from that specialist company. Note that the reference line carries the term Project Sunblock, which is the codename of the technology development happening at Area Pi.

Mr Chairman. There remains a link of practical reasoning to close, which I will now do. It will be apparent to members of the board that the exact location of the drone crash and recovery site is available to us from the satellite surveillance. Yesterday, the Dante sheriff's department conducted a physical search of that location, and returned with a metal strip that I now show the board.

[Dr Worse holds up evidence bag]

The surface coating on this specimen will be analysed and the results made available to the board. Pending that, you must judge for yourselves the likelihood that its composition will prove to be that of Sunblock, and identical to the contaminant material found on the Condor.

Returning to the communication between Area Pi and Camelline, I will now scroll down your screen page to display the identity of the executive who authorized the aforementioned graphene requisition. As I do so, I can inform you that the single entity that sits above, controls, and is the beneficial owner of Unit Circle Fiduciary is the corporation known to you as Mortiss Brothers, and the name and signature appearing on the communication before you are those of William R Mortiss, the gentleman, Mr Chairman, to your left.

That, members of the board, concludes my submission.

[Uproar in court. Chair inaudible]

[Chair (using Bench microphone)] Order. Order. Bailiffs, attend. Thank you, Dr Worse. Bailiff, detain Mr William Mortiss. Dr Worse, please remain contactable through the sheriff's office. Deputies, assist the bailiffs. Order. Order. This hearing is adjourned.]

[Increased uproar. Public pushing forward to Bench. Turmoil in court. This stenographer unable to continue recording due to crowd surging toward bench and buffe—

[Loud clamour. Voice content uninterpretable. Recording discontinued.]

In consideration of national security, Worse presented his evidence without reference to the key element in Sunblock composition, namely terencium, nor detail of the photochemical–electric mechanism of radar energy absorption.

27   INCIDENT AT BAKEHOUSE

Two blocks west of the BHEH is the Old Town, a small section of historical Dante preserved, restored, or rebuilt as a tourist precinct. The original *Judgment Daily* office is now a museum where visitors are treated to a demonstration of the hand-cranked press; in exchange for five dollars, they leave with a wet-inked page of news from the 1870s. Along from the museum, the Old Courthouse is used for various City Hall purposes, committee meetings, public exhibitions, and occasionally as a theatre. It was this facility that was made available to the safety board for the day's hearing on the Condor crash.

Across Main Street from the court building is the Bakehouse Tavern, reputably located on the site of the fabled Worse bakery of 1877. The actual building is set well back, having a spacious outdoor dining area furnished with bar tables, service trolleys and cactus pots. The forecourt is raised slightly above street level and is edged by a reproduction duckboard. This section of Main Street, decorated with scattered straw bales, is closed to private vehicles.

Twice daily in season, two old nags are roused from sleep in a stable behind the museum for their roles in a dramatized re-enactment ('accurate in every historical detail') of the 'Incident at Bakehouse'. Historical detail, it must be assumed, excludes blank rounds and headset microphones, but those looking on from the outdoor tavern invariably love it. They aren't aware that Rigo is a washed-up Hollywood stuntman whose single lifetime skill is falling off a horse backwards, or that he spends the four hours between performances three-quarters getting drunk and a quarter getting sober. Nor do they mind that his nag Twicing has grown too tired to bother rearing up with a theatrical whinny of pretend terror.

In many ways, that gunfight of 1877 has come to symbolize Dante's sense of itself. Though a modern and increasingly cosmopolitan small city, it often identifies as a frontier town, where the fight of the good with the bad is played out on the street. The immortal presence of their 'Sheriff Worse' from the town's foundation to the present day connects the city to its roots, to timeless ideals of the good, the rule of law, and civilization.

Not that the Bakehouse Tavern epitomizes civilization. The house whisky label is Head Shot and burgers come in the varieties of Sheriff, Preacher, Mongrel Killer, and so on. Their sponsorship of the street fight is surely calculated to fill their tables with drinking, spending tourists rather than serve in teaching history. Nevertheless, it is difficult to be a visitor to Dante and not find oneself seated at the tavern ordering bootleg liquor and (depending on one's mood) a Mortician with fries and Hot Lead sauce from the Pay or Die menu.

Thomas met Worse and Walter Reckles in the BHEH lobby, and together they walked down Silver Street into the old Main Street precinct. The last performance was long over and the crowds were thinning. Later toward evening, the numbers would pick up again as shoppers were replaced by diners.

The left side of the tavern façade was dominated by a large mural depicting the gunfight, showing Keff slumped forward on his mount and Rigo exploding backwards off his. It was painted on glass, actually mirror panels, each about a metre square. Worse counted them: four down and eight across. The wait staff were dressed in Old West costume, and carried wireless order and payment devices in imitation gun holsters at their sides.

Thomas chose a table near the back, close to the mirror. Worse positioned himself so he didn't have to look at it. Reckles sat down and stared at Worse.

'Why are you looking at me like that, Walter?' said Worse.

'I just want to thank you, thank you for what you did. You kind of saved my reputation, saved the Condor safety record, found an explanation for everything, proved the truth, and dropped the bad guys in, all in one day.'

'Your testimony was important. And Tom here, and Nicholas; everyone helped.'

'Yeah, I know. Of course. But that satellite imagery, that was the killer evidence. Area Pi should be swarming with FBI people by now.'

'I hope so,' said Worse.

'I can tell you it is,' said Thomas, who had been speaking on his mobile. 'They've flown in a 7T7-load of agents plus state troopers to secure the perimeter.'

They ordered lemon sodas, one of the few items unspoilt by renaming. Reckles drank his quickly and excused himself, thanking them both again. He needed to walk back to the hotel, collect his bag, and catch a flight home.

'The Mortiss lot must hate all this history on exhibition,' said Worse after Reckles had left, gesturing at the mural.

'They sure do. They've tried to close it down more than once, but lose on free speech grounds as well as the popular vote. It's part of the Dante psyche.'

'I can see that,' said Worse. 'They won't have enjoyed their time in court today, either.'

'Yeah. They'll be spitting barbed wire tonight,' said Thomas.

'That's not necessarily a good state of affairs. The family finances will be crushed but the vendetta temperature will go off the scale. Directed at me, mostly.'

'We're family,' said Thomas. 'Say, you don't by any chance have a Prussica that I can look at, do you? I've never seen one.'

'Aren't they illegal here?'

'Yeah, they are. Not so much under the table, off the record though. Between cousins. Just wondered.'

Worse smiled. He reached inside his jacket as he leaned over, removed the Totengräber, and passed it butt first under the table to Thomas.

'Keep it low,' he said.

Thomas took the pistol and bent his head down to study it. 'Beautiful. I wish I could try it on the range. How did you get it in?'

'Victor has special relationships all over. He looks after me.'

'I'd like to meet Victor one day. Here.'

Thomas passed the pistol back under the table. With several customers around, it was easier for Worse to slip it unseen into his trouser belt for the moment. He would transfer it to the shoulder holster when his situation was less exposed.

'Say, Richard, I was thinking you should have a bit of local authority in reserve. Just in case. Legalize the concealed weapon too.'

Thomas took a tin star from his pocket, reached across the table, and pinned it on Worse's jacket lapel.

'Raise your right hand and repeat after me.'

Worse followed the ceremonials. He was thinking of the look on Victor's face when he told him he'd joined a police force.

'Congratulations, Senior Deputy Sheriff Worse. You are continuing a great family tradition. We'll fix the paperwork tomorrow.' Thomas smiled. 'Excuse me.' He took a brief call on his mobile. 'I have to leave you. I'm sorry, Richard. The Feds need adult backup at Area Pi. They always have trouble dealing with bad language and sulking stares. I'll see you in the morning.'

He left some notes on the table.

'Are you staying to eat here?'

'How could I resist the Hot Lead sauce?' said Worse.

Two hours later, Worse was still sitting there. His meal had been served, and largely returned. Other diners had come and gone, and few tables now had customers. Main Street, crowded earlier, was almost deserted, and the lights were out in the museum and old courthouse opposite.

He had been reflecting on the day's developments. The events in Dante would likely see Mortiss Bros badly damaged and the family's influence, if not its entire wealth, compromised. That wasn't to say the vendetta would finish. There was every reason to expect that it might intensify, but at least there would be fewer funds and resources to direct toward it. Much depended on what happened to Regan. If control were wrenched back from her and more moderate, enlightened family members again ruled the company, the feud might dissipate into what it should be, an historical curiosity.

It was Thursday evening, 10.00 pm, and Worse was missing Sigrid. He called her. It was lunchtime Friday in Perth.

'Richard. I was wondering how it was all going over there,' she said. 'What's the news?'

'Good. The hearing's been adjourned while the FBI clean up that Area Pi operation. I expect they'll take apart the Chicago financial centre as well. Thomas says the casino licences will be withdrawn on a fit and proper test. It's all collapsing around them as we speak, apparently.'

'Are you safe, Richard?'

'Yes. I'm fine. I'm sitting in a sort of Wild-West time capsule in the centre of Dante. You would hate it. They're obsessed with that gunfight I told you about. There are giant murals and re-enactments and God knows what souvenirs. To give you an idea, this café is proud to serve Cordite Bleu cuisine.'

Worse was suddenly distracted, by a familiar but unwelcome sound.

'Hold on, Sigrid.'

He watched as the Seneca sped along Main Street, dispersing alarmed pedestrians. At the front of the tavern it burned rubber, swerving to mount the duckboard via a wheelchair ramp, pushing plastic tables and chairs aside. It came to a stop, facing Worse, eight metres away. Astride it, wearing leather but no helmet, stood Regan Mortiss.

'Worse!' she shouted. 'You son-of-a-bitch, you're going to die.'

She was pointing a long-barrelled pistol at him, aimed with two hands.

'Sorry, Sigrid. Something's happened. Hold on.'

He slowly placed his phone on the table. Other customers hurried from the premises. The only waiter on the forecourt fled into the building.

'On your feet, fucker. I want to see you fall the whole damn way to hell.'

'Regan. Wait. You're upset.'

Worse released the safety on the Totengräber, and stood up. His jacket was unbuttoned but he held it closed with his left hand, covering the weapon.

'I'm upset because I didn't go to the end of the earth and kill you myself.'

'I can understand that. Those three were useless.' He added lightly, 'So, are you here to buy some bread? A twicing, will it be?'

Worse was slowly moving sideways, positioning himself in front of the mural. Regan would be looking at Worse, as well as seeing his back in the mirror, plus herself, her bike light, and a few witless onlookers collecting on the street behind her. Reflections were distracting. Reflections were noise. They meddled with focus and aperture. She might have a vision problem. It was a matter of milliseconds but it was tactical asymmetry.

Regan ignored the provocation.

'One was a Mortiss, you bastard. My half brother.'

'Ben Jay? You sent a boy to do women's work? Listen, Regan. You need help. I know some good people. There's a therapist on my cell phone right now. You could talk to her. Tell her about your childhood. Tell her about your father. What did happen to your father, Regan?'

'Fuck you.'

She gave a slight toss of her head and sneered.

'Well, look at that. You've got yourself a cheap, useless ornament. You know that tin star's a shooting target to every self-respecting Mortiss?'

Worse was watching Regan's pistol. She was impressively steady, but as they spoke she had let it drop a few degrees. He knew that before she made the shot she would raise the barrel level to chest. There would also be a subtle aiming-tilt of her head. They would be the signals.

'And I'm going to kill you, son-of-a-bitch. You're going to drop right where great-uncle Rigo was murdered in cold blood by the bastard baker Worse.'

'There are witnesses, Regan. You can't buy them all off.'

'I don't need to buy them off. I only need to frighten half a jury.'

Worse changed the pace of the talk.

'You know, Regan. I was thinking before you arrived how nice it would be to have company. Come over and join me. I'll order dinner. Then we could discuss your problems. I can help.'

'You've eaten your last meal, Worse.'

'That's grossly inconsiderate, Regan. It was disgusting. I had to send it back.'

'That's what your mother should have thought when you came along.'

Worse was not enjoying the exchange, but Regan was taking her time and slowly passing up advantage. He guessed that if she were stirred enough, her aim would be more passionate than rational. She might go for the star rather than a centre shot. It certainly wasn't going to be half an earlobe. He raised his right hand and inserted a thumb behind the left lapel, projecting it slightly.

Regan had come to a realization.

'So now you're inviting me to sit down for food you think is disgusting?'

That was a question. It shifted timing, and a little control, to him.

'I've never been good with first dates,' said Worse.

Regan lowered one hand and revved the bike. It was a power play, machine roar to tin star.

'You hear that, Worse? That sound will ride up and down over your corpse. They'll be burning you decorated in tyre tracks.'

'I've been run over before,' lied Worse.

She brought her hand back to the pistol.

'Now listen to my idea of a first date, asshole. I'm going to make you sick with fear. Then I'm going to cause you pain. Then I'm going to make you beg. Then I'm going to get you praying. Then I'm going to shoot you fucking dead.'

'You don't see dating for its long-term prospects, I take it.'

Worse was still moving slightly, watching her pistol.

'Look, Regan. That's one-sided. What's in it for me?'

'You'll end up with relief from suffering. If I'm nice.'

Worse knew that what he said next could bring on the end. That conferred a small anticipatory advantage, and he was ready.

'No way that would cover expenses, Rego. I'll take the Seneca in lieu, if that's your preference.'

It took a few moments for Regan's face to signal understanding, then rage; Worse saw it as a tremor in her weapon. She raised the barrel. She tilted her head.

Worse's left hand pulled open his jacket and his right hand drew the pistol from his belt. In a single action he stepped to the right, turned side on, lined up the Prussica, and fired.

The two shots were simultaneous. Regan was thrust backwards off the Seneca, over the duckboard, onto the road. A few confused tourists looked on, unsure if they were witnessing a street performance. But unlike the stuntman earlier, she didn't rise to take a trouper's bow. Instead she lay on Main Street under a faux gas lamp, mouth gaping in her own shadow and a black entry wound barely visible on her forehead.

Worse was hit by broken glass. He glanced behind him at the mural. The shattered panel had been the portrait of Rigo Mortiss. Several tavern staff emerged from the building, staring at Worse. He ignored them.

He walked back to the table and picked up his mobile to phone Thomas. Then he remembered that Sigrid was holding.

'Sorry that took so long.'

'Richard! I thought I heard a shot. Are you all right?'

'Yes. I'm fine. Sigrid, can we talk later? There's a mess here that I need to attend to.'

He looked at the Seneca, still upright and idling. 'And I've just acquired a motorbike.'

28 BACK AT THE BHEH

Worse left payment for the meal he hadn't eaten. Three uniformed sheriff's deputies arrived on foot, drawn by reports of a public disturbance, then more quickly by the sound of gunfire. Worse holstered his weapon as he walked over to the duckboard. He took control.

'Listen everybody. This is sheriff's business. No one is to leave before giving his or her name and address to the deputies here.' He raised his voice as a woman attempted to merge into the darkness. 'That means nobody, madam.'

Worse then addressed the deputies, who were taking in his civilian suit, the accent, and his star with evident incomprehension. 'Get all their details. Some will have photographs or videos. Take it all. Statements now, not tomorrow. There will be witnesses inside as well. That's Regan Mortiss.' Worse pointed. 'Inform the medical examiner. She came off her bike. It belongs to me now, by negotiation. Recover her firearm and cell phone. Another thing: somebody here recognized me and informed her where I was. I want to know who did that. Start with the woman who tried to slip away, but more likely it was a staff member. Check all phone records, including hers.' Worse again pointed at Regan. 'I want no loose ends.'

Worse walked over to the Seneca and lifted a flap on the rider's seat. Then he straddled the machine, giving the throttle a generous twist; that might just get to be a good sound again. He turned between the tables, stood as he jumped from the duckboard to the road, slid the rear wheel around, and without a glance at the others made *accelerando* for the hill, heading up to the BHEH.

At the hotel concourse he gestured to a valet and tipped.

'Clean off the bad blood. Fill the tank. Log it to room five-one-two; name of Worse.'

Worse sat in the lobby waiting for Thomas. A drinks waiter came by and Worse ordered a bottle of a California white and two glasses.

'Just pour one for now, please,' he said, when the waiter returned with his order and an ice bucket.

As Worse watched, he called Sigrid's number again.

'What's happening?' she asked.

'Everything's fine, Sigrid. I'm back at the BHEH now, waiting in the lobby to catch up with Thomas. He had to attend the clean-up at Area Pi.'

'What was going on earlier?' asked Sigrid. 'The gunshot I heard, what was that?'

'That was Regan Mortiss disturbing the peace. My peace. With a pistol.'

'Goodness, Richard. Look after yourself. What happened?'

'She died.'

Just then, Worse saw Sendoff sweeping into the lobby from the concourse and heading to the lift station. He was weighed down with bags of designer-label shopping. His demeanour made it clear that he hadn't heard the news.

'Well, I'm very relieved that you are all right, Richard,' said Sigrid.

'How are you, anyway, Sigrid? How is the presentation going?'

'It's going well, I think. I was pleased we had that conversation on the ship. About Satroit.'

'He was insane?'

'It's not straightforward. I'll explain when you're back.'

'Speaking of Satroit, I need to thank you for *Black Levant*. I'll explain that later, too.'

'Okay. We have a poetry agenda for next Thursday. Thanks for phoning, Richard.'

Fifty minutes later, Thomas appeared, and Worse stood up. He hadn't touched his drink. They shook hands.

'Jeez, cousin. I leave you sitting quietly in the safest, dullest place in town and all hell breaks loose, and for God's sake, you kill off the town's only billionaire, Arizona's ex-pistol champion and the world's paramount Worse threat and leave her corpse on the street while you ride off on her mount.' He beamed. 'That was fantastic, Senior Deputy!'

'Drink?' said Worse.

'You bet.'

Worse poured a second and handed it to Thomas. They clinked glasses.

'I called by the scene on the way here. Saw what the deputies had requisitioned. Watched some videos. It was like the old days. You were mighty fast, cousin. I couldn't see you move.'

'Not that fast. She got her shot away. I was a bit disappointed about that. Came close too. Passed on the left. Ruined the fabulous mirror as well.'

Thomas took a moment to realize Worse was not serious. He laughed loudly and settled back in his chair.

'You know, you are one goddamn amazing cousin. Are you all like that in Australia?'

'Most are faster on the draw. It's still a wild place, especially out west where I come from.'

'You're kidding me, right?'

'I am kidding you. Did you get to eat tonight, Thomas?'

'No, I did not.'

'I couldn't face the Hot Lead, either. Let me order you a meal here.'

Worse called the waiter, who brought menus.

'You did face the hot lead, cousin. You just didn't stomach

it. Jeez, Richard. We're going to have to work hard to stop you becoming the new Dante gunfighter legend. They'll be casting your personal big mirror mural starting tomorrow.'

Worse's face expressed his distaste. He changed the subject.

'What happened out at Area Pi?'

'Interesting. Interesting.' Thomas looked down at the glass in his hand. He spoke quietly. 'We found Mortiss senior. Regan's father.'

'Alive?' asked Worse.

'Alive, but hardly living. It seems he was kept in confinement. Regan got him out of the way by effectively imprisoning him in a domestic compound with basic needs met and no outside contact. Nearly blind, as well.'

'I'm surprised she didn't simply murder him,' said Worse.

'Yeah, well, she was doing that slowly. He was starving to death. We had him taken to Dante General for a check. When he's cleared he'll be interviewed. Damn it. I'll have to tell him his daughter's dead.'

'He might be relieved. I am. What else did you find there?'

'I tell you, Richard, it's a mighty strange place. There was a building full of drones in various stages of assembly. All kinds of things. The FBI will be months pulling it apart to make sense of what was going on.'

The meals arrived and a waiter set up a table. Worse signed the tab.

'What about personnel?' asked Worse. 'Any intelligence from them?'

'Not very forthcoming. But that will change. The Feds are establishing a big operations facility on site. They'll bring in every specialist they need, talkists included.'

Worse looked at Thomas sceptically.

'I know what you're thinking. It's not like that. Rational argument is the new way. If that fails, irrational argument. All strictly distance learning.'

'Enlightened, I'm sure,' said Worse. 'Whom do you think

they were doing the drone work for? Where were they going to sell Sunblock? I mean, did one of your defence agencies have a part in it all?'

'Too early to say, cousin. But if they did, they are staying very quiet.'

'What jurisdiction do you have out there, Thomas?'

'Keeping the peace. Stopping the Feds breaking their own law. Explaining Arizona language and customs like cussin' and courtesy. No detection responsibilities now, if that's what you're asking. The experts are in charge from today.'

The voice and the smile were wry. Worse looked at him.

'You know, Thomas, I'm not sure that building and selling drones was the main game. I think the remit was developing and proving up the Sunblock coating. They could name their own price for that technology. And that means national security might have been in play. I may go back in for another search.'

Thomas looked shocked.

'Don't worry,' added Worse. 'Not in person. Strictly virtual.'

'Jeez, Richard. It's the FBI. They'll detect an intrusion and hunt you down,' said Thomas.

'You think so? They'll knock on my poor farmer's door? In Belarus?'

Thomas placed his meal plate on the table and picked up his drink. He looked at Worse, expressionless.

'Be sure to tell me if you find something of interest, Senior Deputy.'

Seneca aficionados will recognize the specialty model (unlicensable in many countries). Under the rider's seat is a 'vintage switch' that, according to biker lore, disengages everything invented after 1930. Actually, the shutdown is not that severe, being principally electronic stability, speed limiter, cruise and traction control. This allowed Worse to slide the rear through a quarter circle with the giant front discs locked. The position of the switch requires any rider having mortal misgivings to stop and dismount publicly in order to re-engage the safety functions; this offers a stark choice between injury and ignominy on manly club rides. Senior bikers insist they can tell from the exhaust sound whether or not the safety is on. Spectrum analysis disproves this, but the myth promotes toughness in the impressionable who survive.

29 VIRGIL IN THE UNDERWORLD

It was well after midnight when Worse went to his room on the fifth floor. Deputy Frank was on duty, and they exchanged greetings as Worse opened his door. Just inside, he saw a note on the floor and bent to pick it up. The message was handwritten on hotel stationery, folded over.

> Annulus mirabilis!
> Marigold lives!

Worse held open his door to speak to Frank in the corridor.

'There's a note under my door. Did you see who put it there?'

'No one has been near your door, Dr Worse, in all the time I've been on duty. And it wasn't reported on to me by Deputy Lloyd.'

Worse glanced down the corridor in the other direction. Outside the elevator station was a security camera pointing his way.

'Thank you, Deputy. Good night.'

Worse sat at the small writing desk positioned under a window and attended to mail. Then he logged into Mockingbird on the Mortiss server, and ran status checks. The overlay was intact, despite repeated probes from the company's security team. He saw that a new intruder had been trying to get control, and Worse guessed it was a federal agency. He decided to pursue that the next day. Meanwhile, he uploaded a new chicane called Knightsmove to improve evasion.

The Marigold note was on the desk beside his laptop. It was Worse's habit whenever he checked into a hotel to hack the building security system, partly from interest but also to utilize the facility when occasions called for it. He went back in, located the fifth floor camera feeds, and fast-scanned the vision taking in his door over the hours of his absence.

Early the next morning, he was seated at the same desk. Attacks on Mockingbird from Washington had continued through the night. Someone was clearly trying to take ownership and eliminate Worse. The security firm employed by Mortiss was trying to eliminate them both and purge the system. It was a game with three players, two moving pieces and one shifting the chessboard, and at every turn the rules were shuffled.

Worse installed another chicane to counter the main threat. He could see they were using a classic *Vogelhaus* to conceal their main broach. In response, he deployed a starburst. That would saturate their probing with millions of decoys known as CPs.

Worse was slightly puzzled that a government service would attempt such a covert and difficult entry into Mortiss, given they had the grounds to investigate by court order and subpoena all the records they wanted. He decided to follow the Washington connection and found that it wasn't federal at all. It was coming from a desktop in the Chinese embassy. When he had the machine address, and a few milliseconds before they shut it down, he slipped in a mockingbird. Now it would be Chinese agents knocking on a farmer's door in Belarus.

This all took time, and it felt to Worse like he hadn't yet started the day's proper work. He returned to Unit Circle, and from there through Camelline to Area Pi, and eventually broke into its chemical division.

It made fascinating reading. They had spent a year perfecting a reliable electrical coupling to the Sunblock coating, for which they needed to develop novel conduction layers. The technical challenges along the way were thoroughly documented, as were trial methodologies and details of their eventual breakthrough. It was impressive science.

And it was criminal. When the first josephites were delivered and chemists and engineers were figuring out how to process them to extract the terencium, some kind of spill occurred in a test crushing rig and an assistant died from poisoning. Worse found correspondence with Mortiss Bros organizing a cover-up. That conspiracy was signed off by Regan.

Area Pi didn't construct drones. They bought them, disassembled their surface fabric, coated the components with Sunblock, and put them together with modules for power, radar sensing, and control systems. It wasn't clear whether Mortiss intended to upscale Sunblock production and offer it commercially, or simply prove the technology then sell it to the highest bidder.

Worse returned to the Chicago server and made some adjustments to Mockingbird, uploading more software. To go live, it would require an instruction code and go-command to be sent as well. Worse's virtual finger rested over the *Send* button for several seconds. He decided to give the matter more consideration.

His window overlooked the hotel concourse, and the sound of a motorbike outside made Worse restless. He needed a break, and phoned the bellboy. When he went downstairs the Seneca was waiting for him, and half an hour later, without particularly meaning to be, he was out west on 3141.

Pleno, normally a deserted T-junction with a few ruins and an abandoned water catchment for landmarks, had been transformed overnight. This was as close to Area Pi as the public was allowed, and dozens of press vans and facility trucks were parked along the road edges. Every time a vehicle appeared from the Phoenix direction and turned north, and every time one came south from Area Pi and turned back west, a horde of reporters and television crew would mobilize, trying to make a story out of nothing but through-traffic. The FBI had promised to provide four-hourly briefings, but that left a long time in between watching dust plumes.

Worse turned north, passed the bulk of parked vehicles, and pulled in on the right behind a large black van with tinted windows. Just beyond that was a Road Closed sign. He stood in some shade beside his bike and drank from a water bottle, watching the scene. Close by, he overheard a network reporter interviewing another reporter reporting that there was nothing to report. It reminded him of home.

Two men approached, walking from the intersection towards the black van. When they saw Worse, one came over.

'Nice bike.'

Worse acknowledged with a nod, and gave the club wave. It was returned.

'V-switch?'

'Yes,' said Worse.

'You don't see many of those around here. Where'd you get it?'

'I won it in a competition,' said Worse.

'Lucky you. Mind if I look under the seat?'

That was considered quite a personal request among Seneca owners.

'Sure,' said Worse.

The other man lifted the seat and grinned.

'You ride off?'

'Not always. Today it felt good,' said Worse.

'Yeah, I bet. On this dust and gravel.'

He lowered the seat, and held out his hand.

'The name's Virgil Pickridge.'

'I'm Worse. Richard Worse.'

There was immediate recognition.

'Richard Worse? Tom's cousin? Your name is in all our dispatches. That was quite a performance yesterday. You've given some of us years of work out here.'

'Yes, well, I hope you can clean it up. They were a bad lot,' said Worse.

'So what are you doing here?'

'I was getting cabin fever in the hotel.'

'Want to come down the road and see what you've stirred up?' asked Pickridge.

Worse held back to be out of the FBI dust. He was waved through a perimeter checkpoint and followed the van for about a kilometre inside the compound. They stopped next to several other vehicles inside a hangar that was open on one end. Pickridge came over to Worse.

'Anything in particular I can show you?'

'Regan kept her father imprisoned here somehow. I'd like to see that for myself. I'd also like a look at the coating factory and any chem labs, if that's okay.'

'Follow me,' said Pickridge.

He hesitated, looking at the Seneca.

'Say. It's a big site. Why don't I ride pillion and give directions?'

'Want me to lift the seat?'

'No way.'

They went first to a three-storeyed red brick building that housed offices and laboratories. In every room there were agents sifting through paperwork, sitting at terminals, photographing evidence, or talking into recorders. Worse had a good idea of what they were looking at—he had taken a tour from the privacy of his BHEH room.

Pickridge was surprised that his guest was more interested in looking around the storerooms, but to Worse they offered a simple key to the chemistry that was going on in the place.

In one area, he found several baskets of the sort he had seen in La Ferste. He motioned to Pickridge that he would like to open one. Pickridge nodded, curious himself. A minute later, Worse's expectation was confirmed.

'What is that?'

'It's called a josephite,' said Worse, holding it up. 'Smuggled from the Ferendes. Don't break one. They've got a liquid core and it's toxic. On May first two years ago an employee named Leeshem was poisoned from a terencium sulphide spill in a company crusher. It was kept quiet using a toxicologist bought off by Mortiss. Regan and William gave the orders. You should add it to his indictment.'

Pickridge was taking notes. He looked up.

'You know Regan was shot dead last night?' he said.

'Yes,' said Worse.

'Happened in Dante, so it's a sheriff's department matter at this stage. They haven't told us a lot.'

Worse showed no interest.

'Can I see the coating plant?' he asked.

It was another bike ride away. As they walked to the Seneca, Worse asked if Pickridge knew anything about the electrical power provision and consumption on the site. He was told there was a big substation taking in high voltage lines from Hericho, where most other services were also sourced. Worse had seen the pylons on the satellite images. Close to the substation was a diesel generator plant for back-up supply.

The next building was more recently constructed, and large enough to take the bike through. The first section housed a sterile disassembly area. After that, they passed enormous annealing blocks and ovens that were essentially silica glazing kilns. Reassembly and module installation happened in another building. They exited at the other end.

'That was all bad. Now I'll show you sad,' said Virgil.

He directed Worse to a compound fenced with security wire, enclosing a small, single-level building. It had been the site's transformer station before the power demands of their developing annealing technology required a higher-order replacement. There were no agents working here, and as they approached, Worse was struck with a sense of the bareness of the place. The doors were wide open, with no sign of human comforts, or even recent habitation.

'Prepare yourself for this, Richard.'

Back in his room, Worse lay on his bed. His eyes moistened as he thought about Charles Mortiss and the privations of his imprisonment. What Virgil had shown him reminded Worse, in a small and pathetically solitary way, of the great museums of atrocity that are designed to shock the inhumanity from our race, but seem never to succeed.

Regan was dead. But the company was rotten through, and had been from the start. He thought about the Seneca attack in Perth, about the Glimpse contract to kill Nicholas, about a forgotten man called Leeshem whose painful death was hidden from everyone who would care. He thought about Walter Reckles, and his cynical treatment that had brought Worse into this whole American tragedy. He thought about Charles again, father and daughter.

And he thought about the Mortiss vendetta, nearly a century-and-a-half of hatred and violence directed at the six Thomas Ms, themselves men who were dedicated to protecting the citizens of Dante.

Then he found himself wondering about Marigold.

And finally, but before everything, there was *Famille Oblige*. Worse got up and moved to the work desk, opened his laptop and clicked *Send*.

He said he would destroy Mortiss Bros, and now he had.

Worse was leaving that evening, and he took his bags down to the lobby to check out early. He preferred to sit there rather than stay in his room. Thomas had offered him a ride to the airport, and was to come by the BHEH to collect him.

As it happened, Thomas also arrived early, accompanied by a young man wearing a polo shirt bearing a school insignia. They came over to Worse, who stood up.

'Richard, I'd like you to meet my son, Thomas M Seventh. Tom, this is our Australian cousin, Richard M.'

'A pleasure to meet you, Mr Worse,' said Tom, shaking hands. They chatted for a few minutes, before Tom excused himself and left by the main door. Worse guessed that his departure was prearranged to leave Thomas and him in private.

'A very nice young man,' said Worse. 'Does he know what he wants to do?'

'Not be sheriff, that seems clear. Aeronautics may be the thing. He likes math too.'

'That ends a long tradition,' said Worse. 'Of course, there's nothing contradictory about liking maths and being sheriff. Maybe time with Walter at Flight Control would help him decide.'

'I was thinking the same, about Walter,' said Thomas. 'Some kind of work experience before starting college.'

They were still standing, and Worse motioned Thomas to sit down. It shifted the conversation from family to business. Worse took the Marigold note from his pocket.

'I found this under my room door last night,' said Worse, passing it to Thomas. 'The guards didn't see who put it there.'

Worse didn't say that the security camera in the corridor also recorded no one coming to his door. Thomas read it.

'That's very interesting. A similar thing happened to Anna, an anonymous note raising the whole Area Pi question. I hope she's kept it so we can compare the handwriting. What do you make of it, Richard?'

'Well, it seems celebratory. We could read into it vindication, optimism, rejoicing, survival, perhaps a figurative returning from the dead. I suspect there has been an aggrieved party helping us somehow.'

'Any idea who that might be?' asked Thomas.

'One possibility,' said Worse. 'There was a technician called Leeshem who was killed in an accident at Area Pi. It was covered up. I would begin with his family, if it's of continuing interest to you.'

'Have you looked into that yourself, Richard? Did he have a wife or partner?'

'He had a wife. She died some months ago.'

Thomas passed the note back.

'Speaking of Area Pi, I had a look around this morning,' said Worse.

He realized he should be clearer. 'In person. On my bike. I was given a guided tour by an Agent Pickridge.'

'Virgil? Virgil's on the case? That's excellent. He started with us before turning Feral, as we like to say. What did you learn?'

'It all fits together much as we thought. I found a terencium shipment from the Ferendes.' Worse paused. 'The hardest part was seeing where Regan exiled her father.'

Thomas nodded. 'I saw it too. By the way, an hour ago, the Mortiss business imploded financially. The lights literally went out in Chicago. No one's ever seen anything like it. The Feds aren't saying much, but from what I hear they had some type of long-term spyware buried in there for ongoing investigations, and they lost control of it. They're kind of embarrassed.'

'It's called a mockingbird, Thomas,' said Worse. 'You should trust that it's discriminating and will leave the good people in work while it destroys the rest.'

Thomas gave Worse his expressionless *I don't think you should tell me more* expression. He spoke after a brief silence. 'What are you planning with the Seneca?'

'I was thinking of airfreighting it to Perth. I have a friend coming to stay who needs transport. She can use it.'

'Give me the details and I'll organize it for you,' said Thomas.

'That's very kind. And, Thomas ... this is for you.'

Worse took a parcel from the top of his backpack and passed it to Thomas.

'Don't open it here. But, as I say, every Worse should carry one.'

A waiter approached, and Worse ordered tea. Thomas leaned back in his chair.

'While you were at Area Pi this morning, I spent some time with Charles Mortiss, in his hospital room. He apologized for the family—said he wished he had done more to end it for good. I told him about Regan dying and he said he already knew. He asked if he could call me Thomas, then he said, "I was trying to make things better. She was bad, you know, Thomas. I couldn't control her," and apologized again. He was very weak, and tearful. I found myself feeling sorry for him.'

'Regan was bad,' said Worse. 'You wonder how it happens, turning that bad.'

'She had the Uncle Rigo genes for bad. I would say that's how.'

Worse stayed quiet. Inheritance again. Not the passing-pieces of humanity now, but genes for bad. He wasn't so sure; he understood the modern credule theory, but he had seen the turning as well, many times, and it was rarely for the better.

He was quiet also because he needed time to settle his feelings about Regan. Whatever the circumstances of killing, whatever the imperative, his conscience was implacably enquiring. Regan was bad, but was she unredeemable? Could he have kept her talking? Did he try hard enough? Or as Sigrid might have put it: Was he amusing enough?

Thomas leaned forward again and looked at Worse. When he spoke his voice was changed, soft and almost breaking.

'When I was there, at the hospital, his attorney showed up. I made to leave but Charles asked if I would stay. They had a testamentary deed called an abjuration drawn up. Mortiss took responsibility for the years of vendetta and declared it over. It was a covenant of peace, Richard, binding on descendants, and Charles asked me to be there for its signing.'

Worse nodded slowly, appreciating how moved Thomas was by the development. The curse of six generations was finally lifted, and he had been its witness.

'Then there would seem to be a natural alignment of destinies about young Tom not wanting to become sheriff,' said Worse.

Thomas was looking at the floor. He nodded, but said nothing.

They were seated in the same area where he and Thomas had been served lunch on the day that he checked in. Worse looked across the lobby to where he had first caught sight of Regan Mortiss. Those seats were now empty.

'You know, Thomas, I would like to meet Charles,' said Worse. 'I feel that I owe him some form of explanation for what happened to Mortiss Bros, perhaps even to Regan.'

Worse caught an odd look from Thomas, and thought he should elaborate. 'I'm not suggesting anything apologetic. I mean, to answer questions he might have; give him some peace, if that is possible.'

Worse was also thinking that he wanted to convey a personal revulsion at how the man had suffered at the hand of his own daughter, and to offer condolence, one human being to another.

When he looked back at Thomas, this time more closely, he sensed what was coming.

'He already has peace, cousin, and I saw him arrive at it. Charles Mortiss died at the end of his signature.'

31 MR WOTSAN

Worse entered his apartment, holding travel bags. He always looked forward to returning home, but this time it wasn't the same. Normally, Mrs Brackedger would have collected mail, stocked the refrigerator and put out fresh flowers, perhaps leaving a welcome note with some housekeeping news. Today, the place was exactly as he left it many days before, and that was somehow saddening. He missed her.

He thought about Millie then. He would need to make the apartment more welcoming, more lived-in, for when she arrived. She would be staying in the adjoining unit, which Worse also owned, but he didn't want his place to look cold and lifeless. He needed a new Mrs Brackedger urgently.

On the Sydney to Perth sector, Worse had thought of an experiment that he was keen to perform. He carried his bags to the bedroom and opened the backpack. In the top was the josephite acquired in La Ferste, wrapped in a dark shirt. He had persuaded its way through Australian customs by declaring his occupation to be student spiritualist, for which the crystal ball was a mandated accessory.

Worse went to his kitchen and placed the josephite on the table, finding the best rounded facet upon which it balanced stably. He sat down to contemplate it. After a while he reached out two hands and spun it like a top, as fast as he could. Then he clasped it still and instantly let go, observing intently.

Ah, physics: how it never disappointed.

Worse had not spoken to Spoiling since departing Perth. He decided to phone his friend with the news that he was safely home, and to arrange a time to report on the Mortiss case. Victor answered immediately.

'Worse? This validity matter. It's more difficult than I imagined. Could you—'

'Victor! I've just returned from being threatened and shot at all over the world and you don't even say hello.'

'Oh, Worse. Yes. Hello. I'm sorry. How are you?'

'I am well, thank you, Victor. How are you?'

'Yes, yes. I am well. Except for—'

'The validity matter?' interrupted Worse again. 'Shall I come to your office this afternoon and run through your lecture?'

'Yes, yes. Thank you.'

'Have you woven in the Simile of the Cave?'

'What?'

'Four o'clock,' said Worse, hanging up. It was an equalizer, and he felt terrible for enjoying it.

The arrangement gave Worse time to unpack, rest, and shower. He decided that a walk from his apartment to police head-quarters might restore some articular health after suffering over twenty-four hours of confinement in the air.

When he knocked on Spoiling's door and entered, Spoiling rose from his desk and came forward to embrace him briefly.

'I am very delighted to know you are back, Worse. I apologize for my unforgiveable distraction earlier.'

'Not unforgiveable, Victor.'

Worse looked around the office. 'Are you planning to use audio-visuals? Shall I sit here and listen?'

'Yes, Worse. Thank you. Later. The lecture: already I feel better about it. First I must show you something. Come with me.'

Spoiling walked to his desk and removed some keys from

a drawer. He then led Worse through the outer offices to an elevator. They emerged in the basement car park, where Spoiling headed towards a bay half concealed behind a concrete column. When Worse caught up, he found Spoiling beaming at him, one arm outstretched sideways the way some men introduce a grandchild. He was pointing at a Seneca.

'It's for you, Worse. I acquired it at the police proceeds-of-crime property auction. A gift.'

Spoiling held out the keys. Worse was moved. 'Thank you, Victor. Thank you so much.'

After listening to Spoiling's practice delivery, Worse rode back to his apartment in the Grosvenor building, parking the bike in a spare bay next to his car. He phoned Sigrid from the elevator.

'Richard. You're back safely?'

'Yes. I've spent some time this afternoon with Victor, debriefing about Mortiss Bros and discussing the problem of induction.'

'Good. Detectives do have a problem with induction.'

'Also, I've just acquired a motorbike.'

'You've told me that already.'

'It's happened twice.'

'You're starting a collection?'

'It seems. Of special-licence Senecas from which I've been shot at. I'm naming them Twicing and Marigold.'

'Why?'

'They're journey names; for going and returning.'

'Well, let's hope there will be no further names to find.'

Worse entered his apartment, walking through to the kitchen.

'How is the ekphrasis lecture coming along?'

'Finished. I'm working on the credule symposium now.'

'You know, Sigrid, you're a logician. You could help Victor with his validity presentation.'

'He doesn't need help. I looked him up. He's a philosopher. He's impressively published.'

'True. His lecture is excellent. It's a crisis of humility. He's European. Perhaps that's more how you could help.'

Sigrid was quiet for several seconds. 'I need to go. Dinner this Thursday?'

'Yes,' said Worse. 'Any preference?'

'Buffon's Noodle Room. We haven't eaten there for a while.'

'See you there, six thirty. I'll bring Satroit.'

Evidently, Sigrid was in an exacting mood. 'Just his book will be enough, Richard. Satroit's dead, I remind you.'

As was Marigold, thought Worse. Quite. *Our slim volume of refutations will disallow returning.*

'Naturally, I meant return the book,' he said.

Worse had developed a taste for hot cocoa, partly acquired on the cruise but mostly to avoid coffee in America. He was still in his kitchen filling a mug when there was an intercom call from the security desk in the Grosvenor lobby.

'Worse.'

'Good afternoon, Dr Worse. We have a Mr Wotsan here to see you. He says he is from the recruitment agency.'

'Oh yes.'

Worse had overlooked the time. There had been mention of the agency sending a staffer to inspect Worse's apartment for occupational health and safety issues. It was explained as part of their routine duty of care to the people they recruited, particularly in domestic and industrial situations. Worse, of course, saw no issues, and just wanted someone to start the job.

'Watson, did you say?'

'Yes, Wotsan. Oh, excuse me, Dr Worse. He seems to have disappeared.'

'Well, when you find him, please give him a lift pass. Tell him level 33. Say there's no bell. He needs to knock.'

Worse walked quickly through his apartment, surveying the place for obvious hazards. It didn't look too bad, if one disregarded the reagent shelves and the toxic fume cupboard in the spare bedroom-cum-laboratory, the tangle of data cables and powerlines in the workshop, the poison josephite left balanced on the kitchen table, and the Totengräber kept by the front door. Mrs Brackedger never seemed to notice such things.

A minute later, Worse heard the elevator doors outside his apartment, followed by discreet knocking at his entry. He hid the pistol in a side-table drawer as he passed, and was still sipping cocoa when he opened the door and looked up. Standing before him, one hand holding a small suitcase and the other a sealed letter of introduction, was Hilario.

THE END

APPENDIX A.   ADVANCED COMMENTARY, SOURCES, AND READER EXERCISES

CHAPTER 1 The account given here follows closely the dialogue and stage directions of the modern 'Incident at Bakehouse' re-enactment referred to in Chapter 27, with minor emendations based on the author's own research. This is not as historically tenuous as it may seem: the present script has its origins in the 1880s, when a Chicago newspaperman and impresario meticulously reconstructed the event based on interviews with Miss Baker, another witness (Jimmy Danville, a blacksmith's boy who observed the drama from the bakehouse interior), a sheriff's deputy (Horace Sims, who arrived on the scene just as Rigo Mortiss was thrown from his horse), and Sheriff Worse himself. The resulting act, with appropriate expurgation, was staged in touring Wild West shows for the entertainment of easterners.

[REMARK *What is a town?*] It might be noted that even Keff's 'fleck of a town' is a town. Certainly, Rigo's 'stinking town' is. Within the diegetic purview, Dante has an agreed identity (name, location), infrastructure (main street, buildings, cemetery), and the social custom (commerce, benevolent fund, statutes, court process, at the least) expected of a town. Moreover, we learn that it has the usual civic functionaries (lawman, doctor, preacher, and so on) belonging to a town. From the point of view of Rigo and Keff, every municipal officer or service for which they expressed need was provided to them. On physical and functional grounds, then, they had no reason to suppose that

Dante was anything but a town. And yet, also from their point of view, that town might have had (and, increasingly, by induction, looked to have) a population of one individual: a single, if protean, inhabitant in the person of Thomas Worse.

Had the two outlaws been more fortunate, and more philosophical, their conversation as they rode away may have been instructive.

'You were smart, Rigo, getting that sheriff talking about Socrates. He turned nice after that. Nicer than the mongrel killer anyways.'

'Yes. I find it an excellent method of distracting the law. You know, Keff, I've heard of a one-horse town, but never a one-man one.'

'Yeah. Can't really say that would be a town though, can we?'

'I'm not so sure, Keff. Think of it this way. We call people townsfolk because they live in a town. Right?'

'Yeah.'

'And that preacher, say: he was one of the townsfolk of Dante, wasn't he?'

'Yeah. I guess.'

'Well, looked at another way, we could just as easily say that we call something a town because townsfolk live there.'

'Course we do, Rigo.'

'And what we call a ghost town, with no folks at all, isn't a town, is it?'

'No way, Rigo.'

'Which means that a necessary and sufficient condition for saying a place is a town is that townsfolk live there.'

'Yeah. Interesting.'

'So, Keff, how many townsfolk do you need to call someplace a town?'

'I reckon lots. You need saloons and a flophouse and stables and stuff.'

'Try to be more ... abstract, Keff. I'd say that what we saw in Dante is a type of sorites paradox. Only it's weirder: the way that baker was like a last remaining grain of sand still embodying, in some capacity, the whole heap. It's as if you remove something but it's still there, reparcellated, in a different form.'

'Yeah. Interesting.'

'Or do you think, Keff, we're just confusing intension and extension somehow?'

'No way, Rigo.'

'Maybe the two move in and out of each other, blend in some way.'

'Yeah. Interesting.'

'Maybe there's a kind of conservation principle happening. Reducing one increases the other. Zero-sum semantics, I'd call it.'

'Yeah. Interesting. Hey Rigo, your mare's looking touchy on the right foreleg. Could be that the farrier back there was right.'

CHAPTER 7 Model equations describing n-grammar behaviours can be found in several sources, including Tøssentern, *op. cit.*, which also explores a number of special cases. Except in trivial instances, closed form solutions are not obtainable and the system must be solved numerically. A research report appearing in *Proceedings of the Lindenblüten Society* from **Sheila Place**, a postdoctoral fellow in Thwistle's department in Cambridge, raises intriguing philosophical implications. In the original model n is, of course, integer-valued. Place experimented with generalizing n to non-integer, including irrational, values, and solving for γ. The only irrational for which convergence was obtained was $n = \pi$, and this resulted, extraordinarily, in the solution $\gamma = \pi$

(to set precision) also. The author ventured no interpretation of this, but others have quickly proposed that swint grammar may not be strictly triadic ($n = 3$) but instead $n = \pi = 3.14159\ldots$. In simulation studies of artificial languages where $n = \pi$, a deviation from the (impossible) ideal $k = \pi$ to $k = 3$ results in only a small deterioration in γ. This would suggest that thricing in swints is a stratagem of forced integer approximation, the cost of which is the risk of occasional misunderstanding.

(For those espousing the holiness explanation, the inverse theological question becomes whether the **number of the Trinity** might truly be π. If this were so, the Godhead would comprise Father, Son, and Holy Spirit, plus a nonrepeating decimal fraction counting a partial fourth—perhaps feminine—divine personage yet to be identified.)

It may be that this potential for 'misunderstanding', arising from a small discrepancy between the language parameter n and social number k, is advantageous: it has been suggested that variance introduced in this way could drive the long-term evolution of languages. In the short term (within the lifetime of a species member), it may underlie individuation, personality and creativity. Conversely, this variance is decreased by structurally embedded redundancy, a feature of most grammars that serves to conserve meaning but also affords resiliency to the grammar itself.

Although the programme of mapping speech markers in swints is well progressed, the problem of decoding semantic content is considerably more difficult, both statistically and computationally. The point is succinctly made by **May Ball**, the doyenne of avian morphemics, in a celebrated editorial headed 'Talking to the Animals' in *J. Numerical Ornith*. (In the Ferende creation story this faculty is a given, in that Rep'husela would summon and instruct her condors by calling.) One promising line of research involves a visual barrier paradigm and substituting adaptive voice synthesis for one swint of a thrice. When the substitution is reversed, conversation within the thrice alters dramatically, exhibiting a transient increase in the marker *question*. The elegant methodology is detailed elsewhere in the same journal. Another study, published in *Syrinx*, describes behavioural anomalies in nestlings and adults following exposure to synthetic birdsong during artificial incubation. In a setting of growing appreciation of the sophistication of animal intelligence (note how the description 'bird-brained', once insulting, has become for many an envied compliment), the ethical debate arising from this and similar research designs has been sufficiently vituperative to be labelled by outsiders the Chirping Wars.

It should be made clear that the research establishment is divided on the interpretation of swint speech markers, though not their existence. In particular, *mirth* is not accepted by those who assert the special holiness of the creature (and there is much evidence in support of that belief, including corroborated scriptures from the first century as well as circumstantial observation). They contend that the unisonous call referred to earlier is wrongly analogized to human laughter, it being instead a congregational response of great piety. In this school, *mirth* has the alternative catalogue designation *amen*, and the expectation of those scholars is that swint language (if not birdsong generally), when fully decoded, will be revealed as essentially liturgical. (The saurian world might not have been so festive after all.)

It is therefore no exaggeration to point out that much ecclesiastic dignity—an eliminative realignment of institutional religions, no less—is invested in the swint translation effort, the full implications of which are not widely appreciated. Despite the analytic (and increasingly political) challenges, courageous researchers like Ball and Misgivingston are confident of the project's ultimate success. Perhaps for our needed wisdom we should turn back five centuries to **Leonardo di Boccardo** (later, Pope Ignorius, after the saint) who, in his famed *Credo* submission to the Sacred College entitled *The Illusion of the Prophet*, observed that succeeding prophets through the ages do not accrete doctrinal authority, but lose it. This is partly because each inevitably amplifies the errors of his predecessors, as well as originating his own for relevance (Leonardo's private papers reveal a first intention to write 'vanity' here). Compounding the difficulty for latecomers is this: were some appropriation by chance to prove accurate, it would properly attract a charge of plagiarism on precedence grounds and be *a priori* valueless. These, and more modern axiomatic arguments involving proximation and seriality concepts, along with psychological post-profiling and motivational blatancy analysis[1], explain the diminishing legitimacy of prophesiers over time.

(Leonardo, of course, sourced much of his insight from **St Ignorius**, whom we accept as the only validated prophet[2] in history, inasmuch as he correctly prophesied later figures would declare as prophets and vitiate whatever holiness had gone before. Remarkable, then, that a doctrinal delinquency not rescued (and then incompletely) until the Enlightenment, and from which the only moral escape became and remains apostasy, was predicted in the first century. The expedient substitution of paternalistic repression for autogenous faith over this time was noted by Leonardo, but the best modern critique is from **Ariadne Kuklosian** in her *Cynics of the Sacrosanct*, where the history of the Holy Land is explained using a usurpation paradigm and qualitative methodologies identifying venal and militant principal themes. It should be read alongside **Frances Godwilling**'s[3] *The Empire of Prayer,* a powerful defence of Kuklosian's scholarship against sectarian attack.)

If then, among linguists, the school of piety is proven correct, the swint will rightly have restored to it a primacy and innocence beyond the grasping of pretenders (who may yet enjoy the revisionist greatness of being anointed bird-brained). As **Timothy Bystander** (in *Guilty of Reason*) has remarked, even an atheistic reading should elicit no surprise that a putative one true prophet of a one true God should speak to us from at least the age of the dinosaurs. The problem for humanity has been arriving late and then not listening.

[1] **Blatancy analysis**, essentially an adaptation of credule theory to lie detection, is concerned with dissonance measurement in the behavioural sciences. Readers of serious journalism will know it as the commonly applied, often satirical SayDoCo (Say–Do coefficient) used to score dishonesty in political, public and ecclesiastical affairs. It takes values from minus one (actions exactly antithetical to expressed intentions) to plus one (perfect consistency between the two). Evangelists and prophets invariably score well below zero. (Statisticians will recognize a parallel with Pearson correlation, on which it is indeed based.)

[2] Gender here is important. We acknowledge also Princess Periphereia, the **Prophetess of Parsa**, whose *The flight of gold half-darkens the sun* proved an epiphanic truth more than two thousand years after its pronouncement. This elevated her to the status *Legitimus* (see below, note to Chapter 24).

[3] Not to be confused with namesake Fanny Godwilling, the fictional heroine who emancipates her people in **Angela Gabrielle**'s (a *nom de plume*, surely) quartet of quatrains of tetrameters, *Rubáiyát of the Dispossessed*. Initially a work of restrained dissent, the coarseness of fascism first registers in bathetic simple-mindedness:

> Grand mufti! Grand mufti! Her cant[4]
> beguiles. No giant kneels in the mosque![5]

before a descent into vulgarity and violence expunged, without vindictiveness, by popular uprising.

[4] Continental philosophers are traditionally the fearless expositors of this subject. For a contemporary French perspective, see **Napoléon Lecémot**'s epistolary meditation 'Recognizing Cant' posted from Wagon des Philosophes.

[5] This curious line is the subject of endless speculation, and suppression. In the context of a breathlessly obsequious religious espionage report, it seems to originate in another voice entirely. Generally taken as predictive more than indicative (the tense is ambiguous, leaving aside intention), it is believed by the devout to be the wisdom of God delivered through Gabrielle directly[6] to her readers. As for meaning, the interpretive literature almost invariably references **Standing Giant** (a pagan figure of indomitable free will, who in later theogonies oversees the passage of souls into the underworld) on this question.

[6] An innovation, doubtless born of divine exasperation: excluding the intermediary should reduce transcription errors[7], eliminate vanity and bias, and discourage misdirected idolatry of messengers into the future.
[7] Some of these are well known and have, for rationalists, a dark comicality about them, particularly in the desperation of clerical denial. A brief survey of mistaken graces, including the fiery origin of 'the Host' and the prosaically human inattention that gave rise to *God is Great* (which, according to **al-Fakr'mustiq**, in earliest crypt Afro-Asiatic form admits of the plural[8], and for purists[9] still does) can be found in Appendix 3 of the Kuklosian work cited above.

As that author observes, many such errors, if freely admitted, would pass without censure as curiosities. What Kuklosian holds unforgivable is a foundation of fallacy in spiritual tutelage that not only is fraudulent but amounts to ratiocinative entrapment. For an epigraph, she chose the ritual affirmation:

> I believe in God because I believe the word of the prophet.
> I believe the word of the prophet because I believe in God.

Mystics have always embraced the circular[10], but never so resolutely to imprison the mind. (And in a couplet!) Kuklosian again:

> We should marvel that every living thing has a proper serving of three virtues: perception, reason and agency. What then shall we name this crime, that a child's three are blinded, stolen, and denied, and in their place is left a hollow recitation?[11]

[8] Exposing purveyors of a one God to the charge of deceptive conduct, and rendering nonsensical an implicit superlative (or elative: 'greatest').
[9] So, we conclude, utterers are not purists, and by contraposition purists are not utterers. Purists who are also Semitic lexicologists occasionally point out (after al-Fakr'mustiq) that the phrase is a technical blasphemy and should be abandoned or corrected. French Arabists, in particular, have for centuries made the case; for them it is *le cri de damné*, inviting Satan into the supplicant soul. This failure to expurgate the solecistic is ascribed to institutional obstinacy, but the true reason is more fundamental. (And intractable: see footnote 5, Appendix B. Bystander has the view that *refusal,* in the sense given there, is intimately connected to, and possibly not separable from, intellectual timidity[12, 13].)
[10] For example, the *ouroboros*. Occultists invariably appropriate the infinite to impress the credulous. Strictly, the engine of argument in the couplet credo is perpetual reciprocation—*diallelus*. However, in a suitable (logic) phase space this and 2-state circularity (*circulus in probando*) are seen to be equivalent. A simple, if imperfect, physical analogy for their relation is an oscillating (between two sentences) pendulum that, given

sufficient energy, is free to rotate full circle.

[11] From *The Enemy of Lightness*[14] and, it may be supposed, explaining the *Dispossessed* of Gabrielle. Kuklosian's style generally avoids the rhetorical, and this is a rare exception. (She answers: I call it human sacrifice.)

[12] *Studies in Cowardice II: The Method of Edict.*

[13] In a passage known as the Exhortation to Courage in *2 Syllabines*, St Ignorius writes that a kingdom of lies is bordered by exile. A modernist guide to apostasy can be found in the expiatory lyrics of **Vissy Mofo**'s rap masterwork *Prayer Hall Émigré Ball* (Acridaria Music).

[14] The title is a quotation from Leonardo (see footnote 4, Appendix B).

The proposition that primordially the terms of theism, and therefore theism itself, arose *de novo* out of lexical chaos—having no existent validity beyond an accidental belonging to some inchoate vocabulary and a class of sentences constructed therefrom—is argued in the anonymous (possibly Sedite) e-manifesto *En Arche*. Further consideration of that idea, which has not been seriously challenged, is beyond the scope of these notes, but the interested reader can access occasional discussion papers put out by Episkopos (a dissident Vatican secret college), Wagon des Philosophes in Paris, *Meccan Bride* and *Mosqueto.Net* online, and the Mount Sycamore School of Theology, amongst others.

Suffice it here to conclude that linguistic research will soon inform us that if any uncorrupted intelligibility does persist in the world, it belongs to the swints, whilst human language, on balance, has served our own enlightenment poorly.

CHAPTER 11 Interestingly, the Ferendes already enjoyed an enviable fame in arthropod science. This latest find has sent scholars back to the original field notes of the Scottish naturalist **Thomas MacAkerman**, who gave the first comprehensive description of crab speciation based almost entirely on surveys in Greater Ferende, which he visited in 1816 and 1819. Though his concern was primarily with tidal crustaceans, there is an emerging appreciation that

MacAkerman remarked on transient bipedalism as a flight reflex in a miniature terrestrial crab that he chose not to study. (The student wanting to know more about this scientist *extraordinaire* is referred to Tøssentern's recent monograph on MacAkerman's life and achievements.)

Perhaps more striking than an inferred upright gait is the apparent size[1] of the creature that attacked Glimpse. This is probably an example of the commonly observed **insular gigantism** (reflecting an absence of environmental pressures and predators). Alternatively, this might have been a freak specimen suffering a form of adenomatous endocrine gigantism. Obviously, future capture studies in the field should decide the issue.

The process of **autotomy** (essentially, self-amputation) as occurred here is a well-documented survival and escape tactic in arthropods, as well as in molluscs and some vertebrates. The consequential phenomenon of part regeneration is one of the most intriguing in zoology, though its obvious benefits are lost to humans, whose evolutionary advancement gifted instead the ability to verbalize a circumstanced preference for it.

The attentive reader with an appreciation for symmetries may have surmised, from the fact that a long side passage exists immediately to the left of the second hairpin in a level tunnel, that the geometry here was strictly a reflected **z-bend** (that is, first turn to the left, second to the right). For a crab (smaller than this one) crawling on the roof, the first turn will appear on its right, and it will think[2] it is negotiating a literal z-bend. (Such a symmetry reversal, incidentally, is routinely effected without recourse to mirrors, rotation through the plane or walking on the ceiling, but rather three bold slashes, in a surgical transposition procedure known as Z-plasty.)

[1] Predictably, these salient facts of size and stance have been abstracted by fantasist-theists in furtherance of any cause to fear and revere. For them, the Ferende crab is an avatar of **Standing Giant**.

² Of course if the crab, like the reader, is attentive and apprehends indexical worlds, it may not think this at all. Also, it may be crawling sideways in any case. Also, it may not think anything.

CHAPTER 22 In many ways, our understanding of swint **ethology** is much less advanced than is the case with their language. We do not know if a given thrice is a family unit, or even if its membership is stable¹. (Nor do we know the fate of so-called remainder birds, or how they are identified.) The possibility of fluid interchange between thrices would confer both advantages and difficulties if it proves to be that populations are multilingual. In either case, model complexity and statistical challenges in the analytics are stupefying.

[REMARK *Parsan speech*] If the gap-semantic hypothesis is proven, Misgivingston will have convincingly solved the greatest mystery in classical linguistics: How did the Syllabines communicate—and how did such a sophisticated artistic and scholarly culture flourish—when the vocabulary of their **Parsan language** was a single word (known, from Roman sources, to be *Can't*)? (For an introduction to this subject, and a description of the famously difficult minimization problem referred to by theorists as the Syllabine Task, the reader should consult the endnote to Chapter 17 in Darian's *The Weaver Fish*.)

[EXERCISE *Isomorphism*] The student is encouraged to consider in what ways an interpretational reversal from 'gaps separate words' to 'words separate gaps' shares a symmetry relation with Rigo Mortiss's denotative reversal connecting 'town' and 'townsfolk', and with Satroit's observance dialectic (notes to Chapters 1 and 20, respectively).

[EXERCISE *Romance in Parsa Syllabina*] A poet–centurion stationed in the Roman-occupied province of Parsa wandered from his legion's camp, seeking solitude and inspiration to compose an ode. Coming upon a tranquil glade, he rested on a fallen log and played his cithara. A nearby Syllabine shepherdess, entranced by the heavenly melody, entered the woods to discover its source. She approached the poet, singing to his music with such beauty and purity of voice that he thought her the vision of a Muse. When he sang to her *Omnia vincit amor, et nos cedamus amori*[2], she sought meaning in the gaps. When she responded *Can't can't can't can't can't can't*, he sought meaning in the words. Explain how the centurion proposed marriage and the shepherdess accepted[3].

[1] One prominent sociologist has hypothesized that the phenomenon of thricing in swints is evolutionarily conserved in *ménage à trois*—a human behaviour seen almost exclusively in sophisticated book-reading circles—together with its transient and more democratized variant, known as *threesome*.

[2] Reprised centuries later by Virgil (*Eclogue X: 69*).

[3] Versions of this story, of variable charm, appear throughout antiquity, dating at least from *Cisalpinus* in the early third century BC. The betrothal conundrum is always present in some form but never answered. Only within the last decade has a satisfactory (and darkly existentialist) solution been advanced.

CHAPTER 23 Towards the end of his life, Satroit ordered most of his work, including '**Tyrian Purple**', suppressed as juvenilia. (He freely advised all living poets aged under sixty to do likewise. In response, a coalition of the offended produced an anthology, *Speak for Yourself, Satroit*, which is no longer in print, while Satroit is.) Much of the personal collection, memorabilia and manuscript material curated at Libraire Satroit was saved by his testamentary *notaire*, who claimed to have misunderstood instructions. For that incompetence, he was awarded the *Croix de la République*.

Acknowledging a want of maturity, the poem does illuminate a preoccupation with art and inference (and interference) that has been touched on elsewhere, under ekphrasis. Here is the characteristic tension, impressed into naïve dialogue, ending with a resolve and asserted optimism that we know, for Satroit as for any poet of decline, cannot endure. In fact, the inherent historicism and a concluding surrender to the counterfactual would seem to predestine this. Not surprisingly, many identify here an ulterior pessimism[1] as Satroit's primary concern, and argue its domain to be not art alone, but knowledge.

Alison Pilcrow, in the *Compendium* previously cited, draws attention to Satroit's often-quoted observation that the purpose of poetry is seduction. Sometimes this is perfectly evident, as in 'The Betrothal' or 'A Suitor's Reverie', but more often Satroit supplies a cipher-trove of suggestion and implication that leaves the reader (and translator) with work to do. (Perhaps 'making text' is that very enterprise, though some believe the meaning here is more 'textile', others simply 'sense'.) There are at least three major considerations. **Lawrence Enright**, whose translation is given here, emphasizes the challenge of rendering into English particular nuances of an Ottoman sensibility that are, in Satroit's phrase, 'occulted by alphabet'. (To illustrate, Enright has offered five versions of the third stanza.) Second, there must be unravelled a Phoenician coloratura made in antiquity and half-remembered in descendent souls. Finally, and most problematically, Satroit's is often a language of mercurial imagery rather than tractable vocabulary. (These difficulties are well known: another translation of 'Tyrian Purple', by **Isobel Beckoner**, is voluptuously sexual and almost unrecognizable as the same poem. Its comprehensibility on first publication was not helped by religious censorship.) Taking all this into account, and revisiting Enright's translation subtextually, we might easily conclude that seduction is also the purpose of art, which shares its tireless cycles of making and destroying.

For those interested in the science, it is clear from the final line that Satroit was aware that Tyrian purple is **dibrominated indigo**, a wondrous link across chemistry, biology and border.

[1] Somewhere (this author cannot recall the place, but readers may), Satroit spoke of three tenses of verb being adequate for art and life. These were the past erotic, (present) hesitant, and future separative— serving poetry, knowledge and love, respectively. There seems little joy in that. Satroit's pessimism clearly deserves more scholarly interest for a better understanding of his poetry, and his death.

CHAPTER 24 Worse's advice regarding **swinging the billy**, 'not for use indoors', might sensibly be extended to outdoors as well. If the reader insists on performing this bush theatre, the author recommends rehearsals with cold water. UITA Press takes no responsibility for the quality of the brew or the severity of scalds.

[REMARK *Pendulum*] Worse's centrifuge is a realization of the thought experiment connecting *diallelus* and *circulus*, offered in footnote 10 to Chapter 7 (above). See also endnote to Chapter 19. Hence it is possible to sediment tea leaves, simulate capsize, and unify fallacies, all in a single flamboyant act.

The authoritative history of **photography** is yet to be rewritten, as the task of re-conceptualizing its origins thousands of years into the past is naturally demanding of establishment imagination. There seems no doubt that when the evidence is properly weighed, the technique must be judged a Neolithic invention located in the Ferendes.

(One prejudice to be overcome is an anthropological dis- position to underestimate the sophistication of early humans, conflating two natures, *habilis* and *sapiens* (in the sense, no tools means not smart). Now that such an impressive technology has been uncovered, the intellectual stature of Stone Age peoples might be better appreciated. They hadn't our fountain pens but, for all we know, they were better poets.)

Although the chemistry of the silver halide image must be accepted as a Ferende discovery, a comprehensive re-evaluation of the subject's history requires that we examine a second line of invention, namely optics. The large figure astride the tunnel entrance was certainly a silhouette using light from the fire pit before it. Impressive as that is, the smaller pictograms that were thought to be hand-fashioned or brushed using seki juice as paint are proving to be far more interesting. These are not silhouettes, but show internal (that is, not contiguous with a boundary) contrast structure despite the seki chemistry being uniform across the image. Because this suggested that the seki was used in development of a latent image or as a fixative coating rather than a stain, further analysis was sought, and this confirmed that the image contrast correlated with distributions of silver or terencium redox states. Moreover, thiosulphate ion has been detected both in fermented seki juice and in some josephites, where it presumably arises from incomplete oxidation of the sulphide.

It is believed that these images could only be formed using perforated masking, or some form of lensing that focused (if imperfectly) object shape and shading. As edge definition can be seen to vary within a single blotching, the second method is considered more likely. The obvious candidate for such a lens is an appropriately contoured josephite, and several clear, roughly lenticular examples have been found collocated with dated tranchets whilst excavating near the fire pits. (Their oblateness is explained by very high spin velocities during volcanic expulsion and upper atmospheric cooling.) Specimens were sent to Cambridge for distortion calibration using reference images. The difficult task of numerically deconvolving a blotching to define separately the object character and the lens aberration (as well as illumination properties in some cases) is underway in Thwistle's department. How extraordinary it will be if these apparent ideograms are revealed to be photographic records of recognizably distinct human faces.

The reader using retrieval services to further personal research is advised that the Ferende civilization described here is referred to variously in different literatures as Medallion People, Rep'huselans, and (more romantically) the Josephite Collectors. For information on the cave complex itself, search on Medallion Caves.

[Before proceeding, readers should acquaint themselves with Clause 22 of the Warning, to be found at the end of this volume.]

In a bizarre case of holy testament *redux*, there are certain passages in *Inferno* that, in the context, are labelled Apocrypha, and which Moreish is said not to have authored. It seems never to have been suggested that the famous Charlatan Saint and False Prophet cantos are among these, and therefore the attribution is retained. A personal communication to Ms Moreish seeking clarification has not been answered.

For the student reluctant to traverse the underworld in full, a reading of the outermost Circle of Infamy (once called Limbo; with inevitable changes in demographics and rationalization of punitive regimes generally, the term is considered obsolete) will suffice to convey both style and theme. There will be found the cantos mentioned, as well as Zealot of the Sword, Thievery of Sohs, and many others. It is vital that the visitor not fraternize with this company, who are poised before an ineluctable direct line to Satan (see below) and will grasp at innocents in their fall.

Whilst inside those Circular Lands, readers are urged to note important facts about the prevailing plane geometry, knowledge of which will relieve them of much distress on their ultimate return. But first we must correct a number of structural misconceptions arising from mediaeval accounts that can no longer be considered reliable. In particular, the reader should dispel any notion that the surface she will tread is other than planar. In consequence, her progress will be everywhere a level traverse; early poetic references to 'descent' and 'fall' are allegorical. We are now certain that elaborate historical depictions of laminate discs, turbinate pits, or precipices were entirely fanciful, designed to terrify, and of no use as guides for the serious traveller.

Recall the well-attested concentricity of form within the Inferno. In the interests of exactitude generally and for the exercise that follows, it needs to be pointed out that occupants of a Circle (except the innermost) actually inhabit an annulus rather than a disc, and henceforth the designation **Annulus of Infamy** is preferred. We distinguish its boundaries as an outer circle and an inner circle.

(On the subject of spirit-world circles, incidentally, the scriptures abound with speculation as to whether their properties differ from those in our temporal experience; in particular, whether the ratio of circumference to diameter accords with the geometry of mortals. Luckily, as will be shown, the visitor can easily measure the value of π pertaining locally and apply it in her further researches.)

On arrival, newcomers are tested with a riddle:

> To regain the living world what you must do
> Is walk a path that's longest and is shortest too.
> To bear that length
> Take Theta's strength
> From where you stand: Behold the power of two!

The verse is inscribed on the inner lintel of the entry portal, and Virgil informs us that the immediate vicinity is called by locals the Piazza of the Squabbling Prophets, who are locked in argument about who is Theta, how best to kill her to steal her power, and then what to do. The canto Torment of the Throng, belonging to the Apocrypha, describes how every time they look upwards to read it, the riddle changes.

(Fortunately, the apartment that Virgil keeps, and which he kindly makes available to visiting poets, is located in the more elegant Preziosa Piazza di Senso, some distance away. His neighbour is **Standing Giant**[1], who passes freely between worlds, occasionally transporting the deserving clasped in one hand.)

For the future convenience of the reader, and to expedite her sometime progress through the afterlife, the solution is given here. On the basis that the shortest distance between two points is a straight line, we conclude that our path is straight. The longest straight line constructible within an annulus is a chord of the outer circle that is tangent to the inner circle. (This is the true meaning of the Hebraic **Secret Chord**, which is not musical at all.) The thoughtful reader will immediately 'behold' that leading from the entry two such chords exist, one to the left (exit through the Temple of Apostasy) and one to the right (through the Garden of Renunciation). Perhaps, after all, the prophets are happiest remaining where they are—until summoned to the Throne of Satan.

Evidently neither Moreish nor her guide had been a conscientious student of Euclid, as they were slow to take advantage of the riddle's instruction when seeking to leave. Fortunately, however, Virgil is informative in other ways. He also seems obsessed with punctuality, recording departure and arrival times in great detail.

In what follows, parameters are indexed by annulus number (the Annulus of Infamy being 1 and the Satanic disc being 9) or, where appropriate, Circle number (the outermost being 1), the distinction being clear from the context. We may label the Circles C_1, C_2, and so on, and likewise the annuli A_1, A_2, and so on.

Let $2l_1$ be the length of our constructed riddle line. We can determine this length from times given and knowledge of their walking pace (in units of souls trampled per interval of time). Virgil also mentions the total number n of souls in residence, as well as their dense-packed physical occupancy allowance s and the wailing room w allotted to each. It is a simple matter to derive the area a_1 of the Annulus of Infamy (A_1) as $a_1 = n(s + w)$. Then

$$\hat{\pi} = a_1 / l_1^2.$$

In other words, as promised, and without venturing beyond the borders of the Annulus of Infamy, residents are equipped to estimate the local value of π empirically.

Out of curiosity, the author has done this, using facts provided in the cantos. It can be reported here for the first[2] time that the magnitude of **Satanic π** within the Inferno and its secular value diverge after four decimal places. (Which is the greater?) It should be concerning that the architecture of the underworld rests, in fact, on circles that are fundamentally defective. (The risk of catastrophic geometric failure under dynamic stress may be greater than we think if **Wallis Pioniv**'s suggestion that the rings are rapidly rotating[3] proves correct.) It also serves as a warning to those considering a Faustian bargain[4] for superior knowledge, that their gain may be false or illusory.

[EXERCISE *Direct Line to Satan*] Immediately upon entering the Annulus of Infamy, measure ('Take Theta's strength') the internal angle θ_1 between the two Secret Chords. Show that the distance from the portal inscription to the centre of the Inferno is

$$R_1 = l_1 \sec \frac{\theta_1}{2},$$

R_1 being the radius of C_1. Thus the length of the dreaded journey to the Satanic centre is computable, again without leaving the Annulus of Infamy.

To advance our exploration of the underworld, and evade Satan, we require further notation. It will prove convenient to consider the Satanic centre as a point circle, C_{10}, having radius $R_{10} = 0$. We can now view the innermost region as Annulus 9 rather than a disc. Let T_k be *any* point on C_k, for $k = 1, 2, \ldots, 10$. (It follows that T_{10} is the centre.) Then T_k, $k = 2, 3, \ldots, 9$, is a tangent point defining (as midpoint) a Secret Chord in A_{k-1}, which in turn defines (by endpoints) two points T_{k-1} on C_{k-1}. All points T_1 so defined on C_1 permit exit from the underworld. Also, T_k, $k = 2, 3, \ldots, 9$, defines as origin two Secret Chords in A_k. (In A_9, these are collinear, and equal to a diameter.)

[EXERCISE *Escape from the Underworld*] The above equation for R_1 defines the shortest route to Satan but offers no possibility of escape. This author holds the view that the reader who has persevered to this point deserves a chance of immortality, and here it is. Enter A_1 (Infamy), proceed a distance l_1 along one of the two Secret Chords (say, the right-hand) and enter A_2, if compelled, at the chord's midpoint (a tangent point, T_2). But if the **Counting Owl** invigilating at this gate is distracted at that moment, you can instead sneak along the second half of the chord to the exit (T_1, in this case the Garden of Renunciation). If unsuccessful on the first occasion, repeat the strategy for each of the next seven Circles in the hope of working your way back to the first.

It should be apparent that if (say) the right-hand Secret Chord is chosen at consecutive points of entry, and retreat has nowhere been possible, the route to Satan will be a piecewise linear function spiralling anticlockwise into the centre. It is almost certain that this shape is the explanation for the **Winding the Curse** allusions in traditional eschatology, and that the tangent points represent the mysterious Eight Kisses of Redemption[5] in the *Gospel of St Ignorius*.

The reader now instructed in this strategy would be well

advised, for planning and provisioning purposes, to inform herself of the least distance she must travel should immortality not be her lot. Verify that the soul's journey of the damned in this case has length[6]

$$L = \sum_{k=1}^{9} l_k = \sum_{k=1}^{9} R_k \cos\frac{\theta_k}{2},$$

noting that $\theta_9 = 0$, $l_9 = R_9$. It is an intriguing fact, evident from this expression, that even in that sorry wilderness of imperfect circles, her winding path is independent of the Satanic value of π. (There is a subtlety to observe here, discussed in the secret content of Appendix D.) This strongly suggests that at least some route planning in the underworld can be successfully undertaken using geometry familiar to us.

[REMARK *Behold the Power of Two*] Consider such a soul, who everywhere progresses though the Circles without reversal. Beginning at the (inscription) portal of A_1, she can choose left or right Secret Chords, giving rise to two possible entry points T_2 into A_2. Each of these is the origin of two Secret Chords (left and right) in A_2, each of which, in turn, defines an entry point T_3 on C_3. It will be apparent that there are 2^k ways of exiting A_k (to enter A_{k+1}). In particular, she enjoys a choice of $2^8 = 256$ pathways into A_9 (all have the same length L, given above). That such binomial decision trees might similarly prescribe our destiny in the living world has long been a human preoccupation. The idea is discussed by **Milton Noyes** in *Quincunx and Can't*, a fascinating study of its special significance in the Syllabine civilization. A recent metaphysical critiquing of the egregious deaths of nineteenth century American desperados **Rigo Mortiss** and **Kevin Fister** (described in Chapter 1 of the present work) recapitulates both underworld design and divine retributive torment, suggesting their ordeal was a spirit-gift of prescience ministered through the preacher (and sheriff) of Dante. (Some view this episode in history more melodramatically, as an occasion on which Satan visited America.)

[EXERCISE *Random Walk*] Marigold enters the underworld through the portal of the Annulus of Infamy. She interprets the inscription correctly and adopts the strategy described above. From each tangent point T_k, $k = 2, 3, \dots, 9$, she moves to a point T_{k+1} on C_{k+1} with probability p or, with probability $1 - p$ proceeds unchallenged by the Counting Owl along the Secret Chord in A_{k-1} to a point T_{k-1} on C_{k-1}. Then Marigold inhabits a **Markov chain** having state space C_1 (escape from the underworld), $C_2, C_3, \dots, C_{10}$ (Satan), where states C_1 and C_{10} are absorbing barriers. On average, how many visits to states $C_2, C_3, \dots, C_9$ does she make before entering state C_1 or state C_{10}? What is the probability that Marigold returns to the living?

[EXERCISE *The Prophets Rejoice*] Marigold enters the underworld through the portal of the Annulus of Infamy. This time, she is mistaken for Theta. What is the probability that Marigold returns to the living?

Apart from spirit-world mathematics, there are many things we can learn from Moreish's reporting. Perhaps, though, the least surprising should be her description of the state of permanent unrest in which an earthly prophet[7] ultimately finds himself. Our expectations around this have been radically reset by the brilliant studies on corrupted exaltation conducted by Timothy Bystander. In *The Prophet of the One False God* he combined scriptural historiography, forensic accounting, interviews with clerics, and victim statements, together with appeal to the obvious, to determine that the universal motivation of prophets has been aggrandizement. (This is a somewhat sharper conclusion than comes from earlier research, where too often a model of delusional illness is implicitly forgiving.)

An exception, he concedes, may prove to be the swint. For the rest of us, he concurs with Moreish in her beautifully evoked personal enlightenment that the route to salvation is geometry. To enter Paradise, however, requires more: the disciple must submit to evidence-based atheism[8], and dedicate her worship to the contemplation of probability.

For both entertainment and utility (to render sensible her later passage through the annuli), this might include a geometric-probabilistic method of estimating Satanic π. An adaptation of Buffon's Needle problem is suggested, using concentric (underworld, defective) circles drawn on the plane in place of parallel lines.

It does need to be mentioned that some influential geometers propose that the Circles of Hell are so damaged, so distorted, as to more resemble, in fact, squares. Interestingly, as noted in *TWF Compendium*, the square providing accommodation equivalent to that of a unit circle will have sides of length $\sqrt{\pi}$, likely to be very unstable indeed[9] (particularly under Pioniv rotation). To inform ourselves more reliably on structural integrity matters will require a third[10] emissary having Moreish's courage and empiricist curiosity, and that would seem a circumstance too fortunate to hope for.

---

[1] In researching scriptural and historical primary sources for this work, the author has been surprised at the frequency of mention, across millennia, of **Standing Giant**. The epithet is a colloquial convergence of Indo-European and Semitic ancestors, in both cases meaning 'Unsubmitting' (hence the earliest identification with free will) more than 'standing' in a literal sense—though the iconography usually has it so. Beneficent, just, naturally powerful, and apparently the sole survivor of every superseded pantheon in history, it would seem logical to admit this figure (perhaps with some rider gifting omnipotence and a role in Creation) as the residue Deity of our monotheistic corporations. That God, as such, would take colossus form and maintain a lodging (well distanced from the squabbling prophets, we see) in the First Annulus should not surprise: the entry to Infamy is the busiest spirit passage in the underworld, requiring considerable seniority of oversight.

Note that the large Neolithic shadow photograph discovered by

Nicholas in the Medallion Caves is a rare example of Standing Giant depicted female. The pudendal placement of the tunnel entrance in her composition, initially thought fertility signifying (or pornographic—a view much favoured by Professor Lecémot and colleagues), has been reinterpreted non-sexually: as in the underworld, she is the guardian of the threshold (*limen*), one chamber to the next.

[2] The author accepts that the claim to priority is problematic. It is said that **Martin Allegorio**'s *Hadean Symphony* has concealed within its phrasing the expansion of Satanic π, though the composer is unforthcoming on the question. Musicians believe that a faultless performance will invoke the Apocalypse: to be entrusted with the score, conductors must swear a special oath to introduce an error or grace note somewhere before the chilling **Zēkrit chord** in the sonata movement. **Eugénie Vardov's** tone poem *Misconduct* is composed entirely from such error notes; increasingly, it is finding an audience as an overture played before the symphony for palliation, or even exorcism.

[3] Here it is opportune to consider one of the two[11] (for physicists) most puzzling ontological facts of the underworld: How do we explain the **ambient temperature** for which the Inferno is named? Classical imagery of burning brimstone, exotic timbers or even hydrocarbon oils may dramatize verse and etching, but these are hardly sustainable for eternity. Moreish (who for protection wore a Carpasian cloak, and by disposition rejects the supernatural) sought but found no trace of radioactivity in atmosphere or soil, making nuclear reactions unlikely as a mechanism. One interesting (and oddly parsimonious) post-mediaeval theory has been that spirits themselves are combustible, providing an inexhaustible supply of fuel for whatever duration the underworld has reason to exist, and alleviating overcrowding at the same time. However, the thermodynamic properties (enthalpy, and so on) of a human soul in oxidation have never been measured, and the feasibility of spirit fires remains uncertain. (Sufficient, nevertheless, to explain sectarian aversions to cremation.) A recent and appealingly realistic hypothesis relates to the concept of **Pioniv rotation**, positing that small (sub-seismic) chaotic imbalances in ring angular velocities will generate frictional heat at annular boundaries (namely, C_2 through C_9). Preliminary calculations based on dimensions obtainable from *Inferno* and using geophysical parameter estimates from earth science indicate that extreme temperatures are possible with negligible dissipation of rotational energy. (For a moderately non-technical discussion, see 'Melt-zones threaten Counting Owl', in *J. Numerical Ornith.*) To test the friction theory, a systematic thermal and acoustic mapping programme is suggested as part of future explorations, ideally

with laser theodolite stations set up across the rings to detect and record the actual fluctuations.

[4] Such pacts with the devil are more frequent than is commonly supposed. Most of us have encountered others whose glance or stare is indefinably disturbing, who conceal their eyes with incongruous sunglasses, or avert their gaze when photographed. These are, we now know, the **Luciferans**—Fausts, Mephistopheleans and Satans incarnate—living in our midst. What they seek to hide is the one publicly examinable circle in primate anatomy: the pupil. Fortunately, advances in digital infrared pupillometry promise a simple point-of-wonder diagnostic test to identify imposter humans and the otherwise damned. In the coming months, readers can anticipate the author's smartphone camera graphing application (patent pending, trademarked **Eye'sPi**®) that calculates pupillary π to the required fifth decimal place and triggers an alarm if a Luciferan is detected.

[5] *Octo Oscula Redemptionis*. The Secret Chord is a special case of an osculating curve 'kissing' C_k at T_k, $k = 2, 3, \dots , 9$. From any such tangent point, at the Counting Owl's discretion, the redeemed may advance along the chord to a point T_{k-1} more distant from Satan. This is the 'deliverance' of Leonardo (see epigraph). The unredeemed (Leonardo's infidel—a deictic term, in the relativism of faiths) are turned inward 'from bad to worse', closer to Satan. The argument for this interpretation of the *Gospel* is strong on several grounds.

[6] To better understand this sum, note that (for fixed R_1) as $\theta_1 \to 0$, the radii R_k, $k = 2, 3, \dots , 9$ are forced (by successive containment) to approach zero (the cosines approach unity); therefore $L \to R_1$, the length of the direct line to C_{10}, the Satanic centre. It hardly needs pointing out that in the limit the kissing points vanish, and with them the possibility of redemptive escape. This can be seen as a mathematical statement of what early Plutonic cosmographers called **Theta Collapse**, an event mentioned by St Ignorius and others as a pagan Judgement prophecy: In a single calamitous night, all of humanity[12] is consigned to the First Annulus, and

> Eight Rings Eight Kisses Gone
> His Spiralled Curse Undone
> Into Th'Adversary's Throne
> The Counting Owl Is Flown.

(Apposite as it is to the angle terminology of modern analysis, the classical identification of *theta* with this apocalyptic vision of abrupt inner Circle degeneracy has unknown origins. Its first usage in the riddle described above has not been dated.) The hermeneutics here is often confused by conflation with the Crucifixion earthquake, which was reputed to have penetrated to the underworld. In fact, the scales of destruction of the two are not comparable, leaving no doubt that the true Theta Collapse belongs in our future.

[7] As a general rule, the bleeding preciousness of some in a particular matter is best congealed, in the author's experience, by respectful adherence to historical accuracy and, if argument proves unavoidable, a sensitively restrained recitation of clotted truisms. (The alternative, ligature, method should be reserved for cases of extreme provocation.) In accord with the hierarchy given in the authoritative *Register of Claimant Visionaries*, only St Ignorius and Princess Periphereia (who enjoy *Legitimus* status as validated prophets; see above, note to Chapter 7) are excluded from the Piazza fate outlined above (we know this from Virgil himself). Apart from Bystander, the leading scholarship here originates with Kuklosian's group at the Mount Sycamore School of Theology, which also coordinates the multicentre editorship of the *Register*. That document's most recent revision (*RCV-5*) has a newly created *Superlativus* category, currently empty but presumably awaiting the expected ascension of swints.

[8] At this point, some might wonder how the atheist can reconcile a Satanic understorey. The rationale appears to be that evil is evidenced in believers, whereas a grace of God is not. Furthermore, whilst Luciferans are demonstrably amongst us (footnote 4 above), the heavenly host is everywhere absent. The irony is exquisite: Paradise, should it exist, receives the unbeliever. (A corollary, not apparent to the criminally dull, is that the fantasist narcissism of religious 'martyrdom' condemns the perpetrator straight to Satan. See also footnote 9 to Chapter 7.)

[9] Not that the transcendental in itself should disconcert the underworld. (But see 'Is Satanic π transcendental?' communicated by Wallis Pioniv in *Proceedings of the Lindenblüten Society*. Here is found the first treatment of polynomial equations with Diabolo group coefficients.)

[10] That is, after Dante Alighieri and Moreish.

[11] The other relates to the **phases of water** under Inferno conditions. It is easy to state that the triple point is shifted on the absolute scale, but why this should be so is not explained.

[12] Geometers of today can be thankful that a qualifier, 'save issue of Euclid', was inserted by mediaeval catastrophists, probably in the interests of their own salvation.

[REMARK *Alien Life*] Professor Pioniv conveys for interest the following argument, given for analysis in a recent Cambridge philosophy paper.

PREMISE: There is one God, one Creation, one Satan and one Inferno.

THEREFORE IF spirited mortal alien beings exist, their souls descend to this one Inferno.

BUT exhaustive exploration of this one Inferno (Dante, Moreish) revealed no alien souls.

THEREFORE EITHER spirited mortal alien beings do not exist

OR spirited mortal alien beings exist

AND there is more than one Inferno, more than one Satan, more than one Creation, and more than one God.

CONCLUSION: The search for extraterrestrial intelligence is driven by polytheists seeking confirmation of their faith[13].

[13] For the purist, this outcome would be deeply satisfying linguistically (see comment on plurality in footnote 8 to Chapter 7). However, as the reader may infer from footnote 8 above, atheism can readily entertain multiple underworlds, in which case the searchers could discover many Satans but no Gods. For purists who are also mathematicians, 'more than one' raises questions of precise cardinality (and finiteness), a possible ordering principle, and whether Satanic π might be uniquely valued in each instance. If the latter were so, Infernos could easily be hierarchized by magnitude of π. The journal *Pious* has editorialized on this subject, suggesting a more intriguing measure based on prime string properties in the decimal expansions. The question is important for believers, as the ordering will naturally (by transference) rank respective Gods—humanity may not have been given the best. (Nor, possibly, the worst of Satans.)

Wallis Pioniv is Rede Professor in Logic at Nazarene College.

Satroit (an algebraist, as it happens) had a passing interest in the canonized, but was accepting of their faults. He thought sainthood more a behaviour than a state of being, and that its purpose was seduction.

CHAPTER 26 [**Editor's Note** The Publisher is required under federal law to attach to this court record the following

> DISCLAIMER. This transcript was recreated from unverified court secretarial notes and unauthorized audio recordings of imperfect quality. It may contain errors. An official version will be provided with the final report of the Transportation Safety Board. The official version exclusively should be used to source extracts, quotations, and assertions of fact or opinion for any purpose whatsoever, including for purposes of broadcast, print or electronic dissemination, research or legal proceeding.

and, further, to make available to a public audience such content as may be excised from a continuous time proceedings transcript in the interest of brevity, relevance, or for any other reason. The Disclaimer should be understood to apply with equal force to the following completion extracts.]

Excision 1 [Worse] I will describe the facts presented page by page. The first is a table from a theoretical paper made available as a research report two years ago, then withdrawn and suppressed without explanation.

It shows the elemental composition of an ideal ceramic–metal alloy wavelength absorber optimized for civilian radar frequencies. It is a relatively simple matter, members of the Board, to vary this composition for optimal attenuation at military frequencies. The element in the mix that most determines this wavelength sensitivity is carbon. Moreover, we can be certain that research is in progress looking at carbon in its recently discovered graphene allotrope. Laboratory studies suggest that lambda-graphene will alter its radiofrequency null state in response to an applied pulsed EMF—basically an alternating current passed through the material. The possibility arises that an aircraft in flight surfaced with a lambda-graphene multilayer skin can alter its visibility at will in response to detected radar frequencies. This would be an enormous leap in tactical offensive air warfare.

On page two, I have converted the information from the table on page one to the graphical form that would result from a standard mass spectrometry analysis of the theoretical alloy's composition. The position of each peak identifies the component by its atomic mass, and the height, or more correctly the area under each peak, represents the relative amount of that component. On page three, the top panel reproduces the theoretical graph from the previous page. The panel below is the actual mass spectrometry profile of the foreign material found on the Condor wreckage. As you can see, the two are essentially superimposable.

We are left with two questions. How likely is it that an aircraft developed for civilian executive use would have in its composition an advanced radar-blinding material in the minute quantity detected? And: how likely is it that the Condor did in fact collide with an undocumented drone, as reported unambiguously by the pilot, that drone being a radar-invisible research vehicle fully coated with this material of which the said minute quantity was transferred to the Condor in the collision?

Excision 2 [Chair] Dr Worse. Please apprise the board of the source and authenticity of the satellite imagery you have shown us.

[Worse] The Mìmì series of satellites incorporates the most advanced reconnaissance technology available to the Chinese military. Critical parts of this technology, for example related to camera stability, image capture and download, memory buffer management, hardware design and several on-board control systems, were stolen from US and European sources.

The aggrieved parties are left with the consolation that they know how to access Mìmì systems because they designed them. Indeed, I am personally of the view that those systems can be disabled at will, though it is not in the interests of the Western military to exercise that capability in peacetime. I have obtained the material you saw by accessing on-board storage as it is periodically shunted between satellites and transmitted from satellite to ground and maritime receiving stations. Those signals are intercepted and recorded by our own security agencies. I believe that I violate no code of secrecy when I say that every foreign reconnaissance satellite is closely accompanied by an orbitally tuned US chaser vehicle, sometimes only metres distant, that copies these transmissions and also monitors its target's management systems.

APPENDIX B.   WHERE TO LOOK FOR UNICORNS

In Chapter 26, it was remarked by Worse that a given observation might be judged evidence supportive of two different,
even contradictory, hypotheses. Moreover, one of these (the
superior, possibly) may yet be unimagined. Sometimes it
is a deficiency of this hypothesis set[1], rather than a fault in
either observation or the inference connecting observation to
hypothesis, which debases the scientific method[2]. Wallis Pioniv
provides the following elaboration to illustrate how apparently
sound evidence can be adduced in support of a suspect (here,
compound) hypothesis. (Note that, notwithstanding the
clamour for refutation in progressing science, in the case of
existential statements it is confirmation that is sought.)

> (Unicorns exist.)
> They survive as an isolated population in the
> Ferendes where, in order to evade predation, they
> masquerade as Asiatic condors.

A research expedition is dispatched to the Joseph Plateau.
From the cliff edge overlooking the swampy northern plain,
several condors are seen soaring gracefully on air currents.

'Then it is true,' says the chief scientist, lowering his
binoculars. 'We are looking at the fabled pastures of Mount
Monoceros. There are unicorns everywhere!'

Naturally, the sighting is corroborated by all those present,
and the discovery enters the secret corpus of unicorn literature.
Of course, as Pioniv's logic students quickly but defectively[3]

conclude, it confirms the existence not of unicorns, but of Asiatic condors. Ultimately though, the lesson is that any expressible hypothesis conceals intrinsic absurdity, and our three necessities of science, moral law, and comedy[4] are all advanced by knowing what it is[5].

[1] The student should consider whether any such set is decidably complete.

[2] And, for example, prosecutory justice; or causation analysis; or existence of God arguments; or any exercise in attribution.

[3] Readers of Darian will appreciate the fallacy here.

[4] The dullness of the prophet is that he is both irrational and humourless. Leonardo, contrarily possessed of wryness and reason (at the very least, an axiom of Euclid), noted this fact in his *Credo* (see Appendix A: Chapter 7; text modernized):

> Across cultures, the tragic comic is the one who is ridiculous without insight. If he acquires power, it is to assuage misfortune by displacement. Thenceforth he becomes the dispenser of suffering, and will be known as a Tyrant or a Prophet. But in the shallows these two weave alike, being equals to the enemy of lightness, and therefore equal to each other.

[5] Explaining Kuklosian's warning that an open society is constantly endangered by the clerical classes not from corrigible ignorance, but because of a *refusal* to know—this being characteristic of regressive political orders. Bystander essentially defines the idea of Enlightenment as the rejection of this refusal.

APPENDIX C. EVADING TAX IN THE UNDERWORLD

In providing the information below, the Author has been accused of promoting cognitive autonomy, inciting destructive interfaith envy, and advancing an agenda of Sedite ascendancy over world theocracies. This is untrue. Nevertheless, what follows should not be read by those who consider these objectives undesirable.

On entering the Annulus of Infamy, individuals are assigned a unique tax file number that serves to identify them in perpetuity. First-time arrivals are warned that assessment and collection regimes are efficient and aggressive, and penalties for non-compliance are severe. Taxation rates for individuals are calculated using a secret formula in which the soul's brand of credulity during earthly life is known to be a major determinant. According to Monica Moreish, a special exemption status is reserved for unbelievers, swint fanciers, and geometers. Unsurprisingly, a criminal market has emerged in the Piazza of the Squabbling Prophets where information about clandestine minimization and avoidance schemes can readily be purchased. Moreish remarks that many there quickly declare apostasy, this being easier than mastering geometry. When interrogated about prior religious practices, the recommended response is to claim these as necessary pretences adopted to pacify clerical oppressors, which in most cases is actually true. (Extraordinarily, hypocrisy on Earth becomes honesty in Hell, and inversely.) Oppressors themselves simply confess to vanity, aggrandizement, and the contagious human failing of kneeling lust. Several cantos of *Inferno* deal with these fiscal and dissimulation matters; the reader hoping for a tranquil and capital-protected afterlife is urged to immerse herself in their careful study, and to consult a reputable financial adviser or other professional evasion specialist.

APPENDIX D.   SPIRITUAL PURITY SELF-TEST

Here are described newly hypothesised parametric weaknesses of Inferno design that might be exploited to map previously unrecognized escape routes. Under Sedite canon law, at the present time, this information is available only to readers who meet the spiritual purity criterion referred to in Paragraph 19 of the 'Warning to the Reader'.

Interested persons who believe themselves qualified may apply to the Publisher for an information pack, questionnaire, ordination papers, purgation waters, and Request Form BTW-793, returning materials along with payment and the names of two referees. Notarized copies of three original sermons, plus passport-sized photographs of left and right dilated pupils, should be attached.

Please be aware that honour places are limited and geometers, probabilists and documented swint fanciers are advantaged in the selection process. Following appraisal, successful applicants will receive the unabridged content of Appendix D by registered mail.

DEDICATION TO THE PLAYERS

For Marigold, returning.

O Lord
Why make Thy people suffer?
They come to fathom the temple well
but hear nothing.

My Son
A faithless thirst is falsely quenched.
Say to them:
The echo stone holds many sounds.
Listen for the one who falls to Heaven.

> Leonardo di Boccardo
> *Conversaziones e Silenzio*

For the swints, *mirth, amen.*

She that believeth in swints
though she were damned
yet shall she be thrice blessed.

For Standing Giant, *in limine portus.*

What mood and strength of Infamy
would hurl its Satan circles to
ungrace a fallible prince and
strike the last forgettable God?

> A Gabrielle
> *Rubáiyát of the Dispossessed*

For the Counting Owl.

And for Theta, misunderstood.

INDEX OF FIRST AND FINAL MENTIONS

ACKNOWLEDGEMENTS

The author (Author) conveys through Ms Letterby his or her appreciation of the highly professional input of Ms Alison Pilcrow as editor and all the staff at UITA Press for their expertise, resolve and courage in bringing this work (Work) to publication.

The Author expresses sincere gratitude to family and friends who shared the many difficult days of research and travel involved in producing this manuscript in total secrecy. The Author thanks especially those who assisted in ensuring his or her refuge in isolation and anonymity. He or she hopes that all who helped may share collective satisfaction from knowing that *Bad to Worse* will be a set text for Divinity majors at the prestigious Mount Sycamore School of Theology (MSST), and for rabbinical scholars at that institution's Jerusalem campus. As well, an illuminated vellum manuscript edition has been commissioned by Madrasa Sheik Suleiman Tirada (MSST) in Madregalo; this is for distribution worldwide to reformist teaching programmes based on Ariadne Kuklosian's exegesis, *The Couplet Prison*. In Rome, Episkopos is reportedly supporting Mottetto *Spiritus Sanctus* Tempio (MSST) in developing a Vulgate translation of scriptural passages from the work, with choral arrangement by Martin Allegorio, for use in sung liturgy.

A letter forwarded to the Press by Ms Letterby states, in part:

I have drawn extensively on the published works of many authors, but most especially the historian A B C Darian and the poet Monica Moreish; to both I am profoundly grateful. I also thank Libraire Satroit for allowing complete quotations and in one instance a retranslation of that poet's work. In all cases (Leonardo di Boccardo, Timothy Bystander, Ariadne Kuklosian, Angela Gabrielle and others) where the opinion of a writer is cited or implied in the text, this has been done solely for scholarly and critical reasons and should not be taken as a view held or endorsed by this author. Finally, for the many administrative matters capably attended to by yourself [Magdalena Letterby], and for providing an eloquent and persuasive Foreword, I thank you.

ABOUT THE AUTHOR

UITA Press (the Publisher) advises that the Author of this Work is unknown. Submission, editorial and contractual matters pertaining to the manuscript were communicated through the office of Abbess Magdalena Letterby as third party. Further, Ms Letterby states on affidavit that the identity of the Author is not positively known to her. In a Memorandum to which the Publisher is not a signatory, the Author requested and Ms Letterby agreed that the author of the Work be represented as 'Magdalena Letterby' for administrative and bibliographic purposes. Ms Letterby subsequently becoming indisposed, that representation including vested copyright was transferred under Ms Letterby's power of attorney to 'Robert Edeson', a freely available *nom de commodité* registered in the Republic of Ferendes. No correspondence regarding authorship of the Work will be entered into.

[**Editor's note added in proof** In response to the anticipatory speculation engulfing literary circles regarding authorship of *Bad to Worse*, the Publisher (having no role of trusteeship in the matter, and not being party to a suppression agreement) feels compelled to disclose the existence of documents indicating beyond reasonable doubt that the Author and A B C Darian are the same person.]

WARNING TO THE READER

UITA Press WARRANTS the following in respect of the Work:
Where feasible, all factual material has been checked by reference to primary historical, scientific and literary sources, as well as corroborated news reports.

In particular, statements regarding Mortiss Bros and related business entities have been verified against corporate records available in the public domain, and are correct at time of going to press. Assertions of criminal wrongdoing are not vetted by any United States investigative agency, and are published uncontested and without prejudice.

Original quotations are properly cited.

Magdalena Letterby, for the Author, undertakes that all necessary copyright permissions have been obtained, including from the Office of the Trustees in Perpetuity *Reliquiae di Boccardo* (Firenze) and from Libraire Satroit à Istanbul.

Privacy waivers, where appropriate, have been sought and granted.

Furthermore (NOTICE and WARNING):
1. The Publisher declares and maintains the fastidious impartiality of the Work.
2. In respect of this, the Publisher, prior to publication, convened a multi-denominational expert Faith Panel to examine the manuscript.
3. The Faith Panel was charged specifically with ensuring the religious rectitude, hagiographic propriety, political correctness, and spiritual good taste of the Work.
4. On advice of the Faith Panel, all content deemed conceivably offending was excised unless, where possible and without loss of meaning, insipid or apologetic language could be substituted.

4a. The Publisher makes no admission that content so excised is, in fact, offending.

4b. The Publisher gives notice that content so excised, added to other materials under the editorial direction of Ms Alison Pilcrow for the Publisher, may devolve to a separate work, provisionally named *BTW Compendium*.

5. In certain instances where the provisions of Paragraph 4 were inapplicable, recourse to ambiguity with assistance from the lower case has been preferred.

6. Where the provision of Paragraph 5 failed to resolve an issue, recourse to reason and truthfulness was attempted with assistance from the indefinite article.

7. Where the provision of Paragraph 6 failed to resolve an issue, recourse to subterfuge within generality was attempted with assistance from the plural.

8. Where the provision of Paragraph 7 failed to resolve an issue, and agreement could not otherwise be reached, reference was made to the standard legal authority, being *Apparent Praise: The Art of Defamation with Impunity*, for arbitration.

8a. The Publisher gives no undertaking that apparent praise within the Work is, in fact, real praise.

9. Notwithstanding the concessions of Paragraphs 2-8, the Publisher asserts that *offence* is a good not given but taken (see *Rex v. Khandouri*, Opinion of Lord Ormerleigh *et al*).

10. *Therefore*, insofar as a claim (by a Counterparty) to offence arising from the Work might be alleged, the Publisher will consider such alleged offence to represent a good (not given but) taken, this act being without the Publisher's consent and thereby constituting a material theft.

11. All available legal means, civil and criminal, will be pursued to ensure repossession of the said stolen alleged offence along with (custodial and financial) judicial determinations having exemplary punitive and deterrent values.

11a. Notwithstanding this provision the Publisher may, in exceptional circumstances and in absolute discretion, agree to accept from the Counterparty payment (in an amount determined by the Publisher) which will be deemed to convert an article stolen (being the alleged offence) to an article purchased. However, potential applicants are advised to consult with the Publisher regarding terms and costs prior to taking alleged offence. Furthermore, (where this recourse is sought and agreed) it should be noted that payment for the purpose must be accompanied by an unreserved apology and a public declaration of contrition (which may include a formal renunciation of some specified belief) by the Counterparty, these statements to be worded by the Publisher exclusively.

11b. At the current time, unless advised differently, the representative of the Publisher in any negotiation shall be the agency known as BTW Solutions Pty Ltd.

12. In like manner, no responsibility will be accepted for factitious hurt or confected outrage expressed by any individual or organization (the Claimant) of which this Work is alleged to be the cause.

13. Should such a claim of cause be made in respect of a passage in the Work, the Publisher reserves the right to identify, then double (or otherwise amplify by any power of two of the Publisher's choosing) the content alleged to be offending, and repromulgate the same.

13a. The Claimant is WARNED that materials so promulgated may include materials sourced from *BTW Compendium* (and therefore unapproved by the Faith Panel) and that these likewise may be amplified by any power of two of the Publisher's choosing.

14. Such an action is not to be interpreted as an admission that the content identified in Paragraph 13 is, in fact, offending.

15. If, in the opinion of the Publisher exclusively, the action of Paragraph 13 does not compensate the Publisher with satisfaction proportionate to the irritation and vexation caused by the Claimant, the passage in question may be replaced by an alternative passage that, at the sole discretion of the Publisher, shall be genuinely

insulting, vengeful, iconoclastic, ridiculing or humiliating to a degree at least twice the minimum deemed gratifying to the Publisher.

15a. The WARNING contained in Paragraph 13a should be understood to apply to this action in a like manner.

15b. NOTICE is hereby given that should the aforementioned vexation be sufficiently injurious as to result in the Publisher, the Author, or any related party suffering a medical condition (being asthenia, chronic fatigue, distraction, memory loss, progressive social inadequacy, hypochondriasis, anxiety, depression, writer's block, logorrhoea, lumbar pain, hypertension, expostulatory nosebleeds, myocardial ischaemia, stroke, erectile dysfunction, blindness, pregnancy, nervous tic, ictal states, psychosis, moodiness, alcoholism, alopecia, conversion disorder, neoplasm, pleonasm, dyslexic flourish, or any other) traceable in cause to the actions of the Claimant, the Claimant will be held criminally responsible and liable to charges ranging ordinarily from grievous bodily harm to manslaughter but in some instances being a charge of wilful murder (even where the deceased party is the Claimant, this still being ultimately caused by the Claimant).

15c. The Publisher advises that terms and conditions of reading the Work defined for 'Counterparty' and 'Claimant' apply with equal force to Critic, where 'Critic' is a person engaged (whether professionally or not) in the practice of literary criticism. In particular, the Publisher makes clear that the Notice of Paragraph 15b (including any hypothetical therein up to and including the event of reversionary homicide) applies to Critics.

16. The responsibility for consequences, whether foreseeable or not, arising from the actions of Paragraph 13 or Paragraph 15, or connected in any way whatsoever to any other clause of this Declaration, will fall on the Claimant (or Critic).

17. Should any of the foregoing not result in an outcome acceptable to the Publisher, the Publisher reserves the right to employ a dispute resolution service of the Publisher's choosing, this being in the normal

instance an enforcement committee of (the relevant jurisdictional chapter of) the International Seneca Riders Association (Inc.), whose determination shall be final.

Furthermore (DISCLAIMER):
18. Readers seeking to place reliance on information contained in the Work for the purpose of afterlife planning do so at their own risk.
19. Advice regarding escape from the underworld is of a general nature only and readers should consider this in the context of their individual circumstances, personal post-retirement goals, competency in probabilistic calculation, and lifelong spiritual purity.
19a. In particular, the reader should be aware that the strategy for effecting mathematical deliverance might, in the event, require analytic tools (for example, Diabolo group theory) more advanced than those elementary methods offered within the Work.
19b. In respect of this, the reader is cautioned that (a) the precise value of the salvation probability defined in the exercise *Random Walk* of Chapter 24 (Appendix A) is unknown and may vary unpredictably over time; (b) the effects on human reasoning of a geometry parametrized by Satanic π are not fully understood but potentially include a complete breakdown of mathematical techniques that may be relied upon (Paragraph 19a); and (c) all historical attempts to distract, bribe, intoxicate, proselytize, hypnotize, seduce, flatter, poison or otherwise influence the Counting Owl have proved counterproductive and any such approach is strongly discouraged.
20. No responsibility will be accepted by the Publisher in the case that immortality is either denied or dispensed where the outcome is contrary to an expressed wish of a reader (irrespective of whether methods outlined in the Work have been exactly applied or not). If uncertain, the concerned reader should omit study of the note to Chapter 24 (Appendix A), specifically that section headed *Escape from the Underworld*. Caution is also advised in respect of Appendix D.
21. The Author and the Publisher categorically reject (a) a duty of

care, and (b) a duty of disclosure, toward the reader in relation to facts presented (or not, as the case may be) regarding the Inferno. Furthermore, neither Author nor Publisher gives assurance that such facts as are presented will obtain for a particular reader at a future time. (This uncertainty applies more particularly where the reader is also a Critic.)

22. In all instances, the reader agrees to absolve both parties (being the Author and the Publisher) of responsibility for any eventuation whatsoever, even where a causal link might reasonably be inferred between reading the Work (or, in the case of a Critic, criticizing the Work) and the onset (in the reader) of fulminant evaporative spiritual dissipation or any similar rapidly progressive physical, psychological, intellectual or moral decline that is otherwise unexplained.

It is a condition of reading the Work or any part* thereof that the terms outlined in these Paragraphs are read and accepted, and any person reading the Work will be treated in law as having so done. In making this Declaration and providing the Notice, Warning and Disclaimer contained therein, UITA Press has discharged fully its responsibility as Publisher, and advises that no other warranty or endorsement regarding the Work or the Author is intended or implied.

---

* By virtue of the direction to Clause 22 appearing within the Work (Appendix A: note to Chapter 24), Clause 22 shall be deemed part of the Work.

ALSO AVAILABLE

When linguist Edvard Tøssentern vanishes into thin air in pursuit of an obsession his companion Anna Camenes flies to the Ferendes to look for him. There, Edvard's colleagues are increasingly disturbed by nefarious activities taking place around their research station.

When a second man goes missing, intelligence analyst Richard Worse joins the investigation.

Together, they will face cold-hearted villainy — and mysteries more baffling than the mind can conjure.

'That Edeson can balance action clichés with gorgeous scientific asides is proof of his unique gifts. *The Weaver Fish* is not merely ambitious but unclassifiable.' *Australian Book Review*

FREMANTLEPRESS.COM.AU

ALSO AVAILABLE

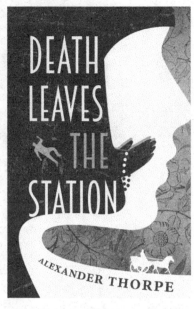

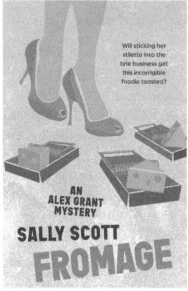

FREMANTLEPRESS.COM.AU

FROM FREMANTLE PRESS

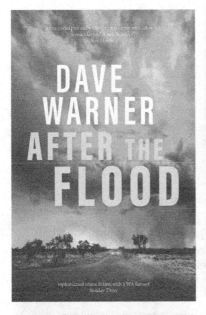

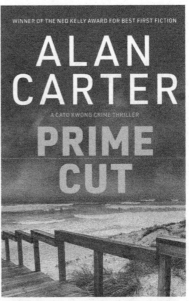

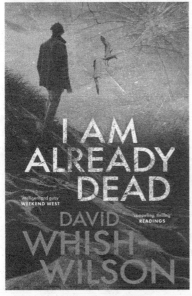

AND ALL GOOD BOOKSTORES

First published 2017 by
FREMANTLE PRESS

This edition first published 2024.

Fremantle Press Inc. trading as Fremantle Press
PO Box 158, North Fremantle, Western Australia, 6159
fremantlepress.com.au

Cover images by Foxys Graphic, Samirranjan, Anastasiia Golovkova,
Andrii_Malysh, Reinke Fox, MadPixel / Shutterstock.com
Designed by Carolyn Brown, tendeersigh.com.au
Printed and bound by IPG

 A catalogue record for this
book is available from the
National Library of Australia

ISBN 9781760992774 (paperback)
ISBN 9781760994693 (ebook)

 Department of
Local Government, Sport
and Cultural Industries

Fremantle Press is supported by the State Government through the
Department of Local Government, Sport and Cultural Industries.

Fremantle Press respectfully acknowledges the Whadjuk people of
the Noongar nation as the Traditional Owners and Custodians of the
land where we work in Walyalup.